DR. MORELLE AND THE DRUMMER GIRL

'Dear Mr. Drummer, Your daughter is safe . . . If you want her back alive it is going to cost you money . . . Don't call the police . . . You are under observation, so don't try any tricks.' A note is left in the girl's flat by her kidnapper. Her father, Harvey Drummer, turns to Dr. Morelle and Miss Frayle to help him secure his daughter's release. The case proves to be one of the most baffling and hazardous of the Doctor's career!

Books by Ernest Dudley
in the Linford Mystery Library:

ALIBI AND DR. MORELLE
THE HARASSED HERO
CONFESS TO DR. MORELLE
THE MIND OF DR. MORELLE
DR. MORELLE AND DESTINY
CALLERS FOR DR. MORELLE
LOOK OUT FOR LUCIFER!
MENACE FOR DR. MORELLE
NIGHTMARE FOR DR. MORELLE
THE WHISTLING SANDS
TO LOVE AND PERISH
DR. MORELLE TAKES A BOW

ERNEST DUDLEY

DR. MORELLE AND THE DRUMMER GIRL

Complete and Unabridged

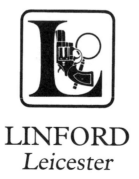

LINFORD
Leicester

First published in Great Britain

First Linford Edition
published 2007

The characters in this book are
entirely imaginary and bear no relation
to any living person.

British Library CIP Data

Dudley, Ernest
    Dr. Morelle and the drummer girl.
    —Large print ed.—
    Linford mystery library
    1. Detective and mystery stories
    2. Large type books
    I. Title
    823.9'14 [F]

ISBN 978–1–84617–752–1

Published by
F. A. Thorpe (Publishing)
Anstey, Leicestershire

Set by Words & Graphics Ltd.
Anstey, Leicestershire
Printed and bound in Great Britain by
T. J. International Ltd., Padstow, Cornwall

This book is printed on acid-free paper

Extract from the *Medical Directory* (current year):

MORELLE (Christian names given) 221B, Harley St., W.1. (Tel. Langham 05011) — M.D. Berne (Univ. Berne Prize & Gold Medallist) 1924; F.R.C.P. Lond. 1932 (Univ. Vienna, Salzburg, Carfax, U.S.A.); Phys. Dept. Nerv. Dis. & Lect. in Neurol. Rome Academy, 1929; Lect. & Research Fell. Sorbonne, 1928; Carfax, U.S.A. Fell. Med. Research Counc. 1930; Research Fell. Salzburg Hosp. 1931; Psychiat. Carlos Hosp. Rome; Psychiat. Horgan Hosp. Baltimore; Pathol. Rudolfa Clin. Berne; Medico-Psychol. Trafalgar Hosp. and Clin. London; Hon. Cons. Psychiat. Welbeck Hosp. Lond. Author, 'Psychol. aspects of prevent. treat. of drug addiction', *Amer. Med. Wkly, 1932;* 'Study of analysis in ment. treat.', Ib.,

1930; 'Nervous & mental aspect of drug addict', *Jl. of Res. in Psychopathol.*, *1931*; 'Hypnot. treat. in nerve & ment. disorder', *Amer. Med. Jnl.*, *1930*; etc.

Extract from *Who's Who* (current year):

MORELLE (Christian names, but no date, place or details of birth given). Educated: Sorbonne; Rome; Vienna. M.D. Berne, 1923 (for further details of career as medical practitioner see *Medical Directory* — current year); Lecturer on medicopsychological aspects of criminology to New York Police Bureau, 1934; Lecturer and medicopsychiat. to police bureaux and criminological authorities of Geneva, Rome, Milan and Paris, 1935–1937. Published miscellaneous papers on medical and scientific subjects (see *Medical Directory* — current year). Writings for journals include: 'Auguste Dupin *versus* Sherlock Holmes — A Study in Ratiocination', *London Archive & Atlantic Weekly, 1931*; 'The Criminal *versus* Society', *English Note-book,*

Le Temps Moderne and *New York Letter, 1933*, etc., etc. See also the Case-books 'Meet Dr. Morelle', 'Meet. Dr. Morelle Again' and 'Menace For Dr. Morelle' (published by John Long.) Address: 221B Harley St., London, W.1. *Recreations:* Criminology and fencing — European fencing champion (Epée) Switzerland, 1927–28–29. *Clubs:* None.

1

Party in Park Lane

'Isn't it a lovely party, Doctor?'

Miss Frayle's face was pink with excitement, her eyes bright behind her horn-rimmed glasses as they roamed round the crowded room. Dr. Morelle stared at her in simulated amazement.

'You perceive some attraction in such a futile waste of time and money?' his voice rasped in her ear. 'I confess I find difficulty in agreeing with you.'

But Miss Frayle refused to listen. She had been looking forward to all this tremendously and she was determined no one, not even Dr. Morelle, was going to damp her enjoyment.

'People must be gay sometimes,' she protested. 'Besides, it isn't as if it's any ordinary party. It's a celebration for Doone Drummer's novel — '

She broke off with a giggle. The Doctor

was deliberately turning his back upon a society photographer trying to creep up on him to add another celebrity to his bag. Rebuffed, the man moved off in search of more co-operative subjects for his candid camera. Dr. Morelle took out a thin gold cigarette-case, lit an inevitable *Le Sphinx* and drew at it irritably.

Miss Frayle's giggle faded as she watched the cigarette-case slipped back to its pocket. It had been presented to the Doctor by a certain young baroness as a token of gratitude for his extricating her from a particularly unsavoury black-mail business. Miss Frayle frowned as she remembered the baroness and her *svelte* allure. She had tried several times to glimpse the inscription inside the cigarette-case, but he never left it lying about and invariably filled it himself. It was only ordinary curiosity on Miss Frayle's part, of course.

'As I was saying,' she continued, 'this is a party to celebrate the year's best seller.' Dr. Morelle's finely-chiselled nostrils fairly quivered in disdain. 'It's all very well for you to turn up your nose like

2

that,' Miss Frayle exclaimed, 'but *The Friendly Enemy* has been raved over by everybody. Look at the terrific sales it's had. It's going to be made into a play, and Hollywood's just bought it. Anyway, I loved it.'

'Which, of course,' Dr. Morelle murmured, 'automatically bestows upon it the *cachet* raising it to the ranks of immortal literature.'

She gave a little shrug, sipped her sherry and turned her attention again to the celebrities jostling around her. She picked out film actors and actresses, famous novelists, journalists and the usual society characters. There was even a champion boxer being mobbed by admirers while he toyed with a sliver of *pâté de foie gras* in an enormous fist.

Her gaze hovered over people with their noses in cocktail-glasses, or munching delicatessen delights, or filling the air with cigarette smoke and high-pitched chatter. For a moment she experienced the oddest sensation that she was watching the antics of a lot of specimens at the Zoo. Resolutely she pushed the absurd thought away. It was not often she found herself at an entertainment like this and she made up her mind unreservedly she was going to enjoy it. She looked round for Doone Drummer.

The author of *The Friendly Enemy* did not, however, appear to have arrived. No doubt, Miss Frayle conjectured, she will wait until the last moment to make her entrance. Miss Frayle had read about her and seen her photographs in the magazines and newspapers, and she had been anticipating meeting her. If her pictures were anything to go by she must be an extremely lovely young woman. Again an involuntary thought obtruded itself upon her enjoyment. It occurred to her that it was Doone Drummer's pulchritude as much as her literary ability which had boosted her into one of the most publicised personalities of the day.

'Do you see Doone Drummer?' Miss Frayle turned to Dr. Morelle.

'Whom?'

'Doone Drummer. She wrote *The Friendly Enemy*. Or are you going to pretend you don't know that all this is in aid of her?'

Whatever crushing reply the Doctor was preparing to deliver was destined to be lost to posterity. At that moment a slim, grey-haired man approached them. His strong, regular features were marred by a slightly strained expression.

'Dr. Morelle? I'm Harvey Drummer, Doone's father. I must apologise for not making myself known to you before. As a matter of fact I've been waiting for my daughter to arrive and introduce us.' He turned to Miss Frayle. 'You're Miss Frayle, of course.'

She smiled at him and then said: 'But the Doctor doesn't know Miss Drummer either. Do you, Doctor?'

'On the contrary,' he surprised her by replying, 'we have met.'

Drummer nodded. 'Doone told me. At the publishers.'

Miss Frayle stared up at the Doctor with a sudden feeling of uneasiness. She had been under the distinct impression that the publishers of some of his scientific works had invited him to the party. The same firm also happened to publish popular literature, and at the top of their list was *The Friendly Enemy*. Miss Frayle found it difficult to believe he had consciously misled her. All the same, she felt fairly certain he had conveyed to her the idea that he had accepted the invitation only because it was from his own publishers. It sounded now, however, as if Doone Drummer, whom she didn't know he had even met, had invited him.

She glanced sharply at that saturnine countenance. Could it be possible that as a result of this chance meeting that heart of ice had melted at last under a woman's spell? Miss Frayle, who was inclined to think sometimes in terms of romantic rhetoric, boggled at the idea. She recalled how he'd accepted the invitation which she had expected him to turn down flat. She dragged her gaze from his inscrutable face as Drummer, giving a swift glance round, turned to them again.

'Your daughter,' Dr. Morelle suggested, 'may be postponing her appearance until the last moment in order to achieve the maximum affect.'

'Frankly that's what I thought myself,' Drummer said. 'Though it would be very unlike her. Success hasn't gone to her head a bit.' The undercurrent of misgiving rose to the surface of his voice as he went on. 'You see I'm giving this party especially for her. Most of the guests are her friends, and she should have been here to receive them.'

'When did you see her last?' Miss Frayle asked.

There was an almost imperceptible pause before the other replied.

'Yesterday evening,' he said.

'Yesterday evening.' Miss Frayle stared at him.

'I assume that your daughter is of a somewhat independent nature?' Dr. Morelle queried smoothly.

'Definitely,' the other replied. 'And since her mother died some two years ago she's lived her own life. She has her own flat, her own car, and so on.'

'She impressed me as having a strongly individual character,' Dr. Morelle murmured. 'I seem to recall a marked resoluteness about the line of her chin.'

Once again Miss Frayle experienced a pang similar to the one she had felt at the apparent revelation that he had been invited to the party by Doone Drummer herself. Talking about the line of her chin! What could have come over him? Involuntarily she touched her own jaw, and then Harvey Drummer was saying:

'By that I don't mean we aren't the best of friends.' His expression relaxed momentarily with a faint smile. 'As a matter of fact her flat's only a stone's throw away, so we can be near each other.' He added: 'I hope you'll forgive me bothering you, only it's nearly an hour since she should have shown up. I suppose I'm — well — rather more anxious than I care to admit.' He forced another smile at the Doctor. 'Your reputation for being able to deal with situations of this sort prompted me to ask your advice.'

'You don't think she might have been taken ill?' Miss Frayle put in.

'If so, why hasn't she got in touch with me?'

'You have of course telephoned her

flat?' Dr. Morelle said.

'Several times. No reply.'

'Isn't there anyone here who might know something?' Miss Frayle said. The room seemed even more crowded, the atmosphere heavy with cigarette-smoke and chatter.

'I've already asked two or three of her friends, but none of them have seen her since yesterday. I can't very well go round tackling everyone; they'd start thinking something was wrong. That's another reason, Dr. Morelle, why I thought I'd ask you what I should do.'

'Have you any idea how your daughter occupied herself since you last saw her?'

'I knew she was lunching with someone today. She told me that this morning.'

'A moment ago you said you hadn't seen her since last night,' Dr. Morelle insinuated.

'Doone 'phoned me about one or two things to do with this party,' the other explained quickly. 'I'd forgotten that.'

'About what time was this telephone call?'

'It would be somewhere around twelve o'clock.'

'So although you had not set eyes on her since last night she had, in fact, spoken to you as recently as midday.'

Harvey Drummer nodded. 'It was then she told me she'd be lunching out. Though she didn't say where or who with. I gathered she'd be returning home to work — she's planning a new novel — until she came along here.'

'That is, of course,' Dr. Morelle murmured through a cloud of cigarette smoke, 'if it *was* her voice you heard.'

2

Where is Doone Drummer?

Dr. Morelle's words caused Miss Frayle to start slightly. Harvey Drummer drew in a sharp breath and muttered jerkily:

'But — but who else could it have been?'

'Dr. Morelle means,' Miss Frayle said, 'it might have been someone imitating her.'

Drummer stared hard at the Doctor.

'Miss Frayle, as usual, has interpreted my meaning admirably. The possibility, however, merits consideration,' he went on. 'Unless, that is — ' Deliberately he left the sentence dangling in mid-air.

'Unless what?' the other asked quickly.

'Unless you are positive beyond all doubt it *was* your daughter's voice.'

'I'm positive.'

Dr. Morelle gave a little shrug and stared abstractedly at the tip of his *Le*

Sphinx. 'In that case we may forget the idea.'

'But how can you be sure, Mr. Drummer?' Miss Frayle persisted.

'Doone's voice is unmistakable. It's low and sort of husky. And her drawly way of speaking — I *know* it was her.'

'I seem to recall the characteristics, you mention,' Dr. Morelle mused, 'upon the occasion of our meeting.'

You seem to recall a lot about it, Miss Frayle commented to herself, considering you only saw her for such a short time! She said: 'I should have thought such an individual voice would have been all the easier to imitate.'

Harvey Drummer shook his head. 'It wasn't only her voice. We discussed matters to do with this party, for instance, which only she could have known.'

'Oh.' Miss Frayle subsided.

'It seems evident that we can reject the theory that anyone else but your daughter telephoned,' Dr. Morelle said.

'Then what's the next step?' Drummer asked.

Dr. Morelle glanced about him before

replying. 'If the next step conveyed us to an atmosphere more conducive to speculation,' he suggested. And the other responded promptly.

'Of course, of course. Let's get away from all this.' He indicated a sparse black-coated figure across the room who was actively engaged in re-filling some glasses. 'I'll just tell Brethers in case I should be wanted.'

A few minutes later found them in a room from which the noise of the party was practically excluded. It was quietly furnished in definitely masculine taste. Sporting prints and trophies. By a leather armchair stood a large bowl of pipes of all shapes and sizes. Some black and worn, some newer. But it was a photograph which attracted Miss Frayle's immediate attention, and she kept stealing a look at it. She hadn't seen this portrait of Doone Drummer before. No doubt, she decided, its composition was too simple and delicate for ordinary magazine or newspaper reproduction.

'Have you considered,' Dr. Morelle was remarking to Drummer, 'that your daughter's absence may be part of a plan designed to publicise her novel?'

'She'd never leave me in the dark, even if she decided to do a thing like that. Which she wouldn't.'

'Someone might have persuaded her to lend herself to such a scheme.'

Harvey Drummer put the drink he had brought with him down on the table, took a cigarette from a large silver box. He said with finality: 'No one could persuade her to do anything she didn't want to do.'

'I should have thought,' Miss Frayle put forward, 'she couldn't get much more publicity than she's had already.'

Drummer nodded over the flame of his cigarette-lighter. 'I think we can rule out any idea of a publicity stunt.'

'She must have been taken ill,' Miss Frayle went on. 'Or — or there's been an accident.'

'But surely someone would have got in touch with me by now? If anything had happened to her when she was out she would have had her handbag with her. Anyone could have checked who she was.'

'Supposing her handbag had been

stolen,' Miss Frayle suggested, 'and she met with an accident afterwards?'

'Even then, the very fact that she's had so much publicity would make it easy to identify her.'

'That's true.' Miss Frayle gave a sigh of defeat.

There was a little silence. Through the open windows came the hum of the evening traffic of Park Lane. As Drummer turned to Dr. Morelle Miss Frayle's gaze was held for a moment by his hand holding his cigarette. It was shaking visibly. She realised that beneath his apparently calm exterior his concern for his daughter was torturing him.

She glanced at the Doctor. He had just turned from the photograph which had attracted her attention, and there was an expression on his face which she found difficult to analyse. She thought she detected the shadow of a smile at the corners of his mouth. But what sort of smile? Of admiration? Of derision? Or was it that he already knew why she had not turned up? She broke off her conjectures as he observed:

15

'Regarding your telephone conversation at midday. A point occurs to me — '

'What is that?'

'Was your daughter speaking from her own flat?'

'You mean,' Miss Frayle broke in excitedly, 'she might have been decoyed and then forced to — ?'

Dr. Morelle subjected her to a withering glance and she relapsed into silence.

'Certainly she was 'phoning from her flat,' Drummer said. 'She would have told me if she was anywhere else, I'm sure.' A sudden thought appeared to strike him. 'Besides, I remember before she rang off I said something about I'd ring her back if I'd anything more to ask her about this evening's arrangements.'

'But you didn't ring her back?' Miss Frayle asked.

'No.' He said to the Doctor: 'I thought of going round to her flat, only it would mean leaving all these people here. And of course I've been hoping she'd turn up any minute.'

Dr. Morelle gave him a slight nod. 'You

mentioned just now that your daughter owned a car. Would she have gone for a drive somewhere, either before or after her lunch appointment?'

The other's reply was prompt enough. 'Her car's laid up at the moment, being overhauled.' He paused, staring down at his glass. Then with a quick gulp drained it and braced himself. 'What shall I do?' he said. 'Call in the police?'

Dr. Morelle had moved to the window. Already the street lamps and car lights glimmered against the bluish-grey backdrop that was beginning to descend over Hyde Park. At that moment the telephone rang. Drummer turned to answer it. But before he could do so the Doctor had whipped away from the window, and with a hawk-like movement pounced on the telephone. With a bland smile he queried:

'Shall I answer it?'

Harvey Drummer hesitated only momentarily. 'Go ahead,' he said.

'Hello,' Dr. Morelle said into the mouthpiece, while the other two watched him intently. There was a pause and they caught the distorted mutter of a voice at the other end. It sounded as if it might be a man's voice.

'This is Mr. Drummer's house,' the Doctor said. 'Do you wish to speak to him personally?'

Drummer made a move to take the telephone. The muttering continued, and Dr. Morelle motioned him to wait. Then the voice at the other end went suddenly silent. After a moment Dr. Morelle replaced the receiver.

'What — what did he say?' Miss Frayle gulped.

'It was a man, wasn't it?' Drummer asked.

The Doctor inclined his head. 'His message was succinct and to the point,' he said. And Miss Frayle caught the speculative look in his eyes. 'He said: 'Tell Drummer if he wants to see his daughter again he'd better follow the instructions I've left at her flat.''

'Oh!' Miss Frayle squeaked.

'What — what does it mean?' Harvey Drummer's voice was low and tense.

'I am not in the habit of generalising on

a situation the details of which are not clear to me,' Dr. Morelle replied. 'But I suggest it means we should proceed to your daughter's flat without delay.'

3

At Dark Lantern Street

Doone Drummer's flat turned out to be on the ground floor of a narrow-fronted, three-storey house in Dark Lantern Street, that cobbled, almost alley-like thoroughfare which cuts through from Park Street to Park Lane. The entrance-hall of the house led to the basement and upper floors, and the flat was on the right as they went in. The main door, heavy and dark-painted, with an arched transom over it, was open. Harvey Drummer explained it was closed after dark. They followed him along the hall, and he let them into the flat with a key.

'We both have a key to each other's front door,' he said.

As the carefully subdued light sprang from two standard lamps, Miss Frayle's glance followed the line of low built-in bookshelves running round the pale green walls. The room was heavy with the scent of flowers.

With long raking strides Dr. Morelle reached the flat-topped writing desk by the tall windows.

'The note!' Drummer exclaimed, as the Doctor bent over the typewriter which was surrounded by note-books and typing-paper. In the machine a half-sheet of paper projected prominently above the keys.

'Do not touch it,' Dr. Morelle said. 'There may be fingerprints.'

The note was typed.

Dear Mr. Drummer, — Your daughter is safe and sound. She is somewhere it will be impossible for you to find. If you want her back alive I am afraid it is going to cost you money. How much I will let you know later. Also how, when and where it is to be paid. Don't call in the police. You are under observation, so don't try any tricks.

Dr. Morelle glanced at the man by his side. Harvey Drummer might have been turned into stone. He stood there speechless. Miss Frayle, who had joined them, gave a low gasp of horror.

'It isn't signed,' Drummer found his voice and muttered automatically. 'I suppose — ' He broke off and then went on again. 'You don't think it could be somebody fooling?'

Dr. Morelle regarded him thoughtfully. 'Can you think of anyone who might be capable of perpetrating a practical joke of this nature?'

The other shook his head. He passed his hand over his face as if to push away the bewilderment that seemed to have stunned him.

'Nobody could be so cruel,' Miss Frayle said.

'It has every appearance of having been written in all seriousness,' was Dr. Morelle's opinion.

'Kidnapped,' Drummer said slowly. 'It's unbelievable.'

There was a heavy silence. Dr. Morelle gazed round the room and asked:

'I presume that your daughter employs domestic help only during the daytime?'

Harvey Drummer made a tremendous effort to pull himself together.

'A sort of housekeeper comes in every morning. Stays to prepare lunch and only comes back in the evening if she's needed.'

'Apparently she was not required tonight,' Dr. Morelle commented. 'Which suggests that your daughter anticipated dining out.'

'Not necessarily. When Doone was working she often preferred to get her own meals.'

The Doctor gave the typewritten message a further scrutiny. Then he moved away from the writing-desk to pause before the bookshelves. They watched him as he peered at the tightly-packed books. His gaze moved along them, then hovered for a moment. 'Freud's *Civilisation and Its Discontent*, he murmured half to himself. 'Adler . . . Jung *and* the other school, I perceive . . . Pavlov . . . Watson . . . ' Over his shoulder he observed: 'Your daughter would appear to be a student of the subconscious.'

'She was very interested in psychology

and that sort of thing.'

Dr. Morelle suddenly picked out a book and flipped its pages. Miss Frayle thought she detected a faint smirk light up his face. She was unable to resist querying artlessly:

'One of yours, Doctor?'

He threw her a side-long glance. 'It does happen to be my collected papers on Lombroso's *L'Uomo Delinquente*,'[1] he replied. 'Pity,' he said, 'had I known she wanted to read it I could have presented her with a copy. Autographed,' he added, and returned the book to its place.

Harvey Drummer made a restless movement.

'Don't — don't you think we ought to do something?'

Dr. Morelle looked at him over his *Le Sphinx*. 'Your view is that the situation

---

[1] Published by Manning & Hopper (London) and Karter (New York). As already stated, Dr. Morelle has disposed of Lombroso's theory that physiognomy has any scientific basis for the determination of character

demands immediate and dramatic action?' As the other started to speak the Doctor proceeded smoothly. 'Accept my assurance that my apparent leisurely attitude is definitely warrantable. It is absolutely essential that the initial moves in this matter should be carefully weighed before putting them into effect.'

'But they may kill her — murder her — '

'Such a possibility at this juncture is so unlikely that we can safely discard it.'

'Why do you think that?'

'I do not think,' Dr. Morelle remarked coolly, 'I *know* that at present your daughter is in no danger of being murdered.'

'You honestly mean that?' The note of relief sounded in Harvey Drummer's voice. 'How *do* you know that?'

Dr. Morelle glanced at him as he tapped the ash off his cigarette. He murmured urbanely:

'Because of the evidence before our eyes.'

'Evidence?'

Frankly mystified Drummer stared

round the room. Automatically Miss Frayle followed his gaze and then turned back to the Doctor.

'Evidence?' she echoed.

Dr. Morelle inclined his head towards the writing desk.

'I do not expect you, my dear Miss Frayle, to see the importance of the most self-evident phenomenon until it has been explained to you in detail.' He turned to the other. 'But surely you, however, have grasped the significance of that message in one vital aspect.'

Harvey Drummer stared at the piece of paper stuck in the typewriter, and then back at Dr. Morelle.

'I — I don't quite see — '

The Doctor compressed his lips into a thin line of impatience.

'Surely,' he said, 'the object of your daughter's abduction is expressed with crystal clarity.'

'To get money, you mean?'

'To extract money from *you*,' Dr. Morelle said. 'The publicity given to your daughter such as, for instance, her recent business transaction with a Hollywood studio, has prompted this kidnapping, from which it should not be difficult to deduce that the kidnapper's aim is to separate her money from her rather than yours from you.'

'Doone certainly has made a terrific amount recently. She's decidedly better off than I am.'

'And her money is, no doubt, banked in her own name?'

'Yes.' Slowly.

'It therefore follows,' Dr. Morelle pointed out, 'that in order for you to obtain the money to effect her release she will be required to authorise you to draw from her bank.'

'That's true.'

'I hadn't thought of that,' Miss Frayle said.

'You amaze me,' was the Doctor's inevitable retort, and Miss Frayle bit her lip and was silent, at any rate for the moment.

'You mean then,' Harvey Drummer went on eagerly, 'that they daren't harm her or she won't be able to give me the necessary authorisation.'

'And that being so,' the Doctor continued, 'it is clearly in their interests, for the present at any rate, to guard her welfare with the utmost care. One would have imagined,' he added as a humorless afterthought, 'that *you* would have been the most appropriate person to abduct.'

'I wish it had been me,' the other declared fervently.

'No doubt,' murmured Dr. Morelle. 'But then criminals as a class are singularly devoid of imagination.'

'Anyway, Doctor, I believe you're absolutely right about her being safe for now,' Harvey Drummer said, optimistic excitement slackening the tension that had gripped him.

Dr. Morelle made no reply, though from his expression he made it obvious that he had no doubts whatever regarding his infallibility. He stood by the green-coloured telephone that was on an upper bookshelf.

'Miss Frayle,' he directed, 'bring me a sheet of typing paper.'

She obeyed with alacrity, and he took the piece of paper from her and curved it in his hand. She remained at his elbow watching him intently. He said to her:

'If I might use some of your face-powder.'

'Face-powder,' she said, puzzled.

Deliberately misunderstanding her he snapped:

'Only a small portion, which considering the amount you waste on yourself you should not miss.'

She continued to gape at him for a moment, then dived into her handbag and quickly produced a compact. She opened it for him, and he tipped some powder into the curved paper. Then he carefully blew the powder on to the telephone while she watched him, puzzled and intrigued by his performance.

'What's the idea, Doctor?' Harvey Drummer asked.

'I'm dusting the instrument in order to ascertain whether the last person to use it left any fingerprints.'

'The chap who 'phoned just now?'

Dr. Morelle was gently blowing away the powder, which covered the telephone receiver in a fine dust, scrutinising its surface closely as he did so.

'Any luck, Doctor?' Miss Frayle queried.

There was no answer for a moment. Both of them watched him silently, and then he straightened himself.

'I can find no signs of it having been used by anyone recently.'

'So he wore gloves, or was smart enough to clean the 'phone afterwards with his handkerchief?'

Dr. Morelle eyed Drummer quizzically.

'Or, alternatively, he telephoned not from here but from a public call box.'

'Funny he should have done that,' the other said slowly, 'when he could have made the call before he left.'

'It is of relatively little importance,' Dr. Morelle shrugged, 'where he made the call from.'

'I suppose so. What ought to be the next move?'

Dr. Morelle made no answer. After a moment it was Miss Frayle who suddenly threw a glance at the door, and said in a tense whisper:

'Doctor — !'

He turned to her slowly.

'What is it?'

'Do you hear what I hear?'

'If you mean the sound of footsteps in the hall,' he said, 'I do.'

'It's someone coming in!' Miss Frayle clutched convulsively at his arm. 'They've stopped outside.'

The approaching footsteps had stopped at the door and they heard a key turn in the lock. Harvey Drummer swung round and was staring as if he expected the appearance of a ghost, as Miss Frayle gulped in another whisper:

'Who can it be?'

The door opened.

4

The Visitor

Miss Frayle's heart was thudding in her throat. She had no idea whom it might be, but she felt it in her bones that the newcomer was bound to be mixed up in some way with the mysterious kidnapping of Doone Drummer. She gave a little gasp at the figure who stood staring at them from behind an armful of flowers.

Miss Frayle's gasp may have been one of surprise or even disappointment, but she had certainly expected a somewhat more sinister figure than this. Anything less sinister than this tallish, good-looking young man who stood framed in the doorway it would have been difficult to imagine. There was also something about his features which she found vaguely familiar. She felt sure she had seen him somewhere, if only she could place him.

'What goes on?' the newcomer queried, taking a few tentative steps into the room. 'Who are you, and where's Miss Drummer?'

'I happen to be her father,' Harvey Drummer said.

'Oh . . . I didn't know.'

'I don't recall the pleasure of having met you,' Drummer said.

'My name's Fulton. Neil Fulton.'

'That's where I've seen you!' Miss Frayle exclaimed. 'The film actor.'

He gave her a faint smile.

Drummer said: 'This is Miss Frayle and Dr. Morelle. Incidentally, might I ask how you happen to have a key to my daughter's flat?'

'She lent it me,' was the easy reply. The young man closed the door behind him, glanced down at the flowers he was hugging, and with a grin that was without any self-consciousness, put them carefully upon a table. 'You see,' he explained, 'Doone knew I might be late from the studio, and we arranged that I should come straight here and duck her party. I'm not very good at parties.'

'You seem to be quite friendly with my daughter.'

'We've been around together a little.' Suddenly he looked at Miss Frayle, then Dr. Morelle, and then back to Drummer with a frown.

'Is there anything wrong?' His voice took an upward inflection. 'Nothing's the matter with her?'

Harvey Drummer turned to Dr. Morelle questioningly. The Doctor, who had remained impassively silent since Fulton's appearance, interpreted the look. He responded with a slight nod.

'I'm afraid something has happened,' Drummer told the newcomer quietly.

Fulton tensed, and Miss Frayle thought he suddenly looked a little wary.

'What?'

'She's been kidnapped.'

The film-actor's mouth fell open. 'Kidnapped!' he said incredulously. 'But this is fantastic.'

Drummer shook his head slowly. 'It may seem like that,' he said heavily. 'But it's true enough.'

'Doone kidnapped? Who on earth

could have done such a thing?'

'That,' Dr. Morelle said at last, 'is what I am in the process of elucidating.'

Fulton stared at him uncertainly.

Drummer said: 'Dr. Morelle has already started the job of trying to find her.'

'I've heard about the Doctor, of course,' the young man said, with, Miss Frayle felt, a shade of doubt in his tone.

'I am suitably flattered,' Dr. Morelle murmured.

Then as Miss Frayle was thinking to herself that he had missed the other's dubious note, Fulton went on:

'But I should have thought — ' He broke off.

'What would you have thought?'

Fulton hesitated at Dr. Morelle's question, and looked somewhat embarrassed.

'I was going to say,' he mumbled, 'I should have thought it was a job for the police.'

'You might care to take a look at the message the kidnapper left,' Drummer cut in. 'It's all right for him to see it?' he said to Dr. Morelle.

The Doctor nodded.

'In the typewriter,' Drummer told Fulton. And as the young man crossed to the writing-desk he added: 'Dr. Morelle doesn't want it touched.'

Miss Frayle watched Fulton's lips moving as he read the message to himself, then he looked up at Dr. Morelle and said:

'Seems as if we daren't call 'em in.'

'If we do . . . ' Drummer left the rest of his sentence unfinished, his mouth a grim line.

'The situation might become dangerous for Miss Drummer,' Dr. Morelle declared, 'if we fail to proceed with the utmost caution.'

'Damn lucky you happened to be around,' Neil Fulton said to him.

'Yes,' agreed Drummer fervently. 'If you hadn't been invited along this evening I don't know whom I should have turned to.'

'If only there was something I could do,' the film actor exclaimed, 'but I can't even think. I feel just as if I'd been hit on the head with a sledgehammer.'

'There is a way in which you might be of assistance.'

Fulton turned eagerly to Dr. Morelle. 'How? What can I do?'

'Answer one or two questions.'

Neil Fulton hesitated, and a faintly guarded expression appeared at the back of his eyes. He said:

'I don't see how anything I can tell you will be of much use.'

'I recall many instances when a seemingly unimportant detail has provided a vital clue.'

Dr. Morelle's tone was smooth, but Miss Frayle wondered if there wasn't a hint of suspicion in his voice. Could it be he suspected the young film-actor himself of being implicated in Doone Drummer's disappearance?

'You mentioned just now,' the Doctor was saying, 'how Miss Drummer lent you a key of her flat.'

'Yes.'

'When exactly did she give you the key?'

'At lunch,' the other said promptly.

'It was you, then, Doone was lunching with today,' Harvey Drummer said.

Fulton nodded. 'We went up to Hampstead to see a film-writer I know. Doone had an idea for a film. There was a part in it which was just what I always wanted to play. I took her up to see this chap and we discussed it over lunch at his house. I had to leave afterwards to get down to the studio.'

'And the name of your friend?'

'Leo Rolf. Lives in Heath Lane, Hampstead Village. He'll confirm what I've just told you.'

Dr. Morelle caught the sting in the other's voice, and replied urbanely:

'I am merely seeking some hint which, while it might have escaped you, could perhaps be the first piece in the puzzle I am trying to solve.'

'I realise that.'

'It was during this lunch,' Dr. Morelle went on, 'that you arranged with Miss Drummer to come back here this evening instead of going to her party?'

'That's why she gave me the key.'

'Did you make this arrangement in the

presence of your friend at Hampstead?'

Neil Fulton nodded. 'Leo made some silly joke about it.'

'What sort of silly joke?'

'Oh . . . ' Fulton looked vague. 'It was just a remark typical of his sophisticated sense of humour.'

'I see.' Dr. Morelle paused for a moment. 'And when you left your sophisticated friend's house Miss Drummer remained behind.'

'That's right. They went on discussing her film idea over coffee.'

'And that was the last time you saw her?'

'Yes,' the other said uneasily, his face clouding over.

'Have you seen this Leo Rolf since?'

'No. I was going to talk to Doone about him this evening to know if they decided anything about this film story.'

'When you left them together at his home in Hampstead you went straight to the film studio where you remained?'

'Till I finished,' the film-actor said emphatically, 'and came on here.'

'Where did you purchase the flowers?'

Miss Frayle's eyes behind her spectacles widened as she waited for Fulton to extricate himself from the trap into which Dr. Morelle had neatly lured him.

'I didn't,' was the answer, accompanied by a glimmer of a smile. 'They've been used in a scene we filmed this afternoon, and I scrounged them for Doone.'

Dr. Morelle took his time, tapping the ash off his *Le Sphinx* before he observed:

'You have, of course, appreciated one small fact which my questions have already brought to light?' He waited for Fulton's response. There was none forthcoming, and he went on: 'We have established that your friend is, according to what we have so far ascertained, the last person to see Miss Drummer before she disappeared.'

There was a little movement from Harvey Drummer. Both he and Miss Frayle stared at Neil Fulton with renewed interest.

'It could certainly look that way. I'll 'phone him at once in case he can tell us something.'

'Do, by all means,' Dr. Morelle said.

The other crossed purposefully to the telephone. Taking a small diary from his inside pocket he found the entry he wanted. He lifted the receiver and dialled.

Miss Frayle could hear the distant burr-burr. Harvey Drummer was tense with anxiety as he waited for the ringing to be answered. Dr. Morelle, on the other hand, dragged at his cigarette and gazed abstractedly round the room.

'Doesn't seem to be any reply,' Fulton said. 'May have got a dinner date or something.' He gave it a few more moments, then, shaking his head, replaced the receiver.

'You've no idea where he may be?' Drummer asked.

'Not the faintest.'

'He wasn't by any chance invited to the party?' Miss Frayle put in quickly.

'No, I'm sure of that. Doone or Leo would surely have mentioned it at lunch.'

'I certainly don't recall hearing his name,' Drummer said.

'I suppose I could 'phone round the various restaurants where he might be,' Fulton suggested. 'I'm trying to think,' he went on with a frown of concentration, 'of any of his friends I know who could tell me where he is. There was some club he was a member of, too. But the name of it's gone.'

Dr. Morelle stirred. Carefully he stubbed out his cigarette and observed quietly. 'I fear you may be attaching too much importance to him. Unless, of course,' with a look at Fulton, 'you have any grounds for suspecting that he might be implicated in this affair.'

'Good heavens, no! If you knew Leo you'd realise that was too fantastic.'

'That being so,' Dr. Morelle said smoothly, 'it seems we can assume that he and Miss Drummer concluded their discussion and she made her departure in a perfectly ordinary way.'

'I feel sure of it,' Neil Fulton agreed.

After a moment's pause Dr. Morelle continued: 'We might acquaint this man at the earliest possible moment of what has transpired,' he said. 'In case he is able to suggest a further clue.'

'I'll give you his 'phone number,' Fulton said promptly. 'You can get in touch with him yourself any time.'

'That would be advisable. Miss Frayle will make a note of it.'

Miss Frayle was perched on the arm of a chair scribbling down the number from Fulton's diary, when the telephone rang again. She gave a startled exclamation, and only just saved herself from losing her balance. She looked up to see Dr. Morelle's sardonic eye fastened upon her. She tried unsuccessfully to stop herself blushing with embarrassment.

'Shall I answer it?' Harvey Drummer said anxiously, 'or would it be better if you — '

Dr. Morelle, however, had already picked up the receiver.

'Is that Dr. Morelle?' a voice said over the wire.

The Doctor at once recognised it as the voice that had spoken to him before. The same curiously muffled tone. The same suggestion that the speaker was deliberately disguising his voice. But this time the caller knew he was Dr. Morelle.

Even as the Doctor wondered how the

other was aware of his identity, the voice said:

'Don't be shy, Doctor. I know it's you. Surprised? May be even more surprises heading your way if you don't watch out.'

Dr. Morelle made no reply. He was quite prepared to let the other do all the talking at this stage. His turn would, no doubt, come later.

'Who is it?' Harvey Drummer at his elbow asked quickly.

Dr. Morelle covered the receiver with his hand. 'Our friend again,' he said.

'The kidnapper?' Fulton exclaimed.

He and Miss Frayle had also moved nearer. They could catch the blurred mutter of the speaker at the other end. Dr. Morelle was listening intently.

'So Drummer's called you in instead of the police?' the voice mocked him. 'I do hope that doesn't mean *you're* going to be so foolish as to try to discover who I am? Or where Miss Drummer is? You will have read the note I left behind for her father — this is a further warning, that unless he does exactly as he's told I shall go ahead and carry out my threat.'

'What's he saying?' Drummer whispered.

Dr. Morelle motioned him to silence.

'I'm simply acting on Mr. Drummer's behalf,' he said into the 'phone. 'This has come as a great shock to him and he sought my help. I have, in fact, dissuaded him from calling the police, in favour of obeying your instructions.'

Despite the fever of excitement which was gripping her, Miss Frayle couldn't help catching a note in the Doctor's voice which she never remembered having heard before. That sarcastic bite, that cutting edge, was tempered now with a soothing quality, as if butter wouldn't melt in his mouth. She realised he was, of course, anxious that the kidnapper's suspicions should remain completely lulled. All the same, this was a new facet of his personality which he had never presented to her before.

'Good for you,' the voice was saying in Dr. Morelle's ear, 'and now get this. If he is prepared to do as I say tell him to put an advert. in the Personal Column of the *Evening Globe*. Just say he'd like to hear about his daughter. That's all. To-morrow's issue. *Evening Globe*. Remember?'

'I have already made a mental note of what you say.'

'Then he'll hear from me how much I want and how it's to be handed over. And don't forget, Dr. Morelle, no funny business. I'm sure we understand each other.'

The speaker hung up.

After a moment Dr. Morelle replaced the receiver, an enigmatic expression on his gaunt face.

5

The Photograph

The man had used a handkerchief over the mouthpiece of the telephone to muffle his voice. He unwrapped it from the receiver and pushed it into his pocket. He pulled off a pair of black, silk gloves, folded them carefully and slipped them into another pocket. He stood motionless and massaged a smooth-shaven chin thoughtfully. His eyes were flat and expressionless. He might have been 'phoning the grocer for all the emotion he showed.

He touched his tie with the tips of his fingers. It was an automatic movement. It betrayed the tension he was putting on his nerves, but there was nothing else to show he was in any way keyed-up. His hands were well-kept and curiously muscular, the muscle between each thumb and index finger making a hard bulge. He could hear his heart beating. Steady, slow, rhythmically.

Suddenly his head jerked round. His eyes narrowed, and with a swift movement he went to the door and pulled it open.

No one.

He relaxed, a little sigh hissing between his clenched teeth. He knew it was almost impossible for anyone to have been out there listening, but it had been risky. He had taken a chance, however small, making the call from here. It was just one of these little risks, he knew, that could trip him. But there wasn't anyone there so it was all right. No one had been listening outside the door.

He crossed back into the room. His gaze went over it, took in the telephone and round about it. He made sure his handkerchief and gloves were safe in his pockets. He closed the door and started back towards that other room he had left a few minutes before. He paused involuntarily as he realised it was only a few minutes and not some immeasurable eon ago. That was the way your nerves played tricks on you. That was the way you knew the strain bit into your resources. The tricks your nerves played on you, like making you feel you'd taken hours over a small thing like a 'phone call.

He gave a little shrug and walked on again unhurriedly.

★   ★   ★

'You think I ought to do exactly what he says, Doctor?'

Dr. Morelle looked up from the telephone book and nodded.

'It is vital to appear to agree with his requests,' he said emphatically, 'not only so that he will refrain from any precipitate action which might imperil your daughter's safety — '

'We mustn't run any risk of that,' Drummer said quickly, his voice heavy with apprehension.

'But at the same time,' Dr. Morelle continued, 'to lull him into a feeling of security.'

It was a few minutes after the man who

claimed to have kidnapped Doone Drummer had rung off.

Dr. Morelle had spoken to the telephone exchange in an effort to trace the number from which the caller had spoken. As he had anticipated, the only information he had obtained was that the call must have come from a dialling telephone which was impossible to check. Dr. Morelle's conjecture that he was pitting himself against no amateur bungler but a cunning and subtly resourceful adversary, was further strengthened.

'I must say, I should have thought — ' began Neil Fulton, only to break off and chew his lower lip moodily.

'What were you going to say?' Miss Frayle asked.

The other hesitated, throwing a look at the Doctor before he went on:

'I should have thought — and I say it with due respect to Dr. Morelle — that in spite of this blighter's threats we could have gone to the police.'

'No!' Drummer turned to Dr. Morelle. 'I agree with what you say. To go to Scotland Yard would risk Doone's life.'

Dr. Morelle closed the telephone book and moved towards them. He said to Miss Frayle:

'The number is Circus 1000. Perhaps you would obtain it for Mr. Drummer.' With a glance at the film-actor he said to Drummer: 'Since you are fully agreeable to my plan — '

'I am. Definitely.'

Dr. Morelle inclined his head. 'Then there remains no more to be said on that score. Unless,' he turned to Fulton, 'you feel your responsibility for the young woman is greater than her father's.'

There was a short silence, during which Miss Frayle, looking up from dialling the number which she had been given, observed Neil Fulton to appear uncomfortable for the first time since his appearance on the scene.

'I — I like her very much,' he finally blurted out. 'That's all.'

He's madly in love with her, of course, Miss Frayle decided at once. She was energetically weaving highly-coloured romances of the film-actor's love, at first unrequited, for the best-selling novelist, when her speculations were interrupted by a voice over the wire.

'*Evening Globe*. Classified Ads.'

'Mr. Drummer,' Miss Frayle said.

Drummer crossed quickly to the 'phone with the slip of paper he carried. The man at the other end was suitably impressed when Drummer guardedly explained to him the vital urgency of the advertisement, and he began to read it out. It had been carefully worded under Dr. Morelle's guidance. After a few minutes he replaced the receiver.

'That's that,' he said. 'In the Personal Column to-morrow all right. They can have my cheque in the morning.' He drew a deep breath. 'Then all we do is wait.' It was as if he were about to sag at the knees, and then by a great effort pulled himself together. 'I suppose I, anyway, should be getting back to my house — all those people there. If anyone asks, I'd better say Doone's been taken ill. Eh, Doctor?'

'Yes.' He had been eyeing the other carefully. 'And I think,' he said, 'I might prescribe a slight sedative for you. It will achieve no good purpose for you to spend a sleepless night.'

'Thank you. Afraid I'll need something like that. I imagine you and Miss Frayle won't be returning to the party now.'

The Doctor shook his head.

'I'd better be getting along home too,' Neil Fulton said. 'Been about as much use as a sick-headache,' he added despairingly. 'But there just doesn't seem anything I can do — devil's got us right where he wants us.' He chewed his lower lip again. 'Like to 'phone you in the morning,' he said to Drummer, who gave him a nod. 'Just in case you've got any news.'

As they started towards the door Dr. Morelle suddenly murmured in Fulton's ear:

'In answer to a question I put to you just now, you expressed a regard for Miss Drummer which it occurs to me was somewhat inadequate.'

Fulton wheeled on him with an involuntary exclamation. 'What d'you mean?'

The Doctor regarded him with the

faintest hint of amusement touching the corner of his mouth. It struck Miss Frayle that it must be decidedly ironic amusement, however, and she promptly felt a surge of sympathy for the young man.

'I was merely pondering the possibility,' Dr. Morelle said coolly, 'of your cherishing a slightly deeper affection for her.'

'I'm damned if I see what it's got to do with you,' the other flared up.

'You force me to remind you that I am attempting to solve the mystery of Miss Drummer's disappearance. I am therefore entitled to any information concerning her.' And Dr. Morelle's jaws closed with a snap.

'Are you in love with her?' Harvey Drummer fired at Fulton point blank.

Neil Fulton paused for a moment. The smoke curled up from Dr. Morelle's cigarette. Miss Frayle's eyes were like saucers behind her horn-rims, as she waited with breathless expectancy for the reply, for she was certain she knew what it would be. It flashed across her mind that of all the characters Neil Fulton had portrayed on the screen, none could have been placed in a more dramatic scene than that in which he now found himself. Inconsequentially she wondered if he was automatically making mental notes of the situation to utilise for a future screen part.

'I suppose I am — well — just a bit crazy about her,' Fulton said slowly. 'Not that I mean a thing in her life,' he added.

'Doone isn't in love with you?' Drummer asked.

'Not yet, anyway.' Smiling ruefully.

'What makes you feel your affection is unrequited?' Dr. Morelle queried.

'How d'you know when it's raining? Besides, I've an idea there's someone else.'

'Someone else?' Drummer exclaimed.

'Whom?' the Doctor asked quietly.

'Only an idea of mine,' the film-actor said hurriedly. 'I may be wrong.'

'But you must have a reason for it,' Drummer insisted.

'I tell you I haven't any reason. It's just an impression I've had most of the time I've known her. After all, that isn't so very long — '

'Did she ever say anything?' Drummer again.

'It was more what she didn't say.'

Miss Frayle flashed Neil Fulton a look of complete understanding. Of course it was what a woman didn't say that often meant more than mere words when she was in love. She gave a tiny sigh, which she hurriedly turned into a cough as she caught Dr. Morelle's derisive glance fixed on her.

'Though, as a matter of fact,' the young man was saying, 'there was something that started me off thinking if there might be someone in the background.' He frowned as if trying to refresh his memory. 'It was after the *première* of some movie, and she asked me in for a drink. I was looking round at her books, and happened to spot one that interested me. As I opened it a picture fell out. A photo of a man. Before I'd time to pick it up and see who it was she snatched it. She seemed a bit flustered, slipped the photo back in the book and replaced it where I'd found it.'

Harvey Drummer's expression was a

mixture of surprise and heavy concern. Obviously, Miss Frayle concluded, his daughter had not confided the innermost secrets of her heart to him.

Dr. Morelle's eyes were heavy-lidded as he brooded over his cigarette. Watching him it seemed to Miss Frayle that the room had become charged with a sudden tension. Could it be that the young film-actor had revealed a clue that was destined to be of vital importance.

The clue of the photograph?

Dr. Morelle's voice cut across the questions that were chasing their tails round Miss Frayle's brain.

'You can recall the book in which the picture was concealed?'

Fulton's brow corrugated as he glanced round the room.

'Somewhere over here, I think.' He moved to the books beside the fireplace. He halted, and ran his eye along the shelves. Harvey Drummer and Miss Frayle followed him.

Dr. Morelle remained where he was, tall, and darkly aloof, his attitude deceptively nonchalant. Suddenly Fulton bent with an exclamation. 'This is it, I'll bet.' His eyes flicked over the title of the book he had picked out. ' 'The Collected Poems of John Donne',' he quoted.

Eagerly he riffled the pages. He stopped suddenly.

'Is it there?'

It was Drummer's voice, a harsh whisper, his jaw jutting forward. The other made no reply. He continued to stare down at the open pages.

'Is it the photo?' Miss Frayle squeaked.

Neil Fulton looked up and nodded. 'Looks as if it's been cut out of a magazine.'

'Who the devil is it?' Drummer queried impatiently, and moved to him quickly. He took the glossy clipping, then he, too, gaped at it unbelievingly. 'Well I'll be damned,' he gulped. Miss Frayle was at his elbow. She, too, stared in turn at the picture.

It was a photograph of Dr. Morelle!

6

The House in Heath Lane

The man tapped on the taxi-cab window behind the driver.

'Stop here.'

The taxi pulled up and the man got out, paid it off and stood watching the taxi until it disappeared round the corner. He always preferred to walk this bit of the way at night. It made a pleasant walk, the narrow grove, dark and shadowed, with at intervals the lamp-light making the trees gold and green oases, and then dark and shadowed again.

He walked slowly up the hill, leaning forward against the incline, and stopping every few yards to gaze around him and take deep breaths of the cool night breeze. It was impossible to believe that the glow away to the right was London; you might be miles from any city, it was so quiet and peaceful. The houses on the opposite side had narrow gardens running down to them, their roofs were below road-level so that he could look straight across Hampstead Heath.

Beneath the brim of his dark hat Leo Rolf was smiling to himself. It wasn't a smile of amusement. More like the sort of look a cat might wear after it had been let loose among a batch of chickens. It was a sleek smile of self-satisfaction.

He stopped at a small house half-way between the pools of light from two street lamps. Directly in front of it a tree trembled and whispered, and the house standing back a little from the houses on either side had the appearance of being drawn in upon itself, as if it were watchful and waiting. The front-door opened on to a few shallow steps to the pavement. He let himself in with one of the keys on his silver key-chain, closed the door behind him.

He walked through slowly into his study. His movements were relaxed as he took a cigarette from the box on his writing-desk and lit it. Then he went to a side-table and mixed himself a bourbon whisky and soda. He had acquired a taste for bourbon whisky during his sojourn in the writing-mills of Hollywood. The mills of Hollywood which, as he had once observed, grind slowly, and such a lot of corn.

He had dined out on the paraphrase for a couple of weeks.

That was when he had first arrived there, when World Wide Films had bought his comedy which had scored a comfortable hit in London, and he had believed every word World Wide told him. It was only when his novelty appeal wore off that he found people not quite so quick off the mark to laugh at his witticisms. Later on it even got so that they turned their back on him the moment he opened his mouth to say anything, even about the humidity. That was when the Hungarian ex-princess hit the place, to be groomed by World Wide. She turned out to be a little Los Angeles hash-slinger, but it didn't matter by then anyway; an aged and nutty screen-struck New York millionaire, who'd had his face lifted and was trying to crash movies, had the place by its ears.

As the man drank his whisky he glanced up at a photo on the wall. It was of his school four, after they'd won the Junior Cup at Marlow Regatta on that glorious summer's day twenty years ago. The fellow on the right bow, was himself. He'd come a long way since then. He took his mind back to that time when he had landed up in Fleet Street as a cub reporter and had quickly realised that unless he wanted to be a newspaperman for the rest of his life, which he didn't — he wanted to be a writer — he'd have to look around for another sort of job. He found one eventually, still in Fleet Street. But with the difference that he was an assistant assistant editor on a women's magazine. It was a pretty boring business; but it gave him his evenings and week-ends, and he was able to start planning what was to be his first play. A comedy. He managed to get it tried out at an out-lying theatre. It was so-so. But though it didn't cut much ice, the mere fact that he'd actually had it produced was encouraging. Seeing his play acted too, taught him a lot.

Resisting the impulse without much effort — he had enough sense to know where his bread-and-butter was — to turn in his magazine job and concentrate on writing a real winner, he went ahead using up his nights and week-ends and wrote four more plays in a row, all of them comedies, without one of them seeing the glow of a single footlight.

This was a stiff jolt, and he was about to chuck in his hand and resign himself to being a fourth-rate Fleet Street hack when he decided to have one more shot, and dreamed up the idea for an autobiographical comedy based on his own experiences on the magazine.

A leading musical-comedy actress, advised by her doctor to give up dancing, chanced to read the play and saw in the leading character of a fashion-editress a part into which she could get her teeth, which happened to be a beautiful crowning job. She got it produced for a suburban try-out tour. Without being a smash it was a nice little proposition, and after the inevitable tinkering around and re-writing, it opened in London and settled down to a comfortable, if unsensational, success.

One of the small-part actors in the play, making his first professional appearance, was named Ned — afterwards changed to the more euphonious Neil — Fulton.

Leo Rolf's gaze drifted towards some of the other photos. Views of his house in Beverley Hills; pictures of him tanned and robust-looking on the beach at Malibu; of him at night-clubs, restaurants, *premières*, with this star; arm-in-arm with that star, this producer, that director. All signed to him most affectionately. He'd had the foresight to build up quite a collection against the time of his return to London. He'd hung on to his American car with its Hollywood number-plate for the same reason; accumulated an awe-inspiring wardrobe of American-made clothes and shoes. He sighed a little and allowed his thoughts to linger over recollections of the blue skies, white houses, Spanish-type, Colonial, mediæval, ye olde English type, and the lush flowers, fruit, and the easy-going Californian scene. The fantastic merry-go-round that was Hollywood. Merry-go-round all right, yes, when you had the in, not so merry when they gave you the out, sign.

But those first few months had been terrific; he'd wallowed in every minute of it. He'd gone out there as the author of London's most tenacious comedy success, the film rights of which World Wide had bought for a nicely boosted sum — largely because he'd played hard to get and two other companies had put up strong competition.

Not only had he worked on the film script of his play, but he'd been called in on an urgent re-write chore, non-stop three days and nights. A musical which had got way behind schedule and simply had to go on the floor *pronto*. Although he hadn't known whether he was standing on his head or his feet, by some miracle he turned in a job which had won raves from the director. He didn't know the director had his knife up to the hilt in the writer Rolf had ousted, and was conditioned to regard anyone on two legs with a mental development a degree above the moronic as a literary genius.

From then on it was like taking candy from a baby. Until he caught up with Bertie. Or, rather, until Bertie caught up with him. Bertie was from London too, but didn't allow any little sentimentality like that to interfere with his purpose, which was to shake Rolf down for a hundred and fifty dollars a week. Bertie was quite pleasant about it and, from his point of view, reasonable. Anyone else might have demanded real money — after all they could have him barred from every studio in Hollywood.

Bertie had discovered that Rolf had employed a 'ghost' to write every word of his last picture for him. Not only the screen-play, but the original idea and story itself which Rolf had sold as his own to World Wide for an extra sum had been the 'ghost's.' Moreover, Bertie was able to inform him, the 'ghost,' who could prove he had previously submitted the identical idea to the company several years before when it had been rejected, was going to sue for plagiarism. Unless Rolf made that weekly contribution to Bertie.

After that things weren't quite the same. It was out of the question for him to use another 'ghost,' and if he'd already guessed the grim truth that he carried too few guns to cope with the skill and dextrous literary box of tricks Hollywood demanded, he knew now he was utterly incapable of tackling any of the assignments handed him. His confidence was crumpled, his nerves battered, and when World Wide omitted to take up their option on him he soon found that the sunshine had grown garish and the blue skies brazen, the flowers and colourful backdrop of California cheap and artificial.

He became homesick for London.

Besides, if he got out now while the going was good he could cash in on his Hollywood trip, and with a bit of luck land on his feet all right back home. In an effort to elude Bertie he folded his tent like the Arabs, and as silently stole aboard a cargo boat from Los Angeles bound for Liverpool.

Somewhat unfortunately for his peace of mind Bertie was also destined to develop nostalgic longings, and about a year after he had settled himself in this house overlooking the Heath this unpleasant memory of his Hollywood trip materialised on Rolf's doorstep.

Over a cup of China tea Bertie chattily outlined his plans for the future. He had one or two projects lined up, lone wolf stuff, but there might be a way, he felt, in which the other could help. Rolf had made it clear that the possibility of his recommencing the weekly contributions was just laughable and — a trifle ill-temperedly — if Bertie couldn't see the funny side of it he could go round spilling the beans about that regrettable lapse in Hollywood, and the hell with him. He hadn't worked on a picture in over three months.

Bertie had smiled understandingly. Of course he had realised Rolf was nothing like so well-heeled as he'd been on the coast, and he was not the sort to put the squeeze on anyone when things weren't going so well with them. Rolf expressed himself with certain lucidness on the subject of the other's magnanimity. Amiably Bertie went on to explain how, without having to put his hand in his pocket, Rolf nevertheless could materially put him in the way of a source of income.

For instance, Rolf had contact with people in the money. The sort of people, too, among whom might be someone likely to own a skeleton in their cupboard, whose past might harbour some indiscretion, some little folly which in their present position they would prefer not to have brought to light. The very sort of person, in fact, with whom Bertie was most anxious to become acquainted in a purely business way. For which favour he was prepared to reward Rolf with his continued silence and, moreover, if such an introduction resulted in his making a really rich haul, Bertie would gladly cut the other in for a slice of the takings.

Two or three weeks later at a first-night Rolf, attracted by what seemed to be an entire battery of flashlights popping, had observed that the object of the press-photographers' attention was Doone

Drummer. With her was Neil Fulton. During the second interval in the bar Rolf had carefully manœuvred himself so that the young actor, returning with a drink for the Drummer girl, was bound to see him. They hadn't met since his return from Hollywood. Judiciously Rolf refrained on this occasion from pushing himself forward to be introduced.

It was as a direct result of this meeting, however cunningly fostered by 'phone calls and invitations for Fulton to drop in for a drink, that he had brought Doone Drummer to lunch today to talk over the idea she had for a picture.

Following that casually-contrived meeting with Fulton at the theatre, Rolf had naturally tipped off Bertie. How did the prospect of making the acquaintance of Doone Drummer appeal to him? he had asked over the 'phone. Was she the sort of proposition he had in mind?

He recalled the little silence before Bertie had answered, almost as if he'd caught his breath, and Rolf had congratulated himself that Bertie was no doubt taken aback by the dazzling prospect that he was dangling before him.

Then Bertie had said quietly:

'Not bad. Not bad at all.'

Rolf hadn't been deceived by the apparent casualness of that response. He knew the other knew that if Doone Drummer could be hooked and played she could be shaken down for something that would really be something. How and when was Bertie's pigeon. All he had to do was to set the ball rolling.

'Take it along,' Bertie had told him. 'Nice and easy. Don't rush it, and let me know how it goes.'

Rolf had said leave it to him; he would take care of every little thing.

He smiled to himself. That same smile that wasn't particularly humorous but was more like the sleek smile of a cat that had been loosed among some chickens. The doorbell rang. And the smile vanished as if it had been sponged off his face. Slowly he lowered the glass that was halfway to his mouth. He put it down and stood up, and moved hesitantly towards the door.

He hadn't 'phoned Bertie yet to give

him the news about Doone Drummer's visit, and it wasn't usual for him to drop in without pre-arrangement. He couldn't imagine who else it could be calling on the off-chance.

Maybe, he thought, Bertie's got something urgent he wants to get off his chest.

He opened the door.

'Good evening,' a voice said to him out of the darkness, a voice he did not know. 'I am Dr. Morelle.'

7

The Intruder

The discovery that the mysterious photograph was of Dr. Morelle himself had completely non-plussed Drummer and Fulton, while Miss Frayle, of course, had been utterly unable to believe the evidence of her eyes. The Doctor however hadn't batted an eyelid, explaining its presence in the book with urbane conviction:

'I don't think I flatter myself unduly when I suggest it is not impossible that, as a result of reading my works, many admirers have on those occasions when it has appeared in print, collected my photograph. As similarly others of lower intellect collect the photographs of their favourite film-star or sports-idol. When the picture fell out of the book,' he'd added, with a glance at Fulton, 'Miss Drummer was no doubt a trifle embarrassed at the idea of her harmless admiration being revealed — a perfectly understandable reaction — and she prevented you from picking up the picture.'

And Harvey Drummer had only succeeded in giving the dagger of growing jealousy a further twist in Miss Frayle's heart when he'd smiled at Dr. Morelle:

'Doone often chatted about you, but I never knew she was such a fan of yours as all that.'

Miss Frayle, as she had watched Dr. Morelle calmly return the cut-out photo of himself to the book and the book to its shelf, felt as if she was looking at a complete stranger. For the first time she was seeing him as a creature of flesh and blood, and not the cold, calculating machine-like figure through whose veins she'd always imagined ice and not blood coursed. As she goggled owl-like at him over her spectacles she'd realised that behind the frosty demeanour to which she had grown accustomed existed a human being whose presence she'd never before suspected. Beneath that austere exterior there beat an understanding heart, that flashing sardonic eye could actually grow warm with kindness. Her brain had reeled as the thought struck home that it was not impossible that his pulses might race, his glance soften with love.

Love for whom?

For Doone Drummer?

The awful suspicion beginning to grow at the back of her mind had been interrupted by Dr. Morelle's announcement that his next step would be to visit Leo Rolf at his house in Heath Lane.

'Wouldn't it be an idea to 'phone again to see if he's back?' Fulton had suggested.

But the Doctor preferred to make it a surprise visit.

And so they had quitted the flat, quiet now, the atmosphere melancholy almost in the darkening shadows, and the air heavy with the scent of flowers. In silence they walked to the Park Lane end of Dark Lantern Street, their footsteps echoing sharply on the worn cobble-stones. Harvey Drummer had hurried away to his house; Neil Fulton, who lived in Kensington, had gone on his way saying he would pick up a taxi.

Hailing a taxi for himself and Miss Frayle, Dr. Morelle maintained on the way back to Harley Street a deep silence.

'Wouldn't you like me to come with you?' Miss Frayle had ventured to ask.

Still silence.

She had put the question to him again, and he had roused himself out of the reverie into which he had apparently fallen, replying that he preferred to go on to Hampstead alone.

'It is possible that I may have to wait some considerable time before this man's return.'

Miss Frayle had subsided. She had felt rebuffed somehow, finding it difficult to believe it was her welfare he was considering, deciding instead that he did not wish the contemplative mood which he was so obviously enjoying to be interrupted by her company.

When they had reached 221B, Harley Street, he had observed that he hoped to be back within two hours, and she was to hold herself in readiness to take notes which he would, doubtless, require to dictate to her.

She had watched his taxi disappear into the gloom with a troubled frown, conscious of the vast difference between her emotions now and only a short while earlier when she had left with him for the party in Park Lane. Then she had felt full of excited anticipation at the prospect of meeting so many famous and interesting people, including the glamorous Doone Drummer, about whom she had read so much, and whose photographs in the magazines and newspapers she had admired so enthusiastically.

She had not expected that she was on her way to be pitchforked into one more of those dark mysteries with which it seemed the Doctor was forever to find himself involved. Another tortuous drama whose end it was impossible to foresee. Most of all she never in all her wildest dreams imagined that she was due to encounter a situation which was to present Dr. Morelle in a totally new light — as a man who inspired the secret admiration of a lovely and celebrated young woman. A young woman, moreover, with whom he himself obviously had more than a nodding acquaintance.

Miss Frayle heaved a profound sigh as she turned the key in the lock and went into the house.

She was not to know that while she was indulging herself in irrational suspicions that Dr. Morelle was interesting himself in the case simply on account of Doone Drummer, the Doctor, hunched in the corner of his taxi, was fuming over the fact that, merely through accepting an invitation to attend some futile party he now found himself investigating a case of kidnapping. He scowled irritably in the darkness as he realised how this would interfere with his new thesis upon the psychological aspects of recidivism, with which work he was most busily engaged.

Dr. Morelle had also stopped the taxi at the beginning of Heath Lane. His decision to walk the rest of the way was not however based on the same reason which had inspired Leo Rolf earlier that evening. The Doctor had been little concerned with the view, delightful as it was, across the Heath; his aim was to make his visit as much of a surprise as possible. He had a high regard for the value of surprise on occasions of this sort.

He had stalked briskly up the dark and shadowed grove, with the lamplight showing up the trees, the ferrule of his swordstick striking metallic taps from the pavement. Outside the house that was withdrawn a little from those on either side, he had paused for a moment. With a feeling of hopeful satisfaction he had observed that the lights were on. It seemed probable that Leo Rolf was now at home. He had mounted the few steps and rung the bell.

Leo Rolf stared at the tall, dark shadowy figure before him.

'Dr. Morelle,' he repeated thoughtfully. 'Name's familiar.'

'A Mr. Neil Fulton is responsible for this unexpected call,' Dr. Morelle said evenly. 'He thought it was possible you might be of assistance to me.'

'Neil Fulton, eh?' There was a little pause while the other stood there indecisively. 'Won't you come in?'

As the door closed behind them Dr. Morelle said:

'He telephoned you earlier, but there was no reply.'

'I've not long been in.'

Rolf took Dr. Morelle's hat and stick and then led the way through to the room in which he had been sitting before the bell rang.

'Where did you meet Neil? Could you use a drink? This is bourbon, but there's Scotch or whatever you'd like.'

'Nothing, thank you.'

'He was in my first play,' the other went on. 'Cigarette? American — don't know if you like 'em.'

'If you will permit me I prefer my own brand.'

Dr. Morelle took out the slim, gold cigarette-case and Rolf lit his cigarette for him, eyeing him curiously from beneath lowered lids. He had heard vaguely of the Doctor's exploits in the field of criminology, and he was trying to figure out what possible errand, as a result of an acquaintance with Fulton, could have brought him unannounced up to Hampstead tonight.

'I met Fulton at Miss Doone Drummer's flat this evening,' Dr. Morelle said.

'Really? Delightful girl. Made a terrific success with that book of hers — what's it called? *The Friendly Enemy*. Haven't read it. Don't go in for novels much — but she's certainly got away with it. She was here to lunch, you know, with Neil. Completely unspoiled, in spite of all the publicity she's had. Don't you think,' he went on with mounting enthusiasm, 'she's one of the loveliest women you've ever met?' Dr. Morelle nodded absently, and the other went on: 'I suppose you were at the party her father was throwing for her?'

'I was there. As it happens her publishers also publish my works.'

'So you're a writer, too,' Rolf said, taking a gulp from his glass.

'I have a number of volumes to my credit,' the Doctor murmured with an air of assumed modesty.

'Fiction?'

'Decidedly not.'

Rolf gave a laugh. 'Scientific stuff. Bit

heavy in the going, eh?'

'That,' retorted Dr. Morelle icily, 'is a matter of opinion.'

But the other merely laughed again.

'So you went back to her flat afterwards?' he queried conversationally.

'I went back to her flat,' Dr. Morelle said, 'but not with Miss Drummer. You see,' pausing to give the other time to shoot him a quizzical glance, 'the young woman failed to arrive at her father's house.'

Rolf's eyes fastened on him in a hard concentrated stare.

'Didn't turn up? Why was that?' His brows met in a frown for a moment and then he said: 'What's happened? Hasn't been taken ill, I hope? Or an accident?'

Dr. Morelle shook his head.

'Neither of those contingencies was responsible for her non-arrival,' he said. He went on coolly: 'She has, in point of fact, been kidnapped.'

Leo Rolf's jaw sagged in astonishment.

'Kidnapped,' he gulped. 'What the devil d'you mean?'

' 'Kidnapped' ' — the Doctor quoted —

"'to steal, to carry off illegally.'"

'But,' the other protested, 'this is London. Not — not New York or Chicago. Things like that don't happen here.'

'Not with altogether the same regularity, I concede. But such crimes are committed even in this part of the world on occasion, I assure you.'

'Even so, who the hell would dream up such a thing about Doone Drummer?'

'That is something I am endeavouring to discover,' Dr. Morelle replied quietly.

The other flopped into a chair, disbelief still plain on his face. 'It's fantastic,' he muttered, 'absolutely fantastic. You're sure,' he said, 'that is what's happened to her? I mean, you don't think it could be an accident? Or lost memory, or something?' And then a look of inspiration breaking over his face he exclaimed suddenly: 'A publicity stunt. Surely, isn't that it? She's just disappeared for a publicity stunt.'

'All those possibilities have been taken into consideration and regretfully rejected. You see,' Dr. Morelle proceeded, 'I have been in conversation with the kidnapper — '

'*What!*'

'On two occasions. Over the telephone, of course.'

The other pushed his hand through his hair. 'This is getting more and more preposterous,' he muttered.

'Not so preposterous as all that.'

Leo Rolf, his face masking a dozen conflicting thoughts, got to his feet and paced up and down. Then he stood and swung round.

'But what's the idea?'

'What is usually the motive for kidnapping someone?'

'You mean they seriously think they're going to hold the girl to ransom? Nonsense!' Rolf expostulated. 'They'd never get away with it. They know they'd never get away with it.'

'They appear to have every intention of attempting to do so.'

'When you spoke to this kidnapper what did he say? — I presume it *was* a man.'

Dr. Morelle eyed him for a fraction of a moment.

'The voice certainly sounded as if it belonged to a man,' he said slowly. 'He informed me to advise her father not to contact the police if he wanted to see her again. Also to place an advertisement in the *Evening Globe* implying we are willing to do business with him, whereupon he would communicate to us the amount of the ransom he will demand, and when and how it is to be paid.'

'It's like something out of a second feature,' the other said. 'The cheapest movie.'

'The situation possesses a certain melodramatic flavour, I grant you.'

'So what happens now? You aren't going to the police? Her old man's going to pay up?'

There was a pause before Dr. Morelle replied:

'That is the impression we are endeavouring to create.'

Rolf glanced at the saturnine features, veiled for a moment in a cloud of cigarette-smoke.

'You mean,' Rolf said, 'you're out to trap him?'

Dr. Morelle inclined his head.

'You appreciate, of course,' he said, thrusting his lean jaw forward, 'that my visit is, in the circumstances, therefore of a strictly confidential nature.'

The other nodded emphatically.

'But of course. I was about to ask you why you'd taken the trouble to tell me all this. After all,' he went on, 'I met her for the first time today. As I expect Fulton told you, she'd got some idea for a film which she thought I might help her with. I probably know less about her than you do.'

'That may be the case,' Dr. Morelle agreed. 'On the other hand, however, you happen to possess one advantage over me.'

'I get it,' the other cut in. 'You're going to say I was the last person to see her before she vanished into the blue.'

'So far as we know,' Dr. Morelle added.

It was at that moment that the 'phone rang.

8

Wrong Number?

The shrill jangle bounced off the walls of the softly-lit room and quivered convulsively on the air hazy with the smoke from their cigarettes. Leo Rolf gave a frown at the telephone, and then with a muttered: 'Excuse me,' he crossed to it and lifted the receiver.

Dr. Morelle watched his brow wrinkle in deeper lines as the other listened for a moment, and then said:

'What number d'you want?'

The caller spoke very quietly. Dr. Morelle couldn't make out from the murmured reply he caught whether it was a man or a woman speaking.

'Afraid this isn't it. You've got the wrong number.'

There was a slight pause then Rolf cradled the receiver and moved back towards the Doctor. With a little shrug he said:

'Just a wrong number. Or,' he added as an after-thought, 'could be someone wanting to know if I was in. You know, this gag housebreakers are supposed to use to check if there's anyone at home? If there is they pretend it's a wrong number and keep away, if the coast is clear they nip along and bust in.' He grimaced. 'See how you've got my mind working.'

'It is indeed a method practised by burglars to aid them in selecting their victims,' the Doctor nodded. 'What is termed, I am given to understand, in underworld jargon as 'Casing a joint'.'

Rolf raised a humorously quizzical eyebrow.

'I can see, Doctor, you've been around,' he said.

'I have, in fact, published what is accepted to be a fully comprehensive glossary of thieves' slang,'[1] was Dr. Morelle's reply.

'Sounds as if it might make amusing

---

[1] 'Dictionary of Underworld Slang and Phrases,' published by Bullen & Joyce (London).

reading — I must look out for it. But, to get back to what we were discussing,' he went on. 'You were going to tell me, weren't you, I'm the very last guy to have seen Doone Drummer before she disappeared — so far as you know, that is?'

'Precisely. Which is the reason for intruding myself upon you without warning this evening.'

'No intrusion at all, my dear Doctor.' Leo Rolf was mixing himself another drink. His manner had become more easy and relaxed. 'Sure you won't join me?' Dr. Morelle again declined the invitation and the other said, his gaze on the rich, liquid amber that sparkled in his glass: 'Only thing is I can't exactly figure out how I'm going to prove of any help. I mean, I can't tell you any more than you must have learned already from Neil Fulton.'

He paused for a drink and looked at Dr. Morelle over the rim of his glass. The Doctor said nothing, merely waited for Rolf to continue.

'For instance, you know she came to lunch with him. We chatted about this and that, her book, my experiences in Hollywood, the film Fulton's working on at the moment, and so on. After lunch he had to dash, get off down to the studio, couldn't wait for coffee — we'd taken rather longer over lunch than we'd realised, matter of fact. He left us to talk round this film idea of hers. We discussed it over coffee. It was quite a bright idea. We kicked it around for an hour or so, and then she pushed off.'

'You employ a servant, I imagine?' Dr. Morelle asked.

The other nodded.

'A Mrs. Fowler. Comes in and gets my breakfast and stays to fix lunch. Took her over with the house. Been here about ten years. If I ask her specially she comes in and organises dinner,' he added. 'Don't think I'd cast her for a kidnapping rôle.'

Dr. Morelle's expression indicated he was in agreement with this judgment. Then:

'About what time did Miss Drummer take her departure?'

'Just on three o'clock. I asked her if I could 'phone for a taxi for her. She said

90

no, she didn't mind walking, and anyhow she'd be sure to get one all right on the way.'

Dr. Morelle drew at his cigarette and exhaled slowly. He was already realising the disadvantage he was under of not being able to enlist police-aid. If only he were free to ring up his old friend, Inspector Hood, all the resources of Scotland Yard would have immediately been brought to bear upon the case. A prompt check-up on every taxi-cab driver in London, for instance, so that almost inevitably the driver who had picked up Doone Drummer would have been found, questioned and his information acted upon accordingly.

With an increased feeling of frustration Dr. Morelle knew it would be impossible for him, operating on his own, to conduct any such large-scale inquiry. However, he consoled himself, there was the possibility that the girl had not, in fact, succeeded in obtaining a taxi. She might have been followed by the kidnapper on foot, or in his car, perhaps, and spirited away on some pretext. Or some cunningly contrived bogus message could have lured her to a place where her captor was waiting in readiness for her.

'I watched her turn the corner,' Rolf was saying, 'and that was the last I saw of her. Not very helpful, am I? But you can't say I didn't warn you.'

'You have no recollection of anything she said which might in any way provide the smallest clue as to her possible whereabouts? No one she mentioned, whom she intended visiting? No appointment planned for this afternoon, or this evening?'

Rolf thought for a moment, then he shook his head.

'Not a thing I can think of,' he said finally. 'I seem to be under the impression she was going back to her flat, and then there was this party later on.'

'She made no reference to any particular guest whom she was expecting at this party?' Dr. Morelle persisted.

'I can't remember anyone,' the other said, frowning thoughtfully. 'Like I told you, Doctor, I just don't seem to have an idea about this fantastic business that's of any help.'

Silently Dr. Morelle tapped the ash off his cigarette. Then he threw in the question: 'Have you any knowledge regarding her relationship with Neil Fulton?'

Rolf's gaze was a trifle narrowed.

'You don't suspect him of being implicated, surely?'

'I have no information about him except what he has himself elected to impart,' was the reply in calculated tones. 'Which was to the effect that he is a film-actor, that he had known the young woman for a short time, also that while his feelings towards her are somewhat warm they are not necessarily reciprocated.'

'Which is enough to make you think he's gone and kidnapped her?'

'I am not in the habit of jumping to conclusions.' The Doctor's voice was like a whip-lash, and Rolf stirred a little uneasily.

'Sorry if I sounded as if I was trying to be funny,' he apologised. 'But this is something new in my life, and I find myself slightly out of my depth.'

'It is not inconceivable that he may be in some way implicated in Miss Drummer's disappearance. The facts are that next to you, he was the last to see her. You have corroborated his story so far as it goes; I have only his word at the moment as to his actions between the time he left here and his arrival at the film-studio. The possibility cannot yet be ruled out that during that time he could have abducted the young woman and carried her off to a place of hiding.'

'Do you know when he got to the studio?'

Dr. Morelle shook his head.

'That is a routine inquiry which I shall, of course, follow up,' he said. 'That he arrived there at about the time he was expected seems evident.'

'You mean otherwise the film people would know he was late, and would give him away when they're questioned?'

'It is an obvious point which must have occurred to him.'

'Assuming he is the guilty guy — if he

isn't, then he wouldn't have to have given it a thought, anyway?'

'Exactly,' Dr. Morelle agreed. 'I have no doubt, therefore, that he arrived there at the time that he told us.'

The other rubbed his chin with a knuckled fist for a moment.

'Can't imagine him doing anything like that,' he said at length. 'Where would it get him?'

'I am bound to admit such an action, on his part, would hardly advance himself in Miss Drummer's estimation, and might well prove disastrous to his career.'

'Which is putting it mild. You're absolutely convinced,' Rolf continued, 'it isn't a publicity gag?'

'All the circumstances indicate otherwise.'

'Then if it isn't Neil Fulton — and we agree he's not much of a bet — who the hell can it be?'

Dr. Morelle regarded him levelly.

'You have no suggestion to offer?'

'Sorry to disappoint you, and all that — but I've told you all I know.'

The Doctor dragged at his cigarette,

and his heavy-lidded gaze was bent on the other. The carefully-tanned face was, he suspected, the result of regular renewals from a sun-lamp. The blond hair, already thinning back from the temples, was carefully brushed to hide an equally sparse crown. The china-blue eyes had a myopic glaze about them. The cinnamon-brown suit with its un-English cut was just a shade too fully draped, the hand-painted tie somewhat over-dazzling, and the dark suede shoes with *crêpe* soles could have been a little less exaggerated in style.

Dr. Morelle caught the gleam of the heavy gold wrist-watch and bracelet, the sparkle of the garnet in the gold ring on the little finger of the curiously powerful-looking left hand. His eyes travelled to the rowing-photograph, then moved round the soft-lit room, over the few tastefully-chosen ornaments, and flickered back to the rowing-photograph and then observed the other photos nearby. Involuntarily it occurred to him how Miss Frayle would have goggled at what were patently various members of

Hollywood's film-colony casually on view. He eyed the tip of his *Le Sphinx* from which the smoke curled in a thin steady spiral, his features smooth and inscrutable.

Leaning against the baby grand piano Leo Rolf took another drink from his glass.

Somehow, he is thinking, this bourbon doesn't taste so good as it did. His eye rests speculatively on the tall, angular figure that now made a move that suggested he was about to leave. The pale face, as if carved in ivory, the finely-chiselled nose, high-bridged to the wide, domed brow. Automatically it crosses his mind what a wonderful type for a film he would make.

Then he is thinking: Does Bertie know about this? Is that why he called him just now? To give him the news? Hope he'll ring him again quickly after Dr. Morelle has gone. He can tell Bertie he's alone now; he can tell him he's got to see him *pronto*.

The run of his thoughts are interrupted; they coil round the little mystery that's been bothering him off and on. The mystery of Bertie's job which he'd somehow fixed himself up with soon after his arrival in London, and which he's held down for the past year. Always refused to say what it was, and so actively disliked being questioned about it — Rolf had given up asking him.

'Permit me to express my gratitude for the information you have given me,' Dr. Morelle was saying with, Rolf fancied, a faintly sarcastic edge to his voice.

'Think nothing of it,' he answered with a good-humoured grin. Then he said seriously: 'If any little thing strikes me which I feel might be any use I'll contact you at once, if not sooner. You'll want all this kept very hush-hush, needless to say?'

'I was about to refer to that. It is vital to the young woman's safety that her disappearance is kept a close secret. I advised her father that his closest friends — even his secretary — should remain completely ignorant of what has happened.'

'Neil Fulton's been warned to keep his mouth shut, too?'

'He is fully impressed with the danger of the news escaping.'

'How did you explain away her non-appearance at her own party? Must have been a bit tricky.'

'Everyone was individually and discreetly informed,' came the smooth rejoinder, 'that Miss Drummer had been urgently called to the bedside of a dear relative suddenly afflicted. This unexpectedly unfortunate event necessitates her being out of town several days.'

'You seem to have thought of everything,' the other told him.

'It is my invariable endeavour in all circumstances to leave as little as possible to that which erring men call chance.'

Dr. Morelle took his swordstick and hat. Rolf stood and stared after the tall gaunt figure as it set off with long raking strides down Heath Lane. He watched until, appearing in the lamplight and disappearing in the shadows, the Doctor finally vanished round the corner. Rolf tapped out a fresh cigarette from his packet. The flame of his lighter glared up into his face, giving it a sudden evil expression. He snapped the flame out and looked out at the glow in the sky that was London.

As he was about to return to the warm light of his house he felt a sudden soft pressure curve round his ankles. He gave a start and then glanced down with a smile at the white cat purring up at him. He bent and scratched the cat's chin and its purr grew louder. After a few moments he straightened himself and went in quickly, closing the door behind him.

9

Inside Information

Dr. Morelle, accompanied by Miss Frayle who was clutching a mid-day edition of the *Evening Globe*, followed the manservant across the small hall of the house in Park Lane. Miss Frayle glanced in the direction of the room where only last evening they had been at the party. Was it really only last evening? she thought. So much drama had been packed into the last few hours, it seemed like days. The manservant — he was the man Harvey Drummer had indicated at the party, only for the life of her Miss Frayle couldn't recall his name — led the way through a door leading into a small but pleasantly-appointed office.

The man behind the desk looked up, blinking nervously from the documents over which he was poring. He stood up quickly.

'Thank you, Brethers,' he said, and rubbing his hands together greeted the Doctor and Miss Frayle. 'I'm Mr. Drummer's secretary. Mr. Drummer is waiting for you.'

The man named Brethers went out, closing the door behind him, as the other moved round his desk. He was a dapper little man with watery eyes behind pince-nez, and a hesitant speech. Miss Frayle noted his remarkably luxuriant hair.

'Will you come in, please?' he said, and opened the door; the upper part of which was of frosted glass. He stood aside for Dr. Morelle and Miss Frayle to enter.

Harvey Drummer stopped his pacing of the thick, fitted carpet, and crossed quickly to them. The man in pince-nez went out. Miss Frayle gazed round the room, richly panelled in light oak, the tall windows of which looked out over Park Lane. She noticed that they were double windows which reduced the sound of the traffic outside to a faint murmur.

'This is the business part of my house,' Harvey Drummer was saying to Dr.

Morelle, 'I keep it shut off as much as possible from the rest. Separate telephone and everything. It's good enough for me.'

'I think it's awfully nice,' put in Miss Frayle.

Drummer smiled at her. 'I rather like being so near my job. As I'm what you might call a freelance financier, I don't need enormous offices or staff. Pearson, the chap you've just met has been my secretary, head cook and bottle-washer for over ten years. Watches over me as if I were a child. Oh,' he smiled, 'don't be deceived by his outward appearance. He's shrewd, sharp and up to all the tricks in the finance world. And there are a few, I can tell you.'

He indicated a chair for Dr. Morelle and pulled one forward for Miss Frayle. He sat down behind a low flat-topped desk and, with concentrated attention, filled his pipe from a large tobacco-jar. Then he went on:

'From here I manage to keep in touch with odd spots of my business, which takes in anything from oil in Persia to oranges in Panama.' He tamped the tobacco down in the bowl of his pipe and lit it carefully. He leaned back in his leather-padded swivelchair and jabbed his pipe at the newspaper on his desk. With a nod at the newspaper Miss Frayle was carrying, he said:

'So the advertisement's in all right?'

Dr. Morelle inclined his head.

Drummer drew his newspaper to him; it was folded at the personal advertisements page, and he read out the advertisement which was circled with a pencil:

"'DAUGHTER'S FATHER agreeable to terms demanded. Advise soon as possible when, where and how matter can be settled satisfactorily and home-coming arranged. — H.D.''

He looked up from the paper, his brows drawn together anxiously.

'Wonder when we'll get a reply?'

'We have no alternative but to await developments,' the Doctor murmured.

'But I didn't drag you round here,' Harvey Drummer went on, 'just to tell you something that you know already.'

'I rather gathered that you had some other motive for your invitation,' Dr. Morelle said mildly.

'I've got a great idea.' Harvey Drummer hunched forward over his desk, stabbing the air with his pipe. 'A great idea to get Doone back unharmed *and* without paying our kidnapping friend a penny.'

'How?' Miss Frayle breathed, leaning forward excitedly.

'This is the way it goes.' The other stuck his pipe between his teeth for a moment, then took it out again and through a thick cloud of smoke continued eagerly. 'Our friend, when he answers the advertisement will, of course, demand money. Whatever amount he has in mind. Five thousand, ten thousand, maybe more. But however much it is we can be sure of one thing. He won't take a cheque.'

'That is a fair assumption,' Dr. Morelle assented, eyeing the other thoughtfully.

'He'll want it in the safest form possible,' Drummer went on. 'Hard cash.

One pound notes will be too bulky, so it'll be five pound notes.'

'If the sum demanded amounts to anything like those you have mentioned even they will be bulky enough,' Dr. Morelle said.

Harvey Drummer nodded in agreement.

'But an ordinary suit-case would carry 'em all right,' he said. 'That's the way I see it. He'll ask for the money to be paid over in five pound notes — to be delivered at such and such a place at such and such a time. In return he'll of course hand over Doone. No reason why he shouldn't. He's got his money, I've got her back, so everybody will be happy.'

'But I thought you hoped you'd get your daughter safely back without having to pay?' Miss Frayle put in.

Harvey Drummer gave her a confident little smile.

'Precisely,' he said. He turned to Dr. Morelle. 'No doubt you've noticed in the newspapers the last few weeks there have been a lot of forgeries?'

'I had noted that.'

'Forged banknotes flooding the country. Been giving the police and the Bank of England a real headache.'

Miss Frayle suddenly clapped her hands together excitedly. 'You mean you're going to pay him with forged notes! How clever of you.'

But Harvey Drummer shook his head.

'I'm going to be a little cleverer than that,' he said, and Miss Frayle subsided. 'As a result of all this forgery business,' Drummer went on, 'the Bank of England plan to take certain steps. I happened to have a word with a banker friend this morning. He won't say definitely, but he hinted very strongly that people in the know, exercising intelligent anticipation, expect all five pound notes to be called in. In about a week's time it'll be, and a new note issued. I don't need to tell you,' he added, 'what that means.'

Dr. Morelle drew at his cigarette slowly.

'It would mean,' he said, 'that the kidnapper would be unable to cash his notes without verification by the bank. As the bank would possess the numbers of

107

these particular notes they would not, of course, be met.'

'What a marvellous idea,' Miss Frayle exclaimed, her face aglow with enthusiasm.

'I must admit I thought it wasn't so bad myself,' Harvey Drummer smiled. His expression clouded, however, as he glanced at the Doctor, who sat in silence gazing apparently abstractedly out of the window. Miss Frayle turned to him.

'Don't you think it's marvellous?'

He brought his gaze round to her slowly.

'It is indeed an ingenious scheme,' he admitted. But his tone was heavy with doubt.

'You don't sound wildly enthusiastic,' Miss Frayle said.

'What's wrong with the idea?' Drummer queried. 'Can you see any holes in it?

'It would appear to be flawless, was the reply in a cool, emotionless voice. 'You may be extremely gratified that you have obtained this useful information. But I prefer to await events before prophesying as to your scheme's success or failure.'

Frowning a little Harvey Drummer leaned back in his chair considerably deflated. Miss Frayle threw him a sympathetic look, then glanced sharply at the Doctor. It was obvious to her that he was reluctant to praise the other's brain-wave simply because it had not occurred to him. She had to admit, of course, in his favour that he hadn't been in Drummer's unique position to obtain that sort of inside information, or no doubt he would have thought of the same idea too. Still that was no reason for his dog-in-the-manger attitude. She shook her head at him rebukingly as he stood up and began to pace slowly towards the window. Over his shoulder he said:

'Nevertheless there are one or two other aspects of this case requiring further investigation while we await the reply to our advertisement.'

'Anything you like, of course,' Harvey Drummer responded.

Dr. Morelle stood for a moment lost in contemplation of the traffic streaming up and down Park Lane. Then he turned slowly and came back to the desk. He said:

'We might obtain some information by questioning the members of your household concerning their movements yesterday afternoon and evening.'

'That won't take you long. There's only Pearson, Brethers and Mrs. Huggins. She's my housekeeper.'

'Shall we start with your secretary. He is the nearest.'

'As good a reason as any for starting with him first,' the other agreed, and pressed a button underneath his desk.

'But Doctor,' Miss Frayle said quickly, 'how are you going to question him without giving the show away?'

Dr. Morelle bent his sardonic gaze on her.

'I am confident, my *dear* Miss Frayle, I shall be able to exercise sufficient ingenuity to avoid that.'

The door opened and Pearson came in. He advanced towards them, an uncertain smile flickering across his thin mouth, and faced his employer.

Drummer gave a cough. 'Dr. Morelle

would like to ask you one or two questions.'

The man turned slowly and raised his eyebrows expectantly over his pince-nez.

'You may recall,' Dr. Morelle began, 'I attended the party yesterday.'

'Of course, of course,' the other responded. 'Many of the guests asked me about you and Miss Frayle.'

'Unfortunately, while I was present,' Dr. Morelle continued, 'I suffered the loss of some scientific notes. I might have dropped them somewhere in the house. Alternatively, someone might have 'borrowed' them — they were loose in my side pocket — with the object of perpetrating a harmless practical joke.'

The secretary clicked his teeth in dismay.

'Dear, dear. How singularly unfortunate.'

'It occurred to me,' Dr. Morelle went on, 'that as you were there the entire time you might have noticed something which would help me to recover the documents. They are of relatively minor importance, but I should like to have them back. You *were* present,' he asked with disarming casualness, 'the entire time, of course?'

'All the time,' was the prompt reply, and with a glance at Harvey Drummer. 'In fact, as Mr. Drummer will tell you, I was in the house all afternoon and evening.'

'That's right,' Drummer affirmed.

'You sleep here?'

Pearson nodded his head.

'It's essential for me to be available at all times; the nature of Mr. Drummer's business demands that.'

'You took care, naturally, that nobody attended the party whose presence was unauthorised?' Dr. Morelle queried.

'Naturally,' was the simple response. 'Everyone, with the exception of the press-photographer, three gossip-writers and two literary critics were personally acquainted with either Mr. Drummer or his daughter.'

'You were perfectly satisfied in your mind as to the *bona fides* of the exceptions you have mentioned?' Dr. Morelle tone was suddenly probing.

'Perfectly satisfied,' Pearson replied.

Miss Frayle was observing the subtle change in the dapper little man's manner. There was a sudden suggestion of a wiry strength in that apparent weak frame. A merest sharpening of the expression, a shrewd narrowing of the eyes behind the ineffectual-looking pince-nez. She remembered Harvey Drummer's remark that despite his exterior the secretary was a man of efficiency and acumen. Her gaze shifted from his carefully brushed and shining hair, to the neatly knotted tie which he had started to finger.

She noticed that the hand, although scrupulously well-kept was deformed, almost claw-like. As she stared at it he caught her gaze and dropped his hand to clasp the other behind his back. Miss Frayle blushed with embarrassment. Poor man, he was obviously sensitive about the appearance of his hands.

'It was obviously an important part of my duties,' he was saying, 'to take care no undesirable persons were able to gain admittance.'

'And I am sure you performed your

duty admirably,' Dr. Morelle observed in a honeyed tone.

'Anyone would have to get up very early in the morning to get past his eagle eye,' Harvey Drummer commented.

'Admittedly I wasn't looking for anyone behaving suspiciously,' the secretary went on. 'But I certainly didn't notice anyone whose behaviour struck me as being out of the ordinary. None of the guests gave the impression of being capable of purloining, even for the fun of it, the papers you mention. I'll run my mind back over the events of yesterday, however, and endeavour to recall any incident which might have been connected with your loss.'

'I am grateful to you for your co-operation,' Dr. Morelle replied.

The other's manner seemed to relax. Once again he was the diffident, almost servile individual with no other thought than to serve his employer. He glanced questioningly at Harvey Drummer.

'Is there anything else, Mr. Drummer?'

Drummer in turn looked at the Doctor.

'There is nothing else I wish to ask,'

Dr. Morelle said urbanely.

Drummer got up and moved round his desk.

'Thanks, Pearson,' he said, and the other went out, closing the door after him quietly.

Harvey Drummer's pipe had gone out and he lit it again. As he expelled a cloud of smoke, he said:

'Looks as if you've drawn a blank there, I'm afraid.'

'You mentioned your housekeeper?'

'Mrs. Huggins? I'll tell Pearson to fetch her.'

He crossed to the door and, opening it, spoke to the man who had just gone out. They heard Pearson reply and the door of the outer office close after him as he went to find the housekeeper. Harvey Drummer did not move from the door. He remained there with his back to Dr. Morelle and Miss Frayle, his attitude suddenly tense.

'What is it?'

It was Dr. Morelle who rapped out the question and moved to the door quickly. Harvey Drummer turned to him, a puzzled frown on his face. He made no reply.

'Something appears to have aroused your interest,' Dr. Morelle persisted. Miss Frayle, with a sudden tingling at the back of her neck, followed him as he added: 'Something of significance?'

'It's nothing,' Drummer smiled unconvincingly. 'I just thought — '

He broke off and the Doctor snapped at him: 'What did you think?'

'It was just — but I must be imagining things. It was just that I thought Pearson closed that drawer in his desk rather quickly. As if I'd surprised him.'

Dr. Morelle had moved into the other office and stood by the desk.

'It's nothing, I'm sure,' Drummer went on. 'I probably startled him. He's a nervy devil. Always has been, and I must have made him jump.' He gave a wry half-laugh, 'Or perhaps it's I whose nerves are jumpy.'

Miss Frayle stood in the doorway and saw the Doctor glance narrowly at the drawer which the other had indicated.

'With your permission,' Dr. Morelle

said, 'I should like to open it.'

Harvey Drummer shrugged. He appeared slightly amused.

'Go ahead, I don't suppose Pearson will have any objections. I imagine he only keeps his pencils and note books and odds and ends in it.'

Dr. Morelle pulled the drawer open.

Miss Frayle's pulse quickened as she saw that familiar tightening of his jaw, that sudden hawk-like expression as he stood staring down. Then with a swift pounce he reached into the drawer, and she gave a sharp gasp.

In his hands he was holding a pair of black silk gloves.

10

The Housekeeper

'What on earth — ?' Harvey Drummer exclaimed as he stared at the pair of black gloves which Dr. Morelle held up for his inspection. 'I don't seem to remember seeing those before.'

'Possibly your secretary is adopting some new sartorial departure,' Dr. Morelle observed.

'He's coming back,' Miss Frayle breathed, as she caught the sound of voices approaching. Dr. Morelle had already dropped the gloves in the drawer and closed it.

'Saying nothing about it for the moment, eh?' Harvey Drummer asked, leading the way back into his office.

'I think we can allow the subject to await later discussion,' Dr. Morelle said, he and Miss Frayle following the other. They heard Pearson come into the outer office and say:

'Wait just a moment, please.'

'All right,' a woman's voice answered.

The secretary appeared at the door. 'Mrs. Huggins is here.'

'Show her in,' Drummer said.

The woman who came into the room couldn't have been less like the mental picture Miss Frayle had conjured up of her. Her name, combined with the knowledge that she was the housekeeper, had created the impression of a middle-aged soul, typical of the popular conception of a woman in her job.

Instead, Miss Frayle found herself staring at an extremely attractive woman no more than thirty years old, whose dress showed off to advantage a charmingly rounded figure. She was a red-head, with a pleasantly pretty face and nice eyes. She gave Dr. Morelle and Miss Frayle a friendly smile. Turning to Drummer she said, with a slight Cockney accent:

'Mr. Pearson said you wanted to see me.'

'Yes, Mrs. Huggins. This is Miss Frayle

and Dr. Morelle.'

'Oh!'

Mrs. Huggins had obviously heard something of Dr. Morelle's exploits. Her eyes were bright with interest as she stared at him.

'They were at the party,' Harvey Drummer went on, 'and the Doctor unfortunately lost something — he'll tell you about it, Mrs. Huggins.'

She turned to Dr. Morelle and said conversationally:

'It's an awful name, isn't it? Not Rosie; personally I rather like that. Huggins. It was my husband's fault, though I suppose he couldn't help it either.' Her eyes clouded for a moment, and she added with a little sigh: 'Poor Bill.' Dr. Morelle regarded her questioningly. 'He died, you see,' she explained. 'Drowned when he was out in a rowing-boat fishing during his holidays. They never found him.'

'How long ago was this unfortunate occurrence?' Dr. Morelle asked her quietly.

'Just on a year ago,' she replied. 'About two years after we'd come here.'

'We?'

'I employed both Mr. and Mrs. Huggins,' Drummer explained. 'He was my manservant.'

The woman turned to Drummer with a little smile. To the Doctor she said:

'Mr. Drummer was marvellous to me.' She spoke with simple sincerity. 'That's why I stayed on. If it had been anybody else I'd had to have got a job somewhere else.'

Drummer made a deprecating movement with his pipe.

'You were much too good to let go, if I could possibly help it,' he said.

'I'm sorry you lost something at the party,' the woman said to Dr. Morelle. 'If there's anything I can do to help find it —'

'I assume you were about while the party was in progress?' Dr. Morelle asked.

There was a slight pause before Mrs. Huggins's answer: 'I wasn't.'

Did she, Miss Frayle wondered, detect a sudden gleam in the Doctor's eye at this unexpected admission? She stared at the woman with quickening interest.

'Indeed?' Dr. Morelle made no attempt to disguise the hint of surprise in his tone. Harvey Drummer was about to say something, but Mrs. Huggins went on:

'It was my afternoon off. The arrangements for the party were in the hands of Fortune's. So there was nothing for me to do, anyway.'

'No,' Drummer said. 'Fortune's did the whole thing. The bits and pieces to eat, drink, and a couple of men to serve.'

Dr. Morelle pounced on him like a cat on a mouse.

'Your secretary,' he snapped, 'gave me to understand that the only people present on the occasion with whom you and Miss Drummer were not acquainted, were a press-photographer, three journalists and two literary reviewers. It would now appear there were two other complete strangers also present.'

'Afraid Pearson and I forgot that,' Drummer said. 'But I really don't think those two were of any importance.'

'I should have thought I was the best judge of that,' was the sharp retort.

Harvey Drummer gave Dr. Morelle a

glance. He was beginning to receive practical demonstration that the Doctor suffered neither fools nor people who forgot things, gladly. 'I'm sorry,' he found himself apologising.

'To return to you,' Dr. Morelle said, eyeing Mrs. Huggins. 'You were not in the house at all during the party? At what time, may I inquire, did you leave the house last evening?'

Instead of replying the woman said:

'If you'd tell me what happened, perhaps it would make it easier for me to help you.'

'It's some notes of the Doctor's,' Miss Frayle said helpfully. 'He thinks he lost them during the time he was here. He's wondering if somebody might have picked them up and not bothered to return them. Or perhaps 'borrowed' them — they were in his pocket — as a sort of joke.'

'Since my assistant,' and Dr. Morelle's voice had a biting ring, 'has so thoughtfully offered you an explanation for my questions, if you would be kind enough to answer them I should be most grateful.'

'You were asking me what time I left,' the woman said. 'It was after lunch. About three o'clock — I was a little late, as a matter of fact, owing to preparations for the party.'

'And you returned at what time?'

'About ten.'

'You will appreciate,' the Doctor went on suavely, 'the object of my questions. I merely wish to ascertain whether you observed anything suspicious which might be connected with my missing notes. However, as you say you were absent during the time in question, there is little purpose in our pursuing the matter further.'

'I'm afraid I'm not much help,' the woman said with a slight frown. 'I went out after lunch, did some shopping, had tea, then went to the Oriental Cinema just in time for the big picture, about five-thirty.'

'That's got the film 'Midnight,' hasn't it?' Miss Frayle said quickly. 'With John Dacre; I thought it was lovely.'

Dr. Morelle rolled his eyes heaven-wards.

'I feel sure you can find other opportunities to discuss with Mrs. Huggins the merits of the film concerned,' he snapped.

'I loved it,' Mrs. Huggins, deliberately ignoring the Doctor's outburst, said to Miss Frayle. 'I love the films though, don't you? The theatre as well. Stage-struck as a kid I was, had ideas of going in for it, as a matter of fact. Did a bit of amateur acting, children's shows, of course. They always made me play the men's parts, because I could put on a deep voice.'

'If,' Dr. Morelle interposed, his tone razor-like, 'you would return to the topic under discussion!'

'So sorry, Doctor,' Mrs. Huggins beamed at him genially. 'Where was I?'

'You were in the Oriental Cinema, enjoying the featured film.'

'That's right. There was a lovely film with it, too. The second picture, I mean. I forget what it was called, but it was all about one of those mad doctors. Lovely scene there was where this doctor straps the heroine on to the operating-table — '

Dr. Morelle snorted impatiently and Harvey Drummer, unable to keep a touch of amusement out of his voice, put in:

'I'm sure it was most entertaining, Mrs. Huggins.'

'You were unaccompanied all the time?' the Doctor put in.

'Yes, I was alone all the time.'

Dr. Morelle eyed her for a moment before he asked: 'What time did you leave the cinema?'

'About nine o'clock. I sat on a bit, you see, and saw some of the beginning of 'Midnight' over again. On my way home I had a meal at the Half-Way House. As I said I was in by ten o'clock. I'm so sorry,' she went on, 'I can't be more helpful. I do hope your notes will turn up all right.'

She smiled sympathetically at Dr. Morelle, then gave a look at Drummer.

'All right, Mrs. Huggins,' he said. 'Thank you very much.'

At the door she turned.

'Funny about doctors, isn't it?' she said. 'You're always reading in the papers about them losing things, leaving poisons in cars, and that.'

And with a beaming look directed at Dr. Morelle, Mrs. Huggins went out.

'Still not much progress, I'm afraid, Doctor,' Harvey Drummer murmured.

'She's rather a pet, isn't she?' Miss Frayle said.

'Doone is very fond of her,' the other nodded, then his face clouded over as if reminded that his daughter was missing. Dr. Morelle lit a cigarette and stared silently at Harvey Drummer who continued in lowered tones: 'What about Pearson?'

Still Dr. Morelle silently puffed a spiral of cigarette smoke ceilingwards.

'Yes,' Miss Frayle whispered to him urgently. 'Aren't you going to tackle him about those black gloves?'

Dr. Morelle quietly asked Drummer:

'Might Miss Frayle telephone the box-office of the Oriental Cinema?'

The other looked at him in surprise.

'Surely you don't suspect Mrs. Huggins was lying?' Miss Frayle squeaked.

'Why, of course,' Drummer told the Doctor. 'If you think it's an idea.'

Miss Frayle crossed to the telephone on

the wide, flat desk. She was about to lift the receiver when she wheeled round and exclaimed:

'But this is ridiculous. Surely Mrs. Huggins wouldn't lie about something which she must know could be so easily checked?'

'I must say, that's what occurred to me,' Harvey Drummer agreed.

'If, when you obtain the number,' Dr. Morelle unmoved instructed Miss Frayle, 'you would be kind enough to ask if the film in question was showing at five-thirty, I should be obliged.'

'Of course it was showing then,' she protested impatiently. 'I saw it myself at that very time only three days ago — '

Miss Frayle broke off and bit her lip as Dr. Morelle directed a baleful stare at her.

'Would that be the occasion,' he observed, 'when you gave me to under-stand you were visiting a woman friend at Notting Hill who had been taken ill?'

Miss Frayle's face flamed a bright pink, and she bit her lip again. Then she said defiantly:

'As a matter of fact what happened was

that I rang her up on my way there. She was feeling better, and so we met at the Oriental instead. And I still think it's wasting time 'phoning when we ought to be getting on about *him*.' Lowering her voice and indicating the outer office.

The Doctor glared at her dangerously, and with a shrug she lifted the receiver and dialled the number. After a few moments she spoke into the mouthpiece:

'The box-office? I just wanted to confirm that you were showing 'Midnight' yesterday evening at five-thirty as usual.'

There was a pause. Miss Frayle's jaw visibly slackened.

'You're sure?' she gulped. 'A sneak pre-view of a new film instead. Oh . . . '

Limply Miss Frayle replaced the receiver. She turned, bracing herself to meet the sardonically triumphant gaze of Dr. Morelle.

11

The Reply

Harvey Drummer was staring as if thunderstruck at Miss Frayle, then he found his voice. 'So she has lied.'

'It would appear so on the face of it,' Dr. Morelle replied.

'Fetch her back,' Drummer choked. He advanced on the Doctor, his face contorted. 'Fetch her back and drag the truth out of her! She's mixed up in Doone's disappearance. She can identify the kidnapper.'

Dr. Morelle regarded him calmly over his cigarette.

'We should be ill-advised to take any precipitate action.'

For a moment Harvey Drummer stood, fists clenched, and Miss Frayle had a sudden fear that he was about to throw himself violently upon the Doctor. She moved forward instinctively with a muddled idea of stepping between the two men; Drummer lowered his clenched hands, however, and swung away.

'If you won't fetch her back,' he flung over his shoulder savagely, 'I will.' And he marched quickly to the door.

Dr. Morelle made no move to stop him. Calmly tapping the ash off his cigarette he asked, without raising his voice:

'Of what will you accuse her?' At the Doctor's words the other hesitated for a moment. Dr. Morelle continued smoothly. 'Do you propose to denounce her merely for stating she was at a certain cinema when she was in fact not?'

Drummer's hand was on the door-handle, but he turned and faced the Doctor.

'It's — it's more than that,' he said.

'That is a matter of surmise.'

'What do you mean?'

Drummer released his grip on the door-handle, his face clouding with perplexity.

'All we know about Mrs. Huggins,' Dr. Morelle pointed out, 'is that she lied to us about her movements yesterday. Why she lied remains at the moment a mystery. If we accuse her of lying because she is concerned in the disappearance of your daughter she may deny it resolutely. What shall we have gained?'

'We can prove she's a damned liar,' exclaimed the other angrily.

'One point appears to have escaped your notice,' Dr. Morelle said patiently. 'Your housekeeper was enjoying time off from her work to which she is entitled. You have no jurisdiction as to how she amuses herself. She is not required to say how she employs her free hours and if she chooses to lie about it, what remedy have you?'

'She's lying,' Harvey Drummer grumbled obstinately, 'for a reason.'

'All of us lie for a reason,' Dr. Morelle replied. 'Even Miss Frayle here lied about her visit to a friend at Notting Hill.' Miss Frayle gave him a tiny grimace and shrugged her shoulders. 'But that Mrs. Huggins's lie is connected with the kidnapping is, so far as we know, only guesswork. Furthermore,' he went on, 'I must point out to you the danger of accusing her at this stage.'

'Danger?' the other queried. He walked slowly away from the door.

'You have wisely agreed to refrain from making known your daughter's disappearance,' Dr. Morelle said. 'If you accuse this woman, the secret will be revealed. She impressed me as being the not exactly reticent type. You could not be sure she would not repeat the story.'

'I see what you mean,' Harvey Drummer muttered, more steadily.

Miss Frayle watched him with a surge of sympathy as he brushed his hand with a weary gesture across his face.

'It is imperative,' the Doctor's soothing tone proceeded, 'that the kidnapper's suspicions are lulled. If he learns that we actively intend to defeat his purpose, I cannot be held responsible for the consequences.'

The other nodded his head heavily.

'Of course,' he said, 'we must be careful. I'm sorry. I'm afraid I lost my head a bit.'

'So far no damage has been done,' was

the response. 'But I think it might have been done had you made that accusation. If the woman is innocent, she might allow the news of your daughter's disappearance to spread. On the other hand, if she is guilty, hastily accusing her could prove nothing. Again if, for instance, she is an accomplice in the crime she might promptly advise her confederate of our suspicions. If we say nothing and she is innocent, we are no worse off. If she is involved she may be the instrument which will lead us to the discovery of the kidnapper himself.'

'This goes, too, for Pearson, I suppose? Those black gloves, I mean.'

'The same applies,' Dr. Morelle acquiesced. 'The fact that he possesses a pair of black silk gloves which he apparently wishes to keep secret may, under the circumstances, appear suspicious. But it is no proof that he is concerned with your daughter's disappearance. Openly to accuse him would achieve no better result than in Mrs. Huggins's case. We must,' he emphasised, 'proceed cautiously if your daughter is to return to you unharmed.'

'A thought occurs to me,' Harvey Drummer said suddenly frowning. 'And that is I don't see why the kidnapper has to have been at the party. As you seem to suggest.'

Dr. Morelle raised a quizzical eyebrow. 'What is there about it which strikes you as being an unreasonable assumption?'

'I don't see what grounds you've got,' the other said bluntly.

Miss Frayle stared at him wide-eyed. The idea of anyone questioning Dr. Morelle's pronouncements was something unusual in her experience. The Doctor, however, bent a magnanimous expression upon Drummer.

'I mean,' the other was continuing, 'how can you be so sure whoever it was must have been present?'

Dr. Morelle drew at his cigarette for a moment before he spoke.

'The evidence happens to be irrefutable,' he smiled thinly. 'How else could the kidnapper have known that I was present when first he telephoned? You will agree he must have known that, otherwise how was he at once aware it was I who answered? I had not announced my identity. He had telephoned your number.'

Harvey Drummer was immediately apologetic.

'Why of course. You're absolutely right.'

'He always is, you know,' Miss Frayle murmured.

'What happened then,' Drummer said thoughtfully, 'was that they must have seen you and Miss Frayle go off with me to my room, and they nipped out and rang from a call-box?'

'The call need not necessarily have been made from outside.'

'What d'you mean?' the other shot at him.

'It could have come through from the telephone in your outer office. You have just informed me it is a separate line.'

'My God, yes!' Harvey Drummer rapped out. 'Wouldn't have taken them a moment to come along here.'

'Which postulates a further probability.'

'What's that?'

'That the kidnapper,' Dr. Morelle pointed out, 'was not only present at the party, but was someone acquainted with the topography of your house.'

Harvey Drummer stared at Dr. Morelle in open admiration.

'You think of everything,' he said. 'Everything.'

Dr. Morelle gave a little smile and turned expectantly to Miss Frayle. But frowning again, Drummer went on thoughtfully: 'Only thing is nobody springs to mind who knows the arrangement here except the people I employ. Apart from myself, of course,' adding with a grim smile, 'and you were witness to the fact that I couldn't have made the call.'

There was an imperceptible pause before the Doctor observed quietly:

'Have you considered some of your friends, business acquaintances? Is none of them aware of your separate telephones?'

'Now you come to mention it,' Drummer conceded, 'there must be several.'

'The circle of suspects therefore is not so narrow as perhaps would at first appear?'

There was a sudden exclamation from Miss Frayle and both of them regarded her questioningly.

'I've just thought of something,' she said.

'Is it in any way connected with what we are discussing?' Dr. Morelle queried sarcastically.

'Yes, yes. Mrs. Huggins.'

'What about her?'

'Aren't you rather presuming that the kidnapper is a man?'

Harvey Drummer stared at her hard.

'Have you any reason for believing it isn't?' he asked slowly.

'It might be someone deliberately putting on a man's voice,' Miss Frayle declared. 'Have you thought of that?'

'I must admit,' Dr. Morelle said, 'the idea of such a grotesque impersonation had not occurred to me. My imagination does not tend to become as inflamed as yours.'

'What are you getting at, Miss Frayle?' Drummer interposed.

'Your housekeeper. Don't you remember? She said she was stage-struck as a child. She used to act in children's shows — *men's parts, because she could put on a deep voice.'*

'She did say that,' exclaimed Harvey Drummer. He turned on Dr. Morelle who was staring at Miss Frayle as if fascinated. 'What do you think of it?'

'There are moments when Miss Frayle's theories leave me utterly bereft of words with which to express myself,' he replied. 'This is one of them.'

'But, Doctor — ' Miss Frayle began to protest. She was interrupted by the door opening. Pearson stood there holding an envelope.

'This has just arrived for you, Mr. Drummer,' he said. 'It came by hand,' he added.

'By hand?' Harvey Drummer took the envelope from the other, frowning at it.

'Brethers found it on the doormat,' Pearson explained. 'He brought it to me at once.'

'Thanks,' Drummer said, and the secretary went out, closing the door behind him. Harvey Drummer glanced at Dr. Morelle, then down at the envelope again.

'Delivered by hand,' he repeated. 'He certainly moves fast. 'Harvey Drummer, Esquire!'' he read aloud. 'Typewritten, of course.'

'It's the reply,' Miss Frayle gulped. 'The reply to the advertisement.'

'Bound to be,' the other agreed, tearing open the envelope. 'Asking for the money to be paid in five pound notes.'

Miss Frayle and Dr. Morelle, his eyes narrowed, his jaw tightened, watched Drummer quickly take out a folded sheet of paper and read it.

'It's typewritten too,' he muttered.

'What does he say?' Miss Frayle breathed.

There was no reply for a moment. Harvey Drummer's face had become a mask of dismay.

'How much money does he want?' Miss Frayle asked in a tense whisper.

'He — he doesn't want money,' came the choked reply.

Dr. Morelle stepped forward with a quick movement, extending his hand for the letter.

'Read it for yourself.' And as the

Doctor took the letter Drummer added in a defeated voice: 'It's not going to be so easy.'

Dr. Morelle's eyes scanned the note, his face expressionless. Miss Frayle heard him murmur:

'Diamond bracelet to the value of ten thousand pounds.'

'Even mentions that Doone says she'll repay me when she's freed,' Drummer muttered.

'A diamond bracelet,' Dr. Morelle mused. He looked up at Drummer and said: 'It would appear that this person also possesses a certain intelligent anticipation.'

'The cunning swine,' Drummer burst out.

The Doctor tapped the letter thoughtfully against a thumbnail.

'Clever. Quite clever,' he said, half aloud. 'An adversary worthy of my steel.'

12

Bertie

Leo Rolf stood in the vestibule of the Marble Arch Hotel scanning the people passing to and fro.

The pink lighting gave their faces a curiously dream-like quality. From the restaurant behind him an orchestra could be heard in faint waves above the clatter of voices around him.

He gave a nervously impatient glance at his gold wrist-watch. Bertie was late. He'd 'phoned again last night after Dr. Morelle had left but only briefly to convey that he was unable to talk from his end, that Rolf would have to wait until they met the next night. He had been desperately impatient to hear what, if anything, Bertie knew about the disappearance of Doone Drummer. There had been nothing for it, however, but for him to wait until tomorrow.

And now his watch said twenty past nine, and Bertie had said he would be here by nine o'clock. Rolf took a packet of American cigarettes out of his pocket and tapped another one out. He was just lighting it when he caught sight of a familiar figure pushing his way through the crowd towards him.

He promptly adopted a slightly peeved expression for the other's benefit.

'Sorry, old chappie,' Bertie apologised, smiling. 'Just couldn't get away.'

'I was giving you up,' Rolf grumbled.

'Never do that,' was the grinning response. 'You know me; I may not be on the dot, but at least I'm worth waiting for.'

'I sometimes wonder,' Rolf said. But the other laughed away the bitterness underlying his voice.

'Drink?' he said. 'There's a bar downstairs.'

They made their way towards the stairs that curved down to the bar below. As they descended there flashed across Rolf's mind for the thousandth time the sense of unreality he always felt whenever he and the other met. Had anyone told him that he could have remained on more or less friendly terms with a man who was blackmailing him he would have thought they were raving. Yet the incredible fact remained that though the other's company was a constant reminder of the hold he had over him, their relationship on the surface at any rate was perfectly friendly.

The bar was full. After they had given their order to a white-coated waiter they looked around for somewhere to sit and talk. By the time their drinks were brought there was still no signs of anyone vacating the few small tables round the walls.

Bertie, however, did not seem to be worried, although Rolf was aware that they couldn't have a great deal of time in which to talk. The other was never able to get away for more than an hour or so.

Bertie raised his glass.

'Keep smiling,' he grinned at Rolf's somewhat doleful expression.

Rolf took a gulp from his drink, but his anxious face did not clear as he glanced round the bar.

'I wanted to talk to you about — about last night,' he muttered. 'We can't talk here.'

The other glanced round the bar as if realising for the first time that it was crowded.

'Bit of a crush,' he admitted. 'Not quite the place for a cosy chat. We'll have to stick to discussing the weather. There's always the weather,' he continued lightly. 'Funny how there's always a general topic of conversation no matter where you are. Hollywood has its humidity, here it's the weather.'

Glancing at him Rolf realised Bertie was in one of his slightly irresponsible moods which added to the air of youthful charm about him. The line of his clean-shaven jaw was relaxed. He scrutinised him carefully. He wondered how old he could be. Must be past forty-five, he decided, and glanced up at his carefully dyed hair with its glossy sheen beneath the bright lights of the bar.

He had noticed that the other's manner had in some subtle way changed since his arrival in London. It was more staid, almost consciously modulated sometimes. It was only on occasions like this that his boyish attitude took command and the near to stagily urbane manner was dropped.

Bertie was saying something to him, but he wasn't listening. The atmosphere seemed to him to have grown stifling. He ran his finger round the inside of his collar to loosen it.

'I don't know about you,' he muttered, 'but I can't breathe in this place. Can't we get some air?' He finished his drink while the other regarded him with faint amusement.

'You're all jumpy tonight, old chappie.'

'You know the idea was we were going to talk,' Rolf said. 'That's why we've met, isn't it?'

'That was the general idea.'

'Not just about this and that,' Rolf went on. 'Besides, you'll have to be pushing off in a little while. You always do.'

'Want to move along, eh?'

'Can't we find a pub somewhere where there's plenty of room? Then we can go into a huddle in a corner.'

Bertie glanced round him and then nodded his head.

'Okay, let's go.'

A few moments later found them in Oxford Street. They stood on the edge of the pavement for a moment with the stream of traffic and people rushing past them noisily. The lights from the cinema across the road glittered in a variety of colours. Rolf took in grateful gulps of fresh air, as they paused indecisively. A string of buses swung out from Edgware Road into Park Lane. Bertie was glancing round him. He said to Rolf:

'Which way?'

'There's a pub along Oxford Street. Over on the other side.'

The traffic lights in front of them changed to green, and there was a surge of people across the road. Bertie grabbed the other's arm.

'Come on. Let's find your dump.'

They paused for a moment beneath the glare of the cinema lights and continued along Oxford Street. Presently they saw a fake-Tudor public house on the corner.

'This is it,' Rolf said.

The long bar was, though fairly full, spacious and at once Rolf spotted a low table in a more secluded corner just being vacated by a young man and a girl. Hurriedly he pushed past some customers towards the corner, Bertie following him at a more leisurely pace. The young couple, the girl trailing a cloud of cheap perfume behind her, edged away from his aggressive approach, and Rolf threw himself triumphantly into a chair.

'Okay.' Bertie called out to him. 'You fight anyone off while I get the drinks.'

Rolf nodded, settled himself and lit a fresh cigarette. He glanced about him. Nobody within a earshot, he noted with satisfaction. At the same time the hubbub of conversation that arose from the half-crowded bar would have made it difficult for anyone to overhear their conversation. He remembered having read somewhere that the best place for a confidential talk was in some crowded place where everyone else was talking so much that they couldn't hear or weren't interested in anyone else's conversation. This seemed to be a pretty good choice.

Bertie arrived with the drinks, and as he sat down the other plunged into the subject that had been on his mind all the evening.

'Talk about a Yogi's bed of knives,' he said; 'it's nothing to what I've been on since last night. This chap, Dr. Morelle, turning up out of the blue with this news about the Drummer girl. Fairly knocked me for a loop, I can tell you.'

Bertie eyed him over his glass.

'You didn't give anything away?'

Rolf snorted and took a drink from his own glass.

'What sort of a dope d'you take me for?'

'I thought he might've caught you off your guard,' the other said. 'That's why I rang you earlier, last night, to warn you. I guessed you might be hearing something. Being linked up with Neil Fulton I reckoned there was every chance you'd have someone come snooping round. That, plus the fact you were the last to see her before she vanished.'

'You seem to know as much about her as Dr. Morelle.' Rolf was frowning at him.

The other laughed gently.

'Come to think of it I know a bit more. You see, chum, I'm the man who saw her even later than you.'

'You?' Incredulously.

'Me,' the other grinned at him broadly. 'The old brain's ticking over, eh?'

Bertie smiled mockingly and for several moments Rolf sat staring at him. He found it impossible to believe what had happened.

'You're — you're kidding me,' he gulped.

'You've just old me yourself I knew more about it than this doctor guy,' the other reminded him.

Rolf found himself shaking all over as if swept by an icy blast. His hands gripped the edge of the table so that the knuckles were dead white. Bertie's voice came to him as from a distance.

'It was a sudden inspiration I got,' the voice was saying, and the calm amusement in his tone seemed to clear Rolf's brain. Instinctively he leaned forward to catch the quietly spoken words. As conversationally as if he were describing how he'd caught a bus Bertie went on:

'I knew she and Fulton were lunching with you, of course,' he said. 'I remembered you'd also mentioned Fulton would be leaving first for the studio. You see I've been thinking this blackmail racket is too cheap for me. Guess I've got a bit more ambitious. So I think to myself, why not pull off something really worthwhile? A big kill in one go, and I suddenly got a mental picture of that girl — worth God knows how many thousands — leaving your place in Heath Lane, all on her little ownsome. I knew it was what I'd been waiting for. Supposing, I asked myself, I meet her, driving a saloon car hired for the job and pick her up with some excuse?'

'Is that what you did?' Rolf queried him in a low voice.

The other nodded, leaning back with a self-satisfied smirk. He took a drink from his glass and then leaned forward again.

'She'd just turned out of Heath Lane when I saw her,' he said. 'I pulled alongside and went into my patter. Told her I'd just come from Park Lane where her father had been taken suddenly ill. We'd tried to 'phone her at your place, I said, but your line must have been out of order. So I'd driven up to fetch her and get her back to her father quickly as possible. She fell for it hook, line and sinker, and we drove off. On the way I pulled up at a furnished house which I'd rented specially, saying I had to call there to pick up her father's doctor who was visiting another patient. Might be a few moments before he could get away, so would she like to come in and 'phone and see how her old man was? She fell for that too. Of course the moment she was inside the door I gave her a shot with the old hypodermic, and there she is all nicely hidden away.'

He took another drink and said:

'Not bad, eh? For a first time.'

Rolf was staring at him, his pale blue eyes suddenly sharp.

'You dirty rat,' he grated through his teeth. 'You've been planning this for months.'

The other's face changed. It was suddenly hard.

'That was the reason for you wanting me to help you,' Rolf went on, his face working. 'You've got me to put the finger on somebody for a kidnapping job. Not blackmail at all. You'd got this in mind all along.'

'Okay. Okay,' the other said lazily. 'I'll come clean. You're a little brighter than I took you for.'

'Thanks,' was the bitter retort.

'So what?' The other shrugged his shoulders. 'You still get your cut and it'll be a bigger one than for just the old blackmail gag.'

'I don't want any cut.'

'Take it easy,' Bertie told him gently. 'You're in this, anyway. Remember?'

Rolf's blood seemed to freeze up as he caught the hint of menace in the other's tone.

'You've got to keep your trap shut, however squeamish you feel about it,' Bertie was continuing. 'So why not earn yourself a little jack at the same time.'

'You must be crazy,' Rolf flared up at him. 'This is London. Not New York or Los Angeles. You'll never get away with it.'

And another spasm of terror shook him as he went on in a choked whisper: 'Supposing anything happens to her? Supposing she — she died — ' He broke off as he caught a sudden look in Bertie's eyes. 'She *is* dead,' he said suddenly, his voice a flat whisper. '*You've murdered her.*'

13

Fear and Trembling

Bertie leant forward with a sudden savage movement. Rolf flinched back as if the other was going to hit him.

'Shut up, you dope,' Bertie grated. 'Of course the girl isn't dead.'

Rolf stared at him, his pale blue eyes wary. After a moment his expression relaxed. Something in the other's tone and expression convinced him that now, at any rate, he was speaking the truth. Rolf said:

'I'm sorry if I blew my top. But I still think you're crazy to believe you'll get away with it. They'll be on to you like a pack of wolves — '

He broke off. From the corner of his eye he saw someone sitting a few yards across from them. It was a man in a check overcoat and bowler hat. The coat was dirty and wrinkled. Rolf hadn't noticed him there before. The man was staring at them curiously until he met Rolf's gaze, when he turned his face quickly away. Again that fit of trembling shook Rolf's frame.

'We can't talk here,' he suddenly muttered.

Bertie regarded him with amused contempt.

'What you scared about?'

'I'm scared, I admit it,' Rolf said. 'You've got yourself in a spot even if you won't realise it.' He added bitterly: 'And you've dragged me in it with you.'

He looked round again. The man in the bowler hat seemed to be concentrating his attention on his glass of beer. But now the whole place appeared sinister. The laughter suddenly had a devilish ring. The faces in the garish light had become cruel, like faces in a nightmare. He fully expected the appearance at any moment of a squad of policemen who would bear down upon him relentlessly. He stood up shakily.

'Come on,' he insisted. 'We'll talk at my place.'

Bertie shrugged and finished his drink and rose to his feet casually.

'Okay,' he said agreeably. 'Let's do that.'

'We can't go to your place, can we?' Rolf put in meaningly. 'I've never had the pleasure of visiting you yet.'

The other regarded him thoughtfully for a moment

'You're not likely to, either,' he said. His voice was still affable. 'Sorry to sound inhospitable, but where I live and where I work is strictly my business. I thought I'd told you that.'

'All right, all right,' Rolf replied hurriedly, and led the way out of the bar.

They stopped a prowling taxi. As Rolf bustled the other quickly into it he glanced round to make sure no one from the pub was following them. Then he got into the taxi and it drove off.

This time when they reached the foot of Heath Lane, Rolf didn't suggest stopping the taxi and walking the rest of the way. In his anxiety to reach the friendly harbour of his own house he had no desire to linger over the pleasure of the view.

He touched the switch and the house glowed in the soft lamp light; he took the other's hat and he contrived to get control of the shakiness that still sapped the strength from his knees. He mixed Bertie a drink and then poured himself a stiff bourbon. Bertie was unconcernedly gazing at the photographs, smiling reminiscently.

'Gee, those were the days,' he said. 'What the hell got into me that made me think of quitting Hollywood? I'll never forgive myself; I tell you that.'

Rolf relaxed enough to mutter his agreement.

'I think you've got something there.'

'Soon as I make this clean-up,' the other went on, staring lovingly at a picture of Rolf and a blonde actress at Malibu, 'London won't see me for dust. First boat for the good old U.S.' He gave a sudden harsh laugh. 'Maybe, I'll *have* to clear out for safety at that.'

Rolf found his glass rattling against his teeth as he took another drink.

'For God's sake, Bertie,' he managed to gulp, 'be careful. Don't forget I'm in this too — '

He broke off with a sudden start and jerked his head towards the door.

'Now what's eating you?' Bertie queried.

'Thought I heard something.'

'Oh, shut up,' the other replied disgustedly.

Rolf, ignoring him, had put down his glass and was moving to the door. He was convinced he'd heard the sounds of footsteps outside. He could feel little beads of perspiration on his forehead. His heart was thudding violently in his throat. For a moment he stood at the door and then, with a tremendous effort, he steadied himself. He pulled open the door and stepped out into the darkness. As he did so he heard Bertie's mocking voice from the room behind him.

'If it's the cops, tell 'em you did it, and I don't know you.'

Rolf stood on the pavement looking up and down the shadowed street. There seemed to be no one about. He must have been mistaken. He pulled out his handkerchief and, wiping his face, turned and went back into the house.

'No cops?' the other greeted him with an expression of mock disappointment. 'Too bad.'

'It's all right for you,' Rolf flung at him. 'You're different; you've graduated in crookery. So far,' he added bitterly, 'I've only been at the receiving end of it.'

Bertie's face darkened a little.

'Now don't let's get unfriendly,' he said. 'Relax.'

Leo Rolf slumped into a chair with his drink at his elbow and tried to fend off the waves of terror that kept on sweeping towards him.

'If we don't lose our heads,' he heard the other saying, 'we'll get away with it. I tell you, pal,' Bertie's voice was supremely confident, 'if I play the cards the way I've got 'em stacked, I'll collect the swag in the next day or two.'

'Swag?' Rolf raised his head questioningly.

'What d'you think I'm doing this for? Excitement?'

'Money, of course.'

'Bull's-eye first time.'

'The way you said 'swag' sounded as if — '

'You don't imagine,' Bertie said easily, 'I'm going to fall for them paying me in five-pound notes, while they take careful records of the numbers? Or,' he sneered, 'were you thinking I'd take a cheque?'

Rolf understood what Bertie was driving at. 'Can you be paid in one-pound notes?' he suggested. 'They're easy to get rid of.'

'Dope,' the other retorted. 'To carry ten thousand in one-pound notes would need a truck.'

'Ten thousand,' Rolf gasped.

'I told you, I'm doing this for money.'

'They'll never pay.'

'No? Drummer's hardly down-and-out, and the girl must have cleaned up around ten thousand herself lately. They can rake it up between 'em.'

'You seem to have got the whole thing taped.'

'Been working on this gag the last year,' the other admitted. He took a gulp from his glass. Rolf looked at him.

'You got her in that house like you said?' he queried.

Bertie answered him with a non-committal laugh.

'She's in a hide-away all right,' he said. 'But the house was only temporary. I moved her later, when it was dark. Somewhere I'd chosen way back. Where it is needn't bother you one little bit. The less you know about this the less you'll know. Get it?'

There was a little pause and then Rolf said slowly:

'In a minute you'll be admitting you *have* bumped her off. You'll get your money, but Drummer will never see his daughter alive.' Suddenly he sprang to his feet. 'I'm not standing for it,' he said, his voice rising wildly. 'You're making me accessory to a murder. They'll hang me as well as you.'

'*Shut up!*'

But the other raved on unheeding:

'I'm going to spill the beans, I tell you. You can't stop me. You can tell 'em what you like about me, but I'm not going to be mixed up in a murder — '

Bertie's fist drove against his mouth. Rolf found himself lurching against the piano, staring down at the shattered whisky glass at his feet. It had been one of a prized set of Jacobean glasses, and he gave a moan of mingled rage and despair. He raised his head to find the the other's gaze boring into him.

'You need your handkerchief,' Bertie said quietly. 'Your mouth's bleeding.'

Automatically Rolf dabbed at the little trickle of blood at the corner of his mouth. Bertie asked:

'You okay?'

Rolf nodded. The punch in the mouth seemed, in fact, to have stopped his trembling, and the shakiness that had threatened to demoralise him completely. Now his brain was working more coolly. He was realising that if he wanted to come out of this business and land on his feet he'd have to take a grip on himself.

'Sorry I had to do that,' the other was saying. 'But it was a case of being cruel to be kind.' His teeth were bared in that old charming grin, and he patted Rolf's shoulder. 'Eh?'

'I was beginning to make a fool of myself,' Rolf admitted. 'I see now you're right,' he went on slowly. 'If we play it the right way we can get away with it.'

'That's the kind of talk I like to hear.'

'I'll follow your example,' Rolf was continuing. 'As soon as the job's done and I get my cut I'll pull out too.'

Bertie's expression assumed a boyish pleasure at the other's change of attitude. He said:

'You'll get your cut all right. I won't let you down over that. All you've got to do is to keep a grip on yourself and your trap shut. Leave the rest to me. Stick to the story you've told this doctor chap; just that and nothing more. Forget about what you've learnt this evening and we'll see ourselves in the clear.' He glanced at his watch. 'Time for me to beat it.'

Rolf got him his hat. As they went to the door the other said:

'If anybody does start nosing around tip me off when I 'phone.'

After Bertie had gone he went back and

poured himself a fresh drink. Carefully and with seething bitterness in his heart he cleared up the pieces of the broken glass. That done, he glanced at his watch. It was ten minutes since Bertie had gone. He got his hat, switched out the lights and went out. He paused for a moment, trying to fix his mind on his next course of action.

He'd just walk around a little, he decided, as he stared across at the darkness and the glow in the sky beyond. That's it. He knew what he was going to do, but he'd walk around a little just so as to fix it in his mind. So that there would be no slip-up.

He gave a startled gasp as something curled round his ankles. He looked down with a muttered curse at the white cat purring up at him. Savagely he pushed it aside with his foot. It sprawled across the pavement before it turned and flashed out of sight. Rolf pulled the brim of his hat over his eyes and set off down Heath Lane.

A few yards away the watching figure detached itself from the shadows and silently followed him.

14

Ring at the Door

'The conclusions I have so far reached,' Dr. Morelle was saying, as he paced his study, 'appear to indicate four suspects, one or all of whom might be implicated in the kidnapping.'

Miss Frayle looked up from her pencil flying across the page of her note-book.

'All of them?' she queried, her eyes wide over her horn-rims. 'D'you mean they might be working together?'

'I have not entirely dismissed such a possibility,' was the reply. 'Though I incline to the theory that the crime was, in fact, carried out single-handed.'

He paused to stub out his cigarette. At the sudden cessation of his steady flow of words, Miss Frayle gave an almost inaudibly expectant sigh. Perhaps he'd reached the end of his dictation for the evening? She threw a surreptitious glance at the clock on the mantelpiece. Just on ten-thirty. He had been talking and pacing up and down before his writing-desk since eight o'clock. Examining the mystery of Doone Drummer's disappearance in all its aspects from the fateful evening of yesterday up to their visit to Harvey Drummer that morning.

Leaving Miss Frayle to catch up with transcribing a batch of dictation concerned with his routine work, Dr. Morelle had gone out shortly after lunch. He had thought it unnecessary to inform Miss Frayle where he was going. She had been left to wonder if he were pursuing some secret line of inquiry or merely walking round and round the Inner Circle of Regent's Park. This was a method he sometimes employed to help his cogitations. She had expected his return for tea, but he had not arrived. She had been left to finish the bread-and-butter she had cut beautifully thin for him all by herself.

Just before dinner he had stalked in without any explanation of his absence. In answer to her query had he had any tea? Miss Frayle had received no reply.

Realising he was not in the mood for questioning she had wisely decided to remain silent, although longing to know what he'd been up to. He had spoken to her only to ask, with the somewhat hypocritical smile she was used to on these occasions, if she would mind doing a little work after dinner.

Now she watched him take a fresh cigarette from the human skull which served him as a cigarette-box, on the desk. She shuddered slightly as she always did whenever her gaze encountered the thing. She glanced round the quiet study, lit only by a large standard lamp and the desk lamp throwing its pool of light on her note-book. Round the walls were row after row of bookshelves fairly sagging with the weight of their contents.

There was one wall of shelves filled with books, the titles of which she knew by heart. She had stared at them often enough in moments of morbid curiosity, though she had never trusted her nerves so much as even to glance through one. Frightening titles they were to her, in German, French and Italian. Such as:

Kriminalanthropologie und Kriminalistik; Technique Policière; Medécine Légale; Kriminalistische Monatshefte; Kriminalpsychologie; Die Technik der Blutgruttenuntersuchung; Manuel de Identificación Judicial; Le Chambre Noir and *L'Enquête Criminelle*, and dozens more. Every volume in no matter what language, devoted to more or less the same theme; criminal violence, murder and sudden death. His own contributions to the subject in English and their various translations were, of course, prominently displayed.

Against another wall were filing-cabinets relating to every imaginable aspect of psychiatry and psychology, including his own notes and papers which formed the basis for innumerable lectures and articles for scientific journals all over the world.

The lighter flamed, illuminating Dr. Morelle's saturnine features and glinted for a moment in his dark and curiously penetrating eyes. As he drew at his cigarette he murmured:

'I should like to check back over the notes I have dictated to you. Especially with regard to the suspects.'

'Starting with Neil Fulton?' Miss Frayle queried. 'After all he was the first we really thought was mixed up in it.'

The Doctor regarded her for a moment without replying. Then, with a thoughtful glance at his cigarette, he said:

'I was under the impression you have never seriously suspected him, Miss Frayle.'

'No, but I thought you had.'

'So far, admittedly, his story rings true,' Dr. Morelle said. 'I have ascertained that his arrival at the film-studio yesterday afternoon was compatible with the time of his leaving Doone Drummer with Leo Rolf at the latter's house in Hampstead.'

'You rang up about it?' Miss Frayle asked, a slightly surprised note in her voice.

Dr. Morelle shook his head.

'My inquiry was conducted much more discreetly,' he said. 'It is imperative no suggestion that he is in any way suspected should reach the young man. In case he is connected with the kidnapping.'

'How did you find out?' Miss Frayle asked.

'By the simple process of calling at the film-studio in question for a casual conversation with the commissionaire on duty at the studio entrance.'

Miss Frayle felt a little hurt. Even if he hadn't sufficient confidence in her to send her on such an errand, he might at least have taken her with him. He knew how thrilled she would have been to visit a film-studio, though she would probably have caught only a glimpse of it from the outside.

'It would appear impossible,' Dr. Morelle was saying, 'that he could have taken an active part in the abduction during the short time between leaving Hampstead and reaching the studio. I am, therefore, disposed to regard him as, at any rate, an unlikely suspect.'

'Good!' Miss Frayle exclaimed involuntarily. She had felt considerable sympathy for the young film-actor. Convinced as she was that he was deeply in love with Doone Drummer, it was fantastic to her that he had been involved in her disappearance. She caught the Doctor's sardonic gaze and glanced in some confusion at her note-book.

'How about Leo Rolf?' she said, looking up.

Dr. Morelle's eyes narrowed behind the cloud of cigarette smoke from his *Le Sphinx*.

'I was not altogether impressed by him,' he mused. 'He was, upon his own admittance, the last person to see the young woman. At the same time he was unable to substantiate the story he told me last night. I have only his word that Miss Drummer left his house safely. I plan to pursue further enquiries regarding him. If necessary, through Inspector Hood.'

Miss Frayle nodded with a little smile.

'He'd help us. I wonder how he is?' she went on. 'It's about time we saw him again.'

'It will be unnecessary for him to call and see me in person,' Dr. Morelle said. 'I shall be able to convey my requirements to him over the telephone.'

Little did Miss Frayle or Dr. Morelle

realise that they were destined to meet Inspector Hood again not only within a very short time, but under dramatic circumstances.

'I have already ascertained that Rolf has been far from fully employed since his return from America. He has apparently been engaged with writing only two films, his work on the last being so unsuccessful that his engagement was abruptly terminated. I am informed that his estimated earnings during the eighteen months he has been here could not have totalled more than one thousand pounds. Not, one would think, sufficient to maintain the mode of living to which he is obviously accustomed.'

'One thousand pounds for eighteen months,' Miss Frayle did some rapid mental arithmetic. 'That's only about twelve pounds a week.'

'I often wonder, my *dear* Miss Frayle, how I should manage without your invaluable assistance on such problems as the one you have just solved.'

Miss Frayle, however, forgot to blush this time. She was wondering furiously how Dr. Morelle had managed to obtain the information he had about Leo Rolf. She recalled various occasions before when he had demonstrated that there was apparently no source of information to which he hadn't access.

'I am in fact assured,' he was continuing, 'that the man is in need of employment. Which in turn, of course, suggests that his financial resources are low. A large sum of money such as he might realise by holding Miss Drummer to ransom could prove more than acceptable.'

'It seems,' Miss Frayle put in, 'he's jolly well our main suspect.'

'You remind me of an ingenuous member of a jury, persuaded first by counsel for the defence to believe the accused's innocence, then swayed by counsel for the prosecution into believing the accused's guilt. I feel confident, for instance, I could now proceed to convince you that Drummer's secretary, Pearson, is equally suspect.'

'There are his black gloves — ' Miss Frayle began, breaking off as she realised that her remark was justifying the Doctor's observation.

'On the other hand,' Dr. Morelle said, 'the fact that he has been long in his present employment and a recipient of Drummer's confidence is not to be gainsaid.'

'But,' Miss Frayle pointed out, 'Mr. Drummer said you shouldn't take him at his face value, remember? Behind that nervous manner of his, Mr. Drummer said, he was a sharp little businessman.'

'Such characteristics might just as easily speak in his favour as against him,' Dr. Morelle replied. 'That he is shrewd and capable suggests to me that in the position he holds he must have amassed a useful nest-egg for himself. Legitimately. It is hardly conceivable that he would jeopardise his career by involving himself in such a risky undertaking as abducting his employer's daughter.'

Miss Frayle recalled the man in the pince-nez with the servile manner with a little grimace of dislike.

'Supposing,' she persisted, 'he hadn't kidnapped her for money? He may be madly infatuated with her, although she of course couldn't possibly care for him, and he's hidden her away so nobody else should get her.'

Dr. Morelle regarded her pityingly.

'My dear Miss Frayle,' he said, 'cannot you for one moment forget your romantic vapourings? Adhere to the facts as we know them. The motive for kidnapping Doone Drummer is ransom to the tune of a ten thousand pound diamond bracelet.'

'Yes,' Miss Frayle muttered. 'Of course.' And she subsided.

'In point of fact,' Dr. Morelle pursued coolly, 'the demand for the diamond bracelet could sharpen suspicion against Pearson. In his position of trust with Drummer, it is possible that he had also obtained inside information regarding the calling-in of the five-pound notes. If he is responsible for the young woman's disappearance it follows he would have taken the very steps to protect himself from discovery as those which the kidnapper has in fact adopted.'

'And there are those black gloves,' Miss Frayle reminded him. 'I'm sure they've got something to do with the mystery.'

'Possibly,' Dr. Morelle replied. 'Though they are suspicious not because they are black as much as because Pearson would appear to be wearing them surreptitiously. Whether they are black, white, or red silk gloves is unimportant. However, the gloves are no more suspicious than another aspect of his personal appearance, which you have doubtless already noted.'

She blinked at him a little puzzled. Then she said: 'You mean his curiously deformed hands?'

But Dr. Morelle made no reply. He merely gave her that irritatingly enigmatic smile. Tapping the ash off his cigarette, he left her desperately trying to recall what else it was about the secretary's appearance that was so obvious but which she had failed to spot.

'Before you reject our main suspect, Leo Rolf,' Dr. Morelle continued, 'in favour of Pearson, let us examine yet another candidate. I feel confident I can in turn persuade you to reject Pearson for her — '

'Mrs. Huggins, you mean?' Miss Frayle put in quickly. 'She did lie about that film, of course.'

Dr. Morelle inclined his head.

'In case you had misheard the information over the telephone' — he gave Miss Frayle a smooth smile — 'I personally checked with the cinema. They confirmed that the film Mrs. Huggins had described as having seen was not being shown at the time in question.'

You have been getting around, Miss Frayle thought to herself. First the film-studio, then finding out about Leo Rolf, and now checking up on the film. No wonder you didn't have time to come back for tea.

'The fact that the woman was lying in this instance,' Dr. Morelle was saying, 'does not necessarily mean she is guilty of, or implicated in, the kidnapping.'

'Of course not,' Miss Frayle agreed. 'There might be two or three reasons why she lied.'

'What reasons suggest themselves to you, my dear Miss Frayle? As one who has had occasion to concoct excuses of a similar nature, you should be able to supply me with some appropriate examples.'

'You do love to nag over things,' Miss Frayle protested. 'In any case I didn't tell you a lie; I explained to you how it came about.'

He regarded her, his expression frankly disbelieving. 'Nonetheless I await suggestions from that inventive mind of yours.'

'Well,' she began vaguely, 'there are a hundred reasons.'

'I require only one,' Dr. Morelle invited.

'One very obvious reason,' she said impulsively — then catching the Doctor's expectantly glinting eye upon her, changed her mind in mid-sentence — 'is that she had a relative in prison. A brother, for instance, whom she doesn't want anyone to know about. Yesterday was the visiting day for her to go and see him.'

Dr. Morelle was eyeing her with a look amounting almost to admiration.

'To my astonishment,' he said, 'you have put forward what might appear to be a perfectly plausible explanation.'

'Shall I get you a glass of water?' Miss Frayle said sarcastically. 'Or don't you think you're going to faint?'

He ignored her thrust, however, and said thoughtfully:

'I foresee the time when it will be necessary to question Mrs. Huggins somewhat more closely.'

'There's that business about her being able to put on a man's voice,' Miss Frayle added.

'That is also receiving due consideration. It is indeed conceivable that she might be linked with Doone Drummer's disappearance in some way.'

The telephone rang and Miss Frayle gave the Doctor a glance. He replied with a nod, and she lifted up the receiver.

'It's Mr. Drummer,' she said, and he crossed and took the receiver.

'Sorry to be 'phoning so late,' Harvey Drummer apologised. 'But I felt you hadn't gone to bed yet.'

'I am at this moment considering various aspects of your daughter's disappearance.'

'Here's an item of news which I

thought you ought to know about. It's to do with the calling in of the five-pound notes. Afraid my banker friend's intelligent anticipation had got a bit out of hand,' Drummer confessed. 'Been having a chat with him tonight, and he now tells me it turns out it was only a rumour. No basis in fact.'

'As it happens it is of little consequence,' Dr. Morelle said.

'Except that it did give us the idea the kidnapper was somebody who had also got the same information. Remember?'

'I remember.'

'Now it seems,' the other went on, 'the kidnapper's demand for the bracelet is nothing to do with having inside information, but sheer cunning. Such as anyone might have. Incidentally, I've bought the bracelet. Got it through a Hatton Garden friend. Secondhand, twenty stones and worth every penny of ten thousand. It's in my safe now.'

'You have not confided your purchase to anyone?' Dr. Morelle queried.

'No one,' Drummer said promptly. 'Even the man I bought it from is regarding it as strictly confidential. He added: 'I shall have to make up some story to tell Pearson. I've had to do a bit of juggling with my investments to raise the money.'

Dr. Morelle said: 'I have been considering the position of your housekeeper in relation to this affair.'

'You mean about her lying about going to the cinema.'

'That may be of no importance,' was the reply. 'I should like to know more about her husband.'

'Her husband?' Drummer sounded surprised. 'But he's dead.'

Dr. Morelle did not reply at once. Then:

'On what sort of terms were they?'

'All I can tell you is that they got on very well. She was terribly shaken by his death. As she said before you, if it hadn't been that she liked her job here so much she couldn't have stayed on.'

'They came to you with impeccable references, of course?'

'First rate,' was the prompt reply. 'From a chap in the north. Been with him several years, but they wanted to come to London for a change. Same reason as Brethers, as a matter of fact. He was with a retired cotton tycoon living in North Wales. By the way,' he went on, 'I'm afraid you upset Brethers by the questioning you gave him this morning.'

'I am extremely sorry to learn that,' Dr. Morelle replied. 'My recollection of the questions is that they were fairly innocuous.'

'He seems to have got the idea you suspect him of being concerned personally with your missing notes,' the other explained. 'After you'd gone he came and told me he'd picked up a letter someone had dropped at the party. He couldn't remember who it was. Some young chap. He'd returned it to him all right. But as he'd forgotten to mention the incident to you he was wondering if you'd noticed it and thought that he wasn't being frank omitting to tell you.'

'You may certainly reassure him on that score,' Dr. Morelle said.

'I'll tell him. He's a decent sort of chap, as I think you'll agree. No point in upsetting him for nothing.'

Miss Frayle pricked up her ears as she heard the Doctor say:

'Miss Frayle was most impressed by him. Though I must mention,' he added, 'her predilections are not necessarily an infallible guide. It has been known in similar instances for her to be impressed by the guilty person.'

Miss Frayle pulled a face at Dr. Morelle from behind her note-book. I suppose they're talking about Brethers, she thought. The quiet-spoken man-servant with his unobtrusive, straight-forward manner had appeared perfectly self-possessed under Dr. Morelle's questioning.

'Do you propose doing anything about Mrs. Huggins?' Drummer was asking Dr. Morelle.

'I shall wish to question her again. But for the moment I am anxious not to arouse her suspicions in any way.'

'There's Pearson, too. That business of his black gloves.'

'He must also be handled carefully,' was the reply. 'I fancy he might jump to the correct conclusion about any closer interrogation unless his suspicions are carefully lulled.'

'He's not given me any hint he suspects what's happened to Doone,' the other replied. 'I saw him before he went out this evening — gone to visit a cousin, I believe, in Fulham. He was his usual nervously chirpy self.'

A few moments later Harvey Drummer rang off. Dr. Morelle stared abstractedly at the spiral of smoke ascending from his cigarette. Miss Frayle watched him silently for several moments. Then she said:

'Wasn't Mr. Drummer your first suspect? Didn't you think he might have kidnapped his own daughter for some mysterious motive?'

Dr. Morelle raised a questioning eyebrow in her direction.

'It was a possibility which I naturally took into account,' he murmured thoughtfully. 'But the evidence so far appears to indicate that he could not have been in two places at once.'

'You mean because he was with us

when the kidnapper 'phoned?' As the Doctor made no reply, Miss Frayle added: 'But the person 'phoning could have been an accomplice.'

'You think of everything, Miss Frayle,' Dr. Morelle replied somewhat irritably. 'Even the most obvious.'

At that moment the door-bell rang. Miss Frayle's eyes widened behind her horn-rims. She asked:

'Who on earth could that be?'

Dr. Morelle offered no suggestion and, putting down her notebook, she hurried out of the study.

The bell rang again as she reached the door. The caller, whoever it was, was certainly of an impatient nature. It was a man who stood before her swaying slightly against the darkness of Harley Street.

'What d'you want?'

His only reply was to stagger towards her. She stepped back with a rising feeling of alarm. Was it some drunk who had rung the bell out of a perverted sense of humour?

Then she saw that his face, as the light

from the hall shone on it, was a ghastly white; the eyes were half-closed. At once she realised he was not drunk, but desperately ill. There came a sudden gurgling sound from the man and, with a convulsive movement, he lurched forward and pitched headlong into the hall. Miss Frayle stifled the scream that rose in her throat as she stared down at the dark stain welling from the man's back. She turned on her heel and ran back calling out for Dr. Morelle.

Appearing instantly in answer to her cries he went swiftly towards the figure in the hall. The door was still half open and, closing it, he knelt and turned the figure over.

It was Leo Rolf.

15

The Man from Scotland Yard

'Here we are again,' the man in the raincoat said. 'Bobbing up like the proverbial bad penny.'

He leaned his burly frame back in the chair in Dr. Morelle's study, balancing carefully a somewhat ancient-looking trilby-hat on his knees and clamped his teeth over the stem of his short black pipe.

'It's very nice to see you again, Inspector,' Miss Frayle replied. 'Though I always think it's a shame that the only times we meet is when something nasty happens.'

Detective-Inspector Hood chuckled, and the charred bowl of his briar bubbled like a witch's cauldron as he drew at it. He blew a cloud of acrid tobacco-smoke ceilingwards and commented:

'I'm a bit like the Doctor here. People

only send for me when there's trouble, just as they only send for you when they're ill. Eh, Dr. Morelle?' And exhaling another cloud of smoke he turned to the silent figure who sat a carved figure behind his desk, the tips of his fingers pressed together as he gazed abstractedly before him.

Dr. Morelle might not have heard the other's little simile. He made no reply, and the Inspector turned back to Miss Frayle with a good-humoured wink.

'Always get given a nice cup of tea, anyhow,' he said, 'when I do come here.' And he took up the cup of tea which was on the desk at his elbow and drank it off appreciatively.

Miss Frayle gave him a wan but grateful smile. The other's genial presence was helping her to wipe away the memory of those dreadful moments when she had answered that fateful ring at the door. The Scotland Yard man's sturdy matter-of-factness had begun to erase some of the nightmarish picture of that ghastly figure stumbling into the hall and collapsing at her feet.

'No doubt,' Dr. Morelle murmured apparently taking a sudden interest in the conversation, 'the reason doctors are not regaled with a cup of tea on their visit is that they are too busy to drink it.'

Inspector Hood gave a deliberately over-acted start, and then grinned at him and said equably:

'Thought you were using up a little nap, Doctor.'

'I,' was the acid retort, 'have been thinking.'

Although to Miss Frayle it seemed like years ago it was, in fact, just over an hour since the late Leo Rolf's dramatic appearance at 221B, Harley Street. It was pure chance that Inspector Hood had been working late when Dr. Morelle had 'phoned Scotland Yard. He was about to shut up shop for the night, as he put it, but on hearing the Doctor's tidings he had promptly volunteered to come along straight away. Accompanying him was a police surgeon who had made his routine examination of the body. The dead man had been stabbed in the back by what was apparently a large clasp-knife. Following soon after the Inspector, a police-car had arrived with the finger-print men and photographers. Their work completed the body had been borne away to the local mortuary.

'Will you have some more tea?' Miss Frayle asked, indicating Hood's empty cup.

'No thanks, Miss Frayle. Must get on with the business.' Hood glanced expectantly at Dr. Morelle who had stood up and, leaning against his desk, was thoughtfully lighting a cigarette. 'First time you've had a murder right on your doorstep, eh?' he said. And as there was no response, went on: 'Oh, well, there's always got to be a first time.'

'I hope it'll be the last,' Miss Frayle murmured fervently.

The Inspector turned to her, his face serious.

'Yes,' he said, 'must have been pretty nasty for you.'

Miss Frayle only half heard him and nodded absently. She, too, was gazing expectantly at Dr. Morelle.

While Inspector Hood had been

occupied with investigating the murder, the Doctor had telephoned the house in Park Lane and told Harvey Drummer of what had happened. Drummer had at once grasped the significance of the dramatic news, and the Doctor had found it unnecessary to explain to him that it was inevitable that Scotland Yard would have to be informed of the kidnapping of his daughter.

'Whether there is any connection between the two crimes,' Dr. Morelle had said, 'remains to be seen.'

'Anyhow,' Drummer had replied, 'you can't, of course, keep Doone's disappearance from the police.'

'I fear not.'

Dr. Morelle had pictured the other's anxiety at this new development. The safe return of his daughter hinged on the very fact that the police should not be informed of her abduction.

'Rest assured,' Dr. Morelle had said. 'The kidnapper will not learn that the police had been taken into our confidence.'

'If you say so,' the other said, his voice

lightening. 'In any case, there's no other way we can meet this new situation.'

Inspector Hood was chewing on his pipe-stem as he gazed speculatively at the dark, silent figure. He wondered just how much longer he'd have to wait before Dr. Morelle started talking.

He threw a sidelong glance at Miss Frayle. She, too, was eyeing the Doctor with a worried frown. The Inspector wondered what strange business Dr. Morelle had become involved in this time. An adventure that had resulted in a murder on his own doorstep. Hardly, it would seem, something simple that was merely part of the Doctor's daily routine.

Inspector Hood was faintly surprised that Dr. Morelle had got so deeply enmeshed in the case without confiding in him, or if not in himself, someone else at Scotland Yard with whom he was on friendly terms. Dr. Morelle was not one of these clever-clever amateur detectives always several steps ahead of the stupid plodding police. Though, as Hood remembered ruefully, there had been one or two investigations during which the

Doctor had somehow contrived to be more than a step ahead of him.

It seemed to Inspector Hood the murder of this Leo Rolf chap was likely to have unusual angles to it, and he was waiting to hear what they were.

'I am grateful to you for your patience, Inspector.'

The sudden quiet words brought the Scotland Yard man's head up with a jerk. He found those penetrating, almost mesmeric, eyes bent upon him intently. Not for the first time he experienced the uncomfortable feeling that Dr. Morelle was capable of reading his very thoughts.

'Part of my job,' he replied easily, and gave Miss Frayle a grin. 'What's on your mind,' he turned back to the Doctor, 'that you want to get off your chest?'

'You have doubtless been considering,' was the response, 'what sort of circumstances in which I have been involved could culminate in the discovery of a corpse in my own house.'

Again Hood felt that those dark, heavy-lidded eyes had been probing the innermost recesses of his mind.

'I must say,' he answered jocularly, 'it isn't quite like you. You've usually kept the bodies at arm's length, so to speak. Not let 'em clutter up your home-life.'

'It's ghastly,' Miss Frayle murmured, and the Inspector threw her a sympathetic look.

'The circumstances have indeed been somewhat untoward,' the Doctor was saying. 'I am sure you will appreciate I never should have interested myself in the case without informing Scotland Yard, unless there was a weighty reason for my reticence.'

Inspector Hood nodded, and Dr. Morelle continued:

'You will further appreciate, moreover, that in a case of kidnapping, the first demand of the kidnapper is, almost inevitably, that the police should not be informed.'

'Kidnapping?'

Inspector Hood grabbed his pipe from between his teeth, stared at Dr. Morelle, then stuck his pipe back between clamped jaws and drew at it furiously.

'This unfortunate man's murder may

be linked with the other crime,' Dr. Morelle went on. 'Nevertheless, I am going to request your secrecy still. It is a vital factor if the victim is to be rescued.'

Inspector Hood gave a non-committal grunt. But Dr. Morelle went on talking incisively. In crisp, telling phrases he drew a picture of the events following the disappearance of Doone Drummer. The other listened raptly, only the bubblings and gurglings from his pipe interrupting his silence.

Graphically Dr. Morelle described the dramatic 'phone call and the first time he had heard the sinister disguised voice of the kidnapper. He gave a description of Harvey Drummer himself, his strong exterior apparently shaken by the news of his daughter's danger. He recounted Neil Fulton's arrival at the flat in Dark Lantern Street.

Vividly he sketched in the personalities of Pearson, whose servile manner, pince-nez and nervous smile concealed a shrewd business brain, and the house-keeper — unexpectedly curvacious Rosie Huggins — lying about her visit to the cinema. He went on to tell of his visit to Leo Rolf at the house in Heath Lane, and of his subsequent significant discoveries regarding the film-writer's circumstances.

One after another Dr. Morelle conjured up the figures so that they seemed to crowd the study before Inspector Hood's and Miss Frayle's eyes.

Miss Frayle noted with a feeling of intense gratification that Dr. Morelle appeared content to confine his picture of the lovely Doone Drummer to a few brief lines. She watched him closely when he related the discovery of his own photograph in the book at her flat; Miss Frayle had to admit to herself she couldn't detect the slightest tremor in his voice, not the faintest hint in his tone to suggest that his feelings for Doone Drummer were anything but coldly detached.

Perhaps, she began to persuade herself, he isn't attracted to her in the slightest. Perhaps, she thought, her fabulous allure made no more appeal to that unemotional, rigidly analytical mind than anyone else who'd figured in the many cases he'd investigated. In fact, from the romantic angle, perhaps Doone Drummer was giving him cause for as few sleepless nights as, Miss Frayle pondered gloomily, she was herself.

'What you're going to ask me to do,' Inspector Hood said heavily as Dr. Morelle concluded his story, 'is to keep this kidnapping dark?'

Dr. Morelle eyed him for a moment before replying.

'I propose,' he said, 'exacting an even more unusual compliance from you.'

Watching the Inspector's thick eyebrows shoot up interrogatively, Miss Frayle gave the Doctor a look that was charged with anxiety. She was fully aware of what was in the Doctor's mind. Would he succeed in persuading the other to fall in with his ideas?

'Blimey,' Hood exclaimed. 'You're not going to ask me to hush up the murder, are you?'

'I had no intention of trespassing upon our acquaintanceship to that extent.' And Inspector Hood was obliged to give a little chuckle at the implied rebuke in Dr. Morelle's retort. 'I merely wish to impress upon you my responsibility so far as the young woman is concerned. I have undertaken to restore her to her father unharmed. As evidence of his faith in me Drummer has, so far as I may judge, shown every co-operation.' The Doctor paused for a moment, then continued: 'If I am to implement my promise, it is imperative no risk is run that the kidnapper will believe that, despite his threat, the police had been called in.'

'I fully understand,' Inspector Hood returned gravely.

'What you have learned,' Dr. Morelle emphasised, 'is in the strictest confidence. But for the fortunate circumstances that you were able to be present here tonight and not some other police-officer, I should have remained silent about the young woman's disappearance.'

Pursing his lips Inspector Hood shook his head.

'Much as I appreciate your confidence in me, I don't think you would have been right to hold back what might be evidence vital towards clearing up the murder. You've got to admit it's the more serious offence of the two.'

'I am fully aware of the relative seriousness of the crime,' Dr. Morelle snapped. 'I am equally aware, however, once the kidnapper learns that the police know about Miss Drummer's abduction you may have not one murder on your hands, but two.'

Hood looked at him, his heavy brows drawn together. He spoke slowly.

'You think there's a danger of that?'

'Oh yes,' Miss Frayle burst in. 'The Doctor's absolutely right. The kidnapper's ruthless. If he knows the police are after him he'll carry out his threat.'

Inspector Hood shifted his gaze from Miss Frayle to Dr. Morelle and back again to Miss Frayle. He chewed at his pipe ruminatively for a few moments before he turned to the Doctor.

'What d'you want me to do?'

'Permit me to pursue my investigation of the kidnapping,' was the prompt response. 'You, of course,' Dr. Morelle added blandly, 'take complete charge of the more serious case of murder.'

'But the two are obviously connected,'

the other protested.

'While that would appear to be the case,' the Doctor agreed, 'it is by no means certain.'

'After all,' Miss Frayle pointed out in prompt support of Dr. Morelle's view, 'the fact that Leo Rolf was the last person we know who saw Doone Drummer alive, and that he's been murdered, could be a coincidence.'

The Inspector smiled at her benignly.

'You're forgetting one little thing,' he commented. 'Dr. Morelle dropped in on Rolf in connection with the kidnapping. Later Rolf intended returning the compliment when he was done in. Seems obvious to me he had some vital information — something he may have remembered, for instance — to give the Doctor, which the murderer was afraid of so he silenced him.'

'I fear,' the Doctor observed, 'Miss Frayle's understandable enthusiasm on my behalf has somewhat clouded her judgment. I readily concede that circumstances indicate a direct connection between both crimes. I merely wish to underline that circumstantial evidence is not always justified.'

'This may be a case in point, I know,' Inspector Hood agreed.

'But,' Dr. Morelle proceeded, 'let us examine my request objectively. If I continue my investigations independently of your valuable co-operation, you will be able to concentrate all your powers on elucidating the homicide. At the same time you are secure in the knowledge that any evidence I uncover which proves to be directly or indirectly relevant to the murder will be placed promptly in your possession. All I demand is that the young woman's life shall not be further endangered. I can assure this only if allowed to continue alone with my plan to her kidnapper.'

Inspector Hood massaged his chin with a broad hand. Miss Frayle glanced at him, her expression full of anxiety. She could not believe the Inspector, who owed so much to Dr. Morelle's brilliant detective work in the past would thwart his wishes over this issue. On the other hand, she realised, Inspector Hood couldn't allow his personal feelings to sway him in an official matter.

It seemed to her the scales hung in the balance, and the Inspector was weighing them with typical impartiality. She turned towards Dr. Morelle expectantly for that final word from him which would clinch the argument in his favour.

'However skilfully I attempt to persuade you, my dear Inspector,' Miss Frayle heard him say, 'you will I know act only according to your sense of duty.'

'You see, I — ' began Inspector Hood dubiously, and Miss Frayle's heart sank. Apparently unmindful of the other's interruption, however, the Doctor concluded:

'Even if it means having to accept responsibility for a second murder which might have been avoided.'

Miss Frayle saw the Inspector's expression change, and she smiled inwardly. Dr. Morelle had produced the final argument all right. It couldn't fail to persuade Inspector Hood to give way to him.

'Put that way,' Hood grunted, 'I

suppose I can't do anything else but agree with you.'

Permitting only the faintest smile of triumph to light his features for a moment, Dr. Morelle inclined his head slightly.

'I can see this is going to be an open and shut case from the word 'Go',' Hood grumbled, heavily sarcastic. 'Just because of you, for instance, how do I interview one witness who could be pretty useful?'

'You mean Neil Fulton?' Miss Frayle put in.

The other nodded lugubriously. He looked at Dr. Morelle. 'I've got to question him about Rolf, and that'll mean he'll be bound to spill the beans about the kidnapping. Then what?'

'He has been suitably impressed,' Dr. Morelle replied, 'with the need for Miss Drummer's disappearance remaining an absolute secret. So far as I know, his acquaintanceship with Rolf has been relatively slight. With your usual admirable discretion you should contrive to restrain him from divulging that secret.'

'It'll be the first time in my experience,'

Inspector Hood growled, 'I'll have ever questioned a witness and deliberately tried to stop him talking.' He caught Dr. Morelle's glance and grinned involuntarily. 'I know what you're thinking. That it won't be the first time I've questioned people when I *haven't* had to go easy and still not made 'em talk.'

'No such thought ever crossed my mind,' was the suave reply.

Inspector Hood's burly frame shook with subdued merriment as he arched one heavy eye-brow distrustfully at the Doctor. Taking out his pipe he prodded the air to emphasise his next observation.

'You realise,' he said, 'apart from Fulton, there'll be the woman who does for Rolf.'

'I shall be singularly surprised if you elicit any worthwhile information from that quarter. Doubtless the woman witnessed both Fulton's and Miss Drummer's arrival for lunch, served them during the meal, and may have noted their separate departure. But no more. Not, I submit, particularly compelling qualifications for an important witness.'

'Maybe,' agreed the other. 'Anyhow, if she does tell me anything useful about the girl I'll tip you off.'

Inspector Hood was about to knock out the contents of his pipe into the ashtray at his elbow when he caught Dr. Morelle's sensitively chiselled nostrils quiver forbiddingly. He was well aware of the Doctor's repugnance for the charred, gurgling briar that was his inseparable companion. With a wry grin he stuck it back between his teeth and heaved himself laboriously to his feet. Gripping his trilby in his thick, stubby fingers, he said:

'Thanks for a nice cup of tea, anyway.' Miss Frayle gave him a smile. 'You can rely on me, Doctor,' he went on as he ambled slowly to the door. 'The Drummer girl business is strictly confidential. You realise, of course, you're going to have a lot of publicity when the newspapers get hold of the murder?'

'Oh dear,' murmured Miss Frayle.

'Nothing I can do about that, naturally,' Hood added.

'I have no doubt,' Dr. Morelle

remarked, 'that those sections of the British press dealing in the more sensational form of journalism will seize upon tonight's tragic event with their usual avidity.'

Inspector Hood gave a little shrug as Miss Frayle opened the door for him.

'I'll see you out,' she said.

The Scotland Yard man turned at the door and, with heavy humour, said to Dr. Morelle:

'If you will get yourself mixed up with a glamour girl like Doone Drummer, not to mention a body on your door-mat, you must expect to find yourself in the papers.'

16

Melody in F

Miss Frayle glanced at the clock on the study mantelpiece. It was a few minutes to ten. The morning sun shone brightly through the window, and the sky above Harley Street was a clear blue, unmarred by any cloud.

Miss Frayle always found it difficult to overcome her feeling of surprise that nature seemed seldom in tune with human events. It was utterly incongruous to her that the morning could appear so bright and cloudless when only a few hours before Leo Rolf had been horribly murdered.

There was Harvey Drummer, too. However blue the sky was in reality, his own particular horizon at any rate must be darkly overcast.

Immediately after breakfast Dr. Morelle had retired to his laboratory, leaving Miss

Frayle to check through his mail, make two or three 'phone calls and attend to various routine matters. He would be expecting her to join him now; there were notes he would be wanting to give her.

She collected her note-book and pencils. She caught sight of the headline splashed across one-half of the folded newspaper which was one of several on the writing-desk. She had read them all earlier. They were full of Leo Rolf's murder. To her disappointment Dr. Morelle had completely ignored the newspapers. He gave the impression he was too preoccupied with work awaiting him in the laboratory. Miss Frayle shrewdly suspected, however, that, his apparent unconcern was a pose for her benefit. Just like him to demonstrate a lofty disinterestedness in what absorbed most people.

Little did she guess that early that morning a tall, gaunt figure in a long dressing-gown had crept cautiously down to the hall. After scrutinising every word about Leo Rolf's murder he had carefully refolded the newspapers and, leaving them artistically sticking through the letter-box, Dr. Morelle had gone back to bed.

Miss Frayle picked up the *Telegram* for the second time, and stared at the headline.

CORPSE ON FAMOUS DOCTOR'S DOOR-MAT!

Once again she skimmed through the racily lurid and not entirely accurate account of the murder. She was fascinated by the imaginative trimmings with which the reporter had decked out his story. She felt she was reading about a lot of people she had never known.

There were photographs of Leo Rolf, Dr. Morelle and herself. She regarded them closely. Rolf looked all right. The Doctor looked extraordinarily attractive: what a pity he hadn't gone on the films, she thought irrelevantly. As for herself, she had to admit it didn't exactly flatter her.

With a sigh she wondered if she really could have looked like that white blob with two circles which she presumed were her spectacles. It occurred to her the photographer responsible must have deliberately touched up the picture under Dr. Morelle's instructions to make her appear as ghastly as possible.

Replacing the newspaper she switched the 'phone through to the laboratory. Dr. Morelle did not look up as she came in, but remained with his eye glued to a microscope, intent on the slide he was examining.

He was investigating the possibility of determining the difference between blood-groups in relation to the criminal tendencies of the persons concerned. He had been for some time considering a theory that any emotional upheaval must give rise to certain glandular reactions which in turn might have an effect on the blood. This effect might remain apparent in the blood for a length of time afterwards. The conclusion, therefore, was that it would be possible by applying an appropriate blood-test to discover whether a suspect had suffered any emotional stress at the time of the crime in question. Such an indicator could prove of inestimable value in the process of determining a suspect's innocence or guilt.[1]

Miss Frayle stood patiently waiting for the figure concentrated over his instrument to condescend to notice her presence. She regarded the array of paraphernalia on the bench at which he was working, then her gaze wandered round the laboratory. It was small, but had been constructed under Dr. Morelle's supervision so that every inch of space was utilised to the full.

The most modern equipment in gleaming steel and glass occupied the shelves, cupboards and benches all around her. In one corner taps shone over a bright sink. There were stacks of basins of varying sizes, in copper, aluminium and porcelain. Beakers, graduated flasks, specimen-jars, miscellaneous pipettes stood

---

[1] See his monograph, 'Chemical Mutations in Blood as Result of Endocrine Reaction to Emotional Disturbance' (Manning & Hopper; London).

in orderly array. A wonderful and complicated apparatus for micro-analysis, with improvements designed by Dr. Morelle himself, took up the entire length of one bench. Mortars and pestles, retorts and bulbs, crucibles and test-glasses winked and glinted from the shelves. Racks of test-tubes, syphons, funnels and condensers filled the glass-fronted cup-boards.

On one wall a synchronous clock silently registered the passing seconds. An electric signal timing clock stood near an analytical precision balance, capable of accurately weighing the minutest portion of a single hair. There was a percentage hygrometer, and a thermograph, towards which Miss Frayle inevitably turned to watch, fascinated, the delicate tracing of the pen.

Dr. Morelle glanced up as if aware for the first time of Miss Frayle's presence. As usual she received — as she did whenever she entered the laboratory — the distinct impression that he was subjecting her to the identical scrutiny he gave one of his specimen-slides.

She gave him a faint, nervous smile, but his expression remained sombre as he produced his cigarette-case and lit an inevitable *Le Sphinx*.

'How's it going?' she queried brightly.

'How is what going?'

She nodded towards the bench at which he was working.

'Why all that, of course.'

He fixed his gaze on her, and then asked through a spiral of cigarette-smoke:

'Miss Frayle, have you the faintest conception of the investigation with which I am at this moment occupied?'

She hesitated, started to say something and then gave it up.

'As I suspected, you have not,' he said. 'I mention the fact merely to point out that your question was purely rhetorical. Had I bothered to answer it I should have been wasting my time.'

Refusing to be snubbed, however, she continued chattily:

'I see none of the newspapers have mentioned anything about Doone Drummer being kidnapped.'

He moved round the bench glancing at

some pages of notes he had picked up before he made any reply.

'Inspector Hood's assurance sufficed me in that respect. There remained the possibility, of course,' he added, 'that you might indiscreetly reveal the secret while gossiping with one of those pestering journalists.'

'Dr. Morelle,' she protested. 'As if I ever would.'

He made no further comment, but gave his complete attention to the notes he was reading. Miss Frayle tried again.

'They've splashed it all over the front pages,' she said. 'With your picture, and mine too.'

'No doubt you extended the afore-mentioned reporters some bribe in order to obtain publicity for yourself.'

An angry retort rose to her lips, but before she was able to utter it the telephone rang.

'I'll answer it,' she said.

'That,' he observed still without looking up from his notes, 'is the first constructive remark you have so far made.'

'Dr. Morelle's house.' And then Miss

Frayle's expression underwent a dramatic change. Her eyes widening behind her horn-rims, she held her hand over the receiver and whispered urgently to the Doctor. 'It's him — '

He glanced across at her with a faint expression of interest.

'He, I presume you mean.'

'Never mind all that,' she breathed agitatedly. 'It's the kidnapper.'

She had hardly completed the word before the Doctor was at her side and had wrenched the telephone from her grasp.

'Dr. Morelle speaking.'

The familiarly disguised voice with its underlying mocking tone greeted him.

'The newspapers tell me someone staged quite a performance for you last night. Though I imagine a little thing like a murder wouldn't bother you at all.'

'I find it difficult to believe you have telephoned me merely to discuss a matter in which you can have no real interest,' Dr. Morelle replied.

There was a slight pause, then:

'Just some opening conversation, that's all.'

'I think we may dispense with any such formalities.'

'Bit touchy aren't we this morning? Okay. I called you to say how pleased I was you didn't take the opportunity to mention our little matter to the cops. And since we are chatting we can talk a little business. Save me having to trouble Drummer. He's got the diamond bracelet?'

'He has.'

'A ten thousand pounds' job?'

'It is.'

There came a malicious chuckle from the other.

'Daresay that took the wind out of your sails, eh? Expecting I'd ask for five-pound notes and give you the chance of taking the numbers.'

Dr. Morelle remained silent.

'Anyway,' the other went on, 'next thing is for you to hand over the bracelet and me to hand over the girl.'

'That is the procedure I was anticipating.'

'Don't worry. You've kept your word with me, I'll keep my word with you. So this is how it goes. Listen.'

Dr. Morelle glanced at Miss Frayle. She stood tensed and taut, every nerve tingling at the recollection of that sinister voice at the other end of the telephone. The Doctor gave a nod at her note-book. In her excitement she let it slip from her hand to the floor. He glared at her as she bent and quickly picked it up.

'There's a small church between Gloucester Terrace and Sussex Gardens,' the voice was saying in Dr. Morelle's ear. 'St. Julian's it's called. Almost directly behind Lancaster Gate tube station. Got that?'

'A small church named St. Julian's,' Dr. Morelle said, and Miss Frayle scribbled quickly. 'Almost behind Lancaster Gate tube station, between Gloucester Terrace and Sussex Gardens.'

'Correct. A passage runs through with the church on one side and a graveyard behind a high wall on the other. Get that?'

Again Miss Frayle bent her nose over her note-book and scribbled.

'At exactly midnight tonight you will be

218

half-way along the passage. Alone. With the bracelet. You'll hear this from the other side of the wall.' The speaker whistled some bars of haunting music.

'Rubenstein's Melody in F,' Dr. Morelle said.

'Is that what it is?' was the slightly surprised reply. 'One lives and learns. Anyway, when you hear that tune from the graveyard you just sling the package containing the bracelet over the wall. Simple as that. Okay?'

'You make yourself perfectly clear,' Dr. Morelle said smoothly.

'If it sounds melodramatic — midnight at the churchyard stuff — don't let it bother you a little bit. I picked the time and place on account of it's where there'll be no one around, and you won't get a chance to see me. Don't make any mistake about that either. Be there alone, and soon as you've chucked the bracelet over the wall, beat it. It can be unhealthy around a graveyard at that hour, and you wouldn't want to catch a chill.'

'And Miss Drummer?'

'She'll be delivered back at her flat

soon as I've checked the diamonds are a hundred per cent. Say within a couple of hours of you doing your stuff.'

'What guarantee do you offer that you will complete your part of the bargain?'

'The guarantee that if I say I'll do a thing I do it,' the voice rasped. 'Take it or leave it.'

Dr. Morelle gazed abstractedly at Miss Frayle for a moment. Her pencil poised she gave him a questioning look. Then he spoke into the telephone again.

'It would appear I have no alternative but to take it,' he said.

17

The Trap

'It's a great idea,' Inspector Hood is saying. 'We'll give you all the co-operation we can.' It is later that morning in Dr. Morelle's study. Stirring the inevitable cup of tea Miss Frayle has produced for him on his arrival, the Inspector glances at the Doctor with frank admiration. Miss Frayle scribbles some hieroglyphics in her note-book, then looks up expectantly.

'I flatter myself,' Dr. Morelle murmurs, leaning back in his chair behind the writing-desk, 'the scheme is fool-proof. There is no risk of the man being scared off, with fatal consequences for Miss Drummer.'

Miss Frayle represses a shudder. She recalls that sinister voice over the telephone. In her mind's eye she holds the picture of the owner of the voice — a dark, vulture-like creature who would revenge himself upon anyone who crossed him with remorseless cruelty.

Inspector Hood jams his pipe into his mouth and gets up from his chair. He stands there, a burly, comforting figure, one hand grasping his trilby, and he gives Miss Frayle and Dr. Morelle a confident smile.

'Be getting along,' he says. 'Set about briefing my chaps for the job. Need around twenty men, I reckon.'

Dr. Morelle smooths his chin thoughtfully.

'What might appear to be the scheme's one slight disadvantage,' he observes, 'is the force of men required to trap a single individual.'

'So long as we nab him,' the other replies, 'and the girl's unharmed. That's all that matters.'

'That is the objective. It must be attained with no risk of failure.'

'Let's check through the plan again,' the Inspector says. 'Though it's simple enough.'

Dr. Morelle nods. 'Having reconnoitred the ground, so to speak, I am convinced the operation can be carried out success-fully.'

Hood massaged his jaw and drew his brows down in a frown of concentration.

'First,' he said, 'we plant one man in the church belfry with his portable combined transmitting and receiving radio.'

'One of those walkie-talkie things,' Miss Frayle put in.

'That's what they're called,' Hood said. 'We've got the newest type. About the size of an ordinary telephone, with a small aerial. Work on a special dry battery.'

'What range have they?' Dr. Morelle queried.

'Two, three hundred yards.'

'I see.' The Doctor tapped the ash off his cigarette with a faintly dubious expression.

'What's wrong with that?' Hood asked. 'That'll be ample range for us.'

'It occurs to me,' was the reply, 'in the case of these portable combined radios — '

'Walkie-talkies,' Miss Frayle smiled at him, knowing his abhorrence of slang terms. Ignoring her the Doctor went on musingly:

'Their range must be governed by the terrain over which they are employed. In open country, for example, obviously it would be much wider than in crowded districts. In the locality in which we shall be operating the range could be reduced to almost nil.'

'All that'll be taken into account,' Inspector Hood told him firmly.

The frown that had clouded Dr. Morelle's face suddenly cleared.

'You may take it,' he went on, 'that your — ah — walkie-talkies — I suppose I must refer to them thus in order to make myself understandable to Miss Frayle — will operate successfully. You would encounter impossible interference only in the vicinity of steel and concrete buildings, and where you had extraneous noises such as traffic with which to contend. You will be employing your device tonight, however, against dwelling-houses for the most part. There are no structures of the type I have mentioned, while traffic at that time of night will be almost negligible.'

Inspector Hood took a moment to

absorb the Doctor's exposition of the conditions under which he would be working. Then he said:

'Fine. Now, where were we?'

'With your man in the church belfry,' Miss Frayle said.

'From which position,' Dr. Morelle said — and Miss Frayle sighed to herself; there were times when he *did* love the sound of his own voice so much — 'he can overlook the wall. Without revealing his presence he can easily observe anyone in the graveyard — their arrival and departure. He will keep his voice down to a whisper as he broadcasts into the special microphone provided for him.'

'It'll be like one of those running commentaries over the radio,' Miss Frayle put in.

'That's the idea,' Inspector Hood grinned at her.

'The object of this commentary is of a somewhat more serious nature than is generally the case,' Dr. Morelle said coldly. 'You have the street map of locality,' he proceeded. 'It should be a simple matter for you to plant the rest of your force at strategic points.'

'About four spots round the church will cover that,' Inspector Hood nodded. 'They'll pick up what the chap in the belfry says. Then, whichever route the blighter takes after he's collected the bracelet, they'll relay the information over their walkie-talkies to my other men in their positions farther away.'

'Those who will not be on the route he takes should of course be able to converge upon the quarry.'

'That's the idea,' Hood said enthusiastically. 'Soon as they know he isn't coming their way, they'll shift over to the streets he does take.'

'So all the way along,' Miss Frayle said, 'somebody will be able to keep track of him. Until he reaches his hiding place.'

Inspector Hood's brow corrugated slightly, his great hand mauled his jaw as he said to Dr. Morelle:

'Think my chap in the belfry will be able to see all right? Be damn dark tonight, don't forget. No moon. If he can't see and this feller's wearing rubber shoes he might make his getaway.'

'I am perfectly aware that the night will be completely dark,' Dr. Morelle replied. 'The conditions favour both sides, however. It will lessen the risk of the presence of your officer in the belfry being detected. And,' he added, 'our friend will announce himself by whistling the tune of Rubenstein's Melody in F.'

Inspector Hood's expression grew dubious.

'Don't expect my man's all that musical,' he said. 'But soon as he hears that whistle he'll know it's him.'

'It goes like this,' Miss Frayle offered helpfully, starting to whistle the melody. She broke off with a blush as she caught Dr. Morelle gazing at her with exaggerated wonder.

'A creature of varied talents,' he observed to Inspector Hood. 'Capable of rendering extracts from the classics upon the slightest provocation.'

Miss Frayle turned away, biting her lower lip.

'I thought she was doing rather nicely,' Inspector Hood said comfortingly. But

Dr. Morelle was continuing:

'I took the precaution personally to survey the graveyard from the belfry.'

'But that was an hour or two ago,' Miss Frayle swung round quickly to remind him. 'In broad daylight.'

'I hardly need reminding of that,' he snapped at her, and she subsided again. He turned to Inspector Hood. 'There is only one entrance to the graveyard, a small gate in Sussex Gardens. It will be the entrance and exit used tonight, for even though the gate is locked it is a simple matter to climb over it.'

'No other entrance?' Inspector Hood queried.

'Positively none,' Dr. Morelle was emphatic. 'The gate,' he went on, 'is well within vision of the belfry, there is a street lamp a few yards away.'

'Sounds a hundred per cent watertight,' the Inspector agreed.

'Once the direction he takes is indicated,' Dr. Morelle said, 'it will prove relatively easy to follow your man. Needless to say you will plant your officers as inconspicuously as possible.'

'Don't you worry. They'll take up vantage-points in gardens, and at the windows of houses. One or two will be on street corners dressed up as workmen coming off night-shifts. Everyone equipped with a hidden walkie-talkie.'

'You have not overlooked,' Dr. Morelle interposed, 'the possibility that he may arrive and depart by car.'

'That'll be taken care of too,' Hood replied. 'If he uses a car there'll be men in taxis and tradesmen's vans waiting to pick up his trail.'

'You will know on his arrival what form of transport, if any, he will be using. Your officer in the belfry will have time to send out a warning accordingly.'

'Supposing he turns up and makes his getaway on a bicycle,' Miss Frayle put in suddenly.

'My dear Miss Frayle,' Dr. Morelle returned with biting sarcasm, 'no doubt the Inspector plans to engage a fleet of trained cyclists straining at the leash against such an eventuality.'

Inspector Hood chuckled, but Miss Frayle refused to be snubbed.

'But supposing he does use a bike?' she insisted.

'If,' Dr. Morelle pointed out assuming an air of unsurpassed patience, 'he used a bicycle he would still travel at a speed which would require a car, following inconspicuously, to keep him in sight.'

'True enough,' the Inspector agreed and turned to Miss Frayle with a sympathetic smile. 'Even if he uses a bike,' he said to her, 'we can keep him in view from one of the taxis or vans trailing him at just the right speed.'

Producing a box of matches Hood proceeded to light his pipe which had got cold while they'd been talking. He appeared not to notice Dr. Morelle's sensitive nostrils twitch as clouds of acrid smoke began to fill the study. Satisfied by its gurglings and bubblings that his pipe was going nicely, Inspector Hood moved to the door.

'That's the way it'll go,' he declared. 'I'm very much obliged to you, Doctor, for dreaming up such a bright idea.'

'Trust Dr. Morelle to do that,' Miss Frayle said as she opened the door.

'Yes,' Hood conceded, giving her a portentous wink, 'there are times when we flat-footed cops have to hand it to your boss.'

He shot a grin of heavy humour at Dr. Morelle leaning against his desk, an unmistakable smirk of self-satisfaction on his saturnine face. Then the Inspector took his pipe out of his mouth and scratched his chin with its stem.

'One thing, though, you may not have thought of,' he said slowly.

'What is that?'

'Going to this church all on your little ownsome, aren't you?'

Dr. Morelle inclined his head. 'That is part of the bargain between this individual and myself.'

'Has it occurred to you he may be just setting a trap for you, yourself?'

Miss Frayle glanced at the Inspector, her eyes wide with alarm.

'I fail to comprehend your meaning,' was Dr. Morelle's answer.

'Supposing when you get there this chap isn't behind the wall? You're waiting and he slides up, sticks a gun in your back and not only takes the bracelet but you too.'

'And then,' Miss Frayle gasped, 'holding the Doctor to ransom?'

'Just that,' the other said heavily.

'Dr. Morelle,' Miss Frayle exclaimed, a hand flying to her throat in apprehension.

But Dr. Morelle wore a sceptical smile at the corners of his mouth.

'I cannot envisage anyone contemplating kidnapping me,' he observed quietly.

'Why not?' Hood demanded.

'For obvious reasons.'

'I was always under the impression,' the other got in, 'you rated yourself pretty highly.'

'Not, I am obliged to admit, from a material point of view. Though I flatter myself I am of some value to science and those members of the community whom it benefits.'

'What d'you mean?' Miss Frayle queried.

Dr. Morelle examined the tip of his *Le Sphinx*.

'Were I one of your favoured grimacing film-stars,' he said to her, 'my value would be reckoned in many thousands of pounds. Regrettably, however, as Society would rate me, my value is comparatively negligible. Certainly of no size to attract the attentions of a kidnapper.'

'I suppose you're right,' Hood said.

'Do not misunderstand me,' Dr. Morelle added. 'I do not consider it undesirable that my worth is not estimated in terms of vulgar cash.'

'In a minute you'll have me offering to lend you the price of your next meal,' Hood remarked, and Miss Frayle burst out laughing. But her laughter vanished as the Inspector went on more seriously: 'All the same, if you take my tip you won't turn up tonight altogether alone.'

'You mean I should go with him,' Miss Frayle said quickly.

Inspector Hood gave her shoulder a paternal pat.

'I'm sure you'd be an enormous help, Miss Frayle,' he said, avoiding Dr. Morelle's sardonic eye. 'What I mean,' he turned to the Doctor, 'is you'd better carry a gun.'

'Oh!' Miss Frayle exclaimed, facing Dr.

Morelle to see what his reaction would be.

The Doctor drew at his cigarette and then replied slowly:

'Touched as I am by your concern for my welfare, have no fears on my behalf. Although I do not in fact anticipate any trouble of the nature you describe, I intend carrying my swordstick.'

Inspector Hood shrugged his heavy shoulders.

'Have it your way,' he said. 'But I think a gun's more persuasive than a swordstick any time.'

'I quite agree,' Miss Frayle put in. 'I think you ought to take that automatic of yours, Doctor.'

Dr. Morelle merely gave her a smile of supreme self-confidence. With a sinking feeling she realised he was obviously determined to disregard Inspector Hood's advice.

'And all you'll trust me for,' she burst out, 'while you go to meet this dreadful man, is to just sit here and wait?'

'You could not have anticipated my wishes regarding yourself with more commendable accuracy,' Dr. Morelle complimented her.

'Don't you worry,' Inspector Hood consoled Miss Frayle. 'He'll come back all right.'

'Perhaps,' Dr. Morelle insinuated, 'that is precisely what Miss Frayle fears.'

18

When Midnight Strikes

A few minutes to midnight Dr. Morelle tapped on the window behind the taxi-driver.

The taxi drew up on the corner of a street and Sussex Gardens, about thirty yards from St. Julian's Church. Instructing the driver to wait, Dr. Morelle strode briskly towards the church, his swordstick making sharp raps on the pavement. Apart from there being no moon, the night sky was starless. The only light came from the street-lamps. Sussex Gardens appeared completely deserted. A faint smile of satisfaction touched his face. In the apparently deserted streets Inspector Hood's men were at their posts waiting for the voice of the watcher in the church belfry.

He reached the church and paused to gaze about him.

Opposite him a gap of waste land melted into a number of condemned houses beyond. The dark tumbledown huddle lent a sinister and eerie atmosphere to the scene.

The clock above him began striking midnight. He turned into the passage-way between the church and the high wall of the graveyard. The plane trees, like grey sentinels, lined the walls at intervals, their branches soughing gently in the night breeze.

Dr. Morelle's footsteps echoed hollowly on the flagstones. He stopped halfway along the passage. Ahead of him a few steps ascended into Gloucester Terrace. He was aware from his careful reconnaissance made earlier that day, how shrewdly the man he was to meet had chosen their rendezvous. Two lines of approach and escape lay open to him. One on either side of the church, with streets, alley-ways and mews which would afford him every opportunity for concealment. It was for this reason so many of Inspector Hood's men had been recruited. Whichever direction their quarry took through the surrounding maze of streets, the watchers would be strategically deployed so that they could keep on his trail.

The last stroke of midnight reverberated on the air as Dr. Morelle lit a cigarette. The flame from his lighter illuminated for a brief moment his face as if carved in ivory watchful lines beneath his dark hat. The lighter flame died and once again he stood in darkness.

Behind him loomed the quiescent mass of the old church. The belfry tower was almost directly above, overlooking the wall he was facing.

Dr. Morelle stood still, listening intently.

Except for the rustle of the leaves there was silence. From the direction of Paddington Station came the ghostly shriek of a train. The tip of his cigarette glowed reddishly for a moment as Dr. Morelle filled his lungs with smoke. He exhaled slowly, the cigarette smoke wreathing his head in a wraith-like vapour before it melted into the darkness.

The moments dragged by, and he glanced at the luminous face of his wrist-watch. Two minutes past midnight. The thought was barely beginning to grow in his mind that perhaps the other was not going to keep the rendezvous when he suddenly tensed. From the other side of the wall arose the softly whistled notes of the haunting Melody in F.

Dr. Morelle's fingers closed over the package in his pocket. He had collected the diamond bracelet that evening from Harvey Drummer, giving him an outline of the plan for the rescue of his daughter. He took the small package out of his pocket, held it for a moment as he measured the distance, and then threw it over the wall. The whistling broke off abruptly, and he caught a faint sharp thud from the other side. There followed a sound of someone scuffling.

Then complete silence.

Dr. Morelle waited for a few seconds, then he swung on his heel. His footsteps echoed as he walked back the way he had come. He turned into Sussex Gardens and proceeded towards his waiting taxi. So far as he was concerned everything had gone exactly as he had anticipated.

As the sound of the taxi died away a small, slim figure materialised out of the shadows of a garden on the opposite side of the road a few yards distant from the church.

It was Miss Frayle.

As the time arrived for the Doctor to leave for his rendezvous, Miss Frayle had grown more and more apprehensive. She was convinced Inspector Hood's warning of the danger Dr. Morelle risked was only too well founded. Twice she had tried to persuade him at least to carry his automatic. But without any success. After his second brusque rejection of her advice she had offered another plan.

'Don't you think it would be a good idea if I followed you in another taxi? Keeping well behind you, of course — '

'The idea,' had been the icy response, 'has every earmark of blundering stupidity typical of your earlier suggestions.'

'But supposing it is a trap? I shall be worrying myself frantic — '

'If you wish to enliven the tedium of awaiting my return, why not rest your overworked imagination by transcribing those shorthand notes which appear to fill your note-book, still undeciphered?'

Hiding her tears of vexation Miss Frayle had turned away. He knew perfectly well that as a result of Doone Drummer's disappearance routine work had been considerably interrupted, not only for him but for herself. Just as he knew she would give every moment she could to catching up on any work which, through no fault of her own, remained unfinished.

Anyway, that was that, she told herself angrily. So far as she cared he could stick his silly neck into trouble and she hoped it would strangle him. He couldn't say he'd not been warned. Not only by her but by Inspector Hood as well.

Then there rose in her mind the suspicion that far from running into danger he planned to trap the kidnapper single-handed. Simply to impress Doone Drummer. Miss Frayle writhed mentally as that dagger of jealousy twisted yet again in her heart.

Thus the seeds of revolt were sown.

She would show the Doctor that

though she may not be all that alluring, she was not quite the hopeless idiot he pretended to believe her to be.

Setting her jaw determinedly she had begun to make her plans. She had contrived to arrange for a hired car to be ready at the time Dr. Morelle left the house *en route* for his midnight rendezvous.

The moment he had gone she had grabbed the automatic, cold and sinister from his desk-drawer, and slipped it into her coat pocket. Hurrying across to her car waiting on the other side of Harley Street she glimpsed Dr. Morelle getting into a taxi.

Feeling like a character from any film melodrama she had told her driver to follow the taxi, and then sat hunched forward in her seat beside him, her spectacles an inch or two from the windscreen. She had stopped the car as it was about to turn into Sussex Gardens. Telling the driver to wait she had hurried after the tail-light of the Doctor's taxi. Swinging into Sussex Gardens just as the taxi was pulling up she'd hidden herself behind the pillar of a gate opening on to a front garden. She had no plan of action, except stick as close to Dr. Morelle as she dared.

She had heard the tap-tap of his sword-stick fade as he approached the church. She had stood clinging to the shadows, heart in mouth, waiting. The church clock had struck midnight, then presently she had caught the low whistled signal. The Melody in F.

Tensed, hardly daring to breathe, she had peered cautiously round the gate pillar. This was it. The dramatic climax had arrived. It was with almost a sense of disappointment that the familiar tap of the sword-stick returning reached her, and she had ducked back out of sight. Soon she heard the taxi drive off.

Now Miss Frayle was experiencing a feeling she had been decidedly let down. It had all seemed so uneventful. Dr. Morelle hadn't apparently been in the slightest danger. Realising, however, she ought to feel delighted, even if it was a bit of an anti-climax, Miss Frayle began to retrace her steps towards the car.

It was essential for her to arrive back to Harley Street before the Doctor. She was relying on the car's extra speed to get her there before his taxi. She had already made up her mind to confess to him that she had flagrantly disobeyed his orders. She felt confident his anger would melt like snow when he realised she had behaved as she had simply in order to be there in case anything *had* gone wrong. If danger had threatened him she would have been ready — she could tell him with every sincerity — to sell her life dearly on his behalf.

Could Doone Drummer, with all her brains and beauty, offer more?

Something made her stop suddenly.

Behind her came the sound of someone clambering over a gate. She turned, her heart beating quickly. A dark figure appeared out of the shadows by the church. A man. She recalled Dr. Morelle's words that the only way anyone could get in and out of the graveyard was over a locked gate. That was obviously where the man had just come from.

It must be the kidnapper!

She drew back into the protecting shadow of an overhanging hedge. With fascinated eyes she watched the figure on the other side of the road walking quickly towards her. She glanced up and down Sussex Gardens. No sign of anyone else. No detective disguised as an old woman or a working-man. No police-car camouflaged as a tradesman's van to be seen.

Suddenly Miss Frayle experienced one of those flashes of intuition which in the past had been the subject of Dr. Morelle's sardonic disdain. For some inexplicable reason she sensed that the plan for trapping the kidnapper had somehow gone awry. She threw another glance around her. Still no signs of the police. Now the man across the road drew level with her.

She felt the pressure of Dr. Morelle's automatic in her pocket. A wave of determination surged through her. In case that intuition of hers was right she made up her mind to keep the man in sight for as long as she could. She thought of her waiting car. She guessed the driver would, however, only wait so long before returning inevitably to let Dr. Morelle know she had not come back. Which, she told herself, might be all to the good. If she ran into danger she would be assured that Dr. Morelle, however angry he might be with her, would come swiftly to the rescue.

The figure on the other side of the road was now about thirty yards ahead. Silently Miss Frayle went after him. She kept one hand tightly round the automatic, as much to prevent it banging against her leg as for its reassuring feeling. The man was walking very quickly, and she soon found herself being forced to quicken her pace into a half-run.

She cast a glance over her shoulder. Still no sign of anyone. A stray cat darted across the road in front of her, but Miss Frayle felt it reasonable to assume that in no conceivable way could it be a detective in disguise.

The figure ahead suddenly vanished around a corner. Miss Frayle promptly tore across the road, slowing up when she herself gained the turning. She adjusted her horn-rimmed spectacles which had slid down her nose and peered cautiously round the corner.

Some thirty yards away a small van was drawn up in the shadows between two pools of lamp-light. The man she had been following had vanished. Then she saw the way he must have gone. Farther down on the other side she spied the dark narrow opening of an alley. He must have ducked into it.

As she was about to cross over after him someone appeared beside the van. It was a man, and he was looking up and down the road. One of Inspector Hood's detectives, she told herself. She changed her mind and hurried towards him. Apparently he had missed seeing the other man disappear into the alleyway.

He stood there staring at her as she approached.

'You're with Inspector Hood?' she said breathlessly.

He was wearing dark glasses, she realised. There was something vaguely familiar about him. She must have met him before with Inspector Hood.

'Who are you?' he asked her curiously.

'Miss Frayle,' she said promptly. 'Dr. Morelle's assistant.' She went on hurriedly: 'Didn't you see which way he went? That man?'

'No,' the other responded. 'Which way did he go?'

She pointed across at the alley.

'I followed him round the corner. He must have dived down there — '

She broke off and caught her breath. Something in the man's attitude sent a warning bell ringing at the back of her brain. Suddenly in the darkness she was aware of his quiet regular breathing. She glimpsed the line of his shadowed jaw — hard, cruel. Then he was moving towards her, both hands reaching out.

'You're not a detective,' she gasped. 'You're — '

With a desperate sob she pulled the automatic from her pocket and levelled it at him.

'Stop where you are.' Her voice hit an hysterical note. 'Or I'll shoot.'

But it was as if the other couldn't stop himself. He seemed to loom over her.

Closing her eyes, Miss Frayle pulled the trigger.

19

Grim News

Dr. Morelle closed the front door of 221B Harley Street behind him.

He experienced a sense of weariness as he took off his coat and hat. He realised the strain of the night's events had taken its insidious toll of him. He frowned a little as he made his way towards the study. He had expected Miss Frayle to be awaiting his return with her usual breathless interest.

She was probably preparing an inevitable cup of tea for them both. He greeted the idea with anticipatory pleasure. He would find a cup of tea more than refreshing.

He went into the study and switched on the light. He stood at the door for a moment, then stepped back into the hall and called Miss Frayle. There was no reply. With a faintly puzzled frown Dr.

Morelle called again. Still no reply. He glanced at his watch. Just on half-past twelve.

Perhaps, he thought, she too had been feeling the effects of the last day or two and had gone to bed. He reached this conclusion with somewhat mixed feelings. Surprise on the one hand at her having adopted such a sensible course, disappointment on the other at her not being there eager for his account of what had occurred at St. Julian's Church.

Besides, he could have done with a cup of tea.

He closed the door of his study and lit a fresh cigarette. He went through to the laboratory, filled the electric kettle from the tap in the corner, and plugged it in. He got a cup and saucer and then, muttering irritably to himself, went back through the study and along to the kitchen for a lemon. By the time he returned to the laboratory he fancied the kettle was beginning to simmer, and he cut some slices of lemon. He stood staring at the kettle, smoking reflectively while he waited for the water to boil. He heard the echo of one of Miss Frayle's typical remarks to the effect that watched kettles never boiled, and turned away involuntarily to pace the laboratory.

He calculated that at any moment Inspector Hood would be telephoning with the news of the kidnapper's capture. In his mind's eye he pictured Harvey Drummer also anxiously awaiting news. Dr. Morelle had promised to telephone him immediately on hearing from Inspector Hood. He wondered if by now Inspector Hood's triumph was complete. With not only the kidnapper of Doone Drummer, the young woman herself, but also the murderer of Leo Rolf in his hands? The Inspector's independent investigations into Rolf's murder had been on purely routine lines. He was convinced the kidnapper and the murderer were the same person which was why his co-operation on the plan put into operation that night had been so whole-hearted.

Dr. Morelle dragged at his cigarette as his mind wandered over the various aspects of the case. A case amounting now to much more than the abduction of Doone Drummer. While it remained possible there might be no connection between the girl's disappearance and the murder of Leo Rolf, he had little doubt in his mind that both crimes had been committed by the same person. If so, then his method of dealing with the kidnapper would be justified. By gaining the ruthless criminal's confidence he had undoubtedly reduced the chance of Doone Drummer's life being endangered.

In what way had Rolf been concerned in the abduction, and why had he been murdered? The answer to that question was something he anticipated with interest. He wondered if it would implicate Neil Fulton. The film-actor had telephoned twice asking for news of the missing woman. The second time Miss Frayle had told him he would be advised as soon as there was definite news.

The kettle bubbled over suddenly, interrupting his ruminations. While he waited for the tea to brew he considered his theory that the kidnapper must be familiar with the house in Park Lane. A picture of Rosie Huggins formed in his mind. Would he soon know the reason for her deliberate lies? Was she implicated in the crime?

The picture of Rosie Huggins was obscured by that of the man in the pince-nez. Pearson. Where did his black silk gloves enter into the puzzle? Was the person who should by now be fast in Inspector Hood's grasp none other than Harvey Drummer's secretary?

For a moment there flashed across his mind the image of Doone Drummer's father. He toyed again with the possibility that he himself was responsible for his daughter's disappearance. He pictured Inspector Hood's reaction if the kidnapper turned out to be Harvey Drummer. Then it occurred to him that even if he had not actively participated in the crime, the possibility that Drummer had instigated it might yet remain.

He heard the telephone ring in his study and, his face set in grim lines, he went quickly out of the laboratory.

'Dr. Morelle speaking,' he said, anticipating Inspector Hood's familiar voice in reply. What jarred against his eardrum, however, was a woman's high-pitched squawk.

'So sorry to disturb you at this hour. But I rather felt you worked late — '

'Who is it?' the Doctor snapped.

'I'm Miss Widgewood. You've never heard of me, of course, but I've heard so much about you. It's my cat, you see, Doctor. Ptolemy. That's his name, you know. He's utterly vanished. I'm sure something dreadful will happen to him unless you — '

Dr. Morelle gave a snarl and, speechless with rage, slammed down the receiver. Muttering angrily to himself he paced the study. He stubbed out his cigarette and was deciding whether or not to return, to the laboratory and pour himself another cup of tea when the telephone jangled again. He eyed it warily for a moment, then lifted the receiver.

A man's voice answered him, and for a brief moment he thought it was Inspector Hood. Once again he was disappointed.

'Dr. Morelle? I'm the driver for Welbeck Car Hire.'

'Are you about to inform me,' Dr. Morelle interrupted him sarcastically, 'that you have lost a car?'

'Eh?' Puzzled. 'Lost a car — ?'

'Never mind,' Dr. Morelle snapped. 'What do you want?'

'I wondered if Miss Frayle's got back all right?'

'Miss Frayle? Got back? I was not under the impression that she had been out.'

'Oh yes. Took her myself. About an hour ago. Behind Lancaster Gate I dropped her.'

'What nonsense is this?' Dr. Morelle exploded. 'You are obviously confusing Miss Frayle with someone else — '

'Hold on, Doctor,' the other begged him. 'I tell you, Miss Frayle ordered me to be waiting outside your house at half-past eleven. Other side of the street I was to be. I got there on the dot. Saw you come out. Miss Frayle nipped out after you, and we followed your taxi to Lancaster Gate.'

Dr. Morelle could hardly believe his ears.

'There must be some error,' he replied. 'Miss Frayle has been here all the evening.'

'All right. It's none of my business, only rang up because when I dropped her she told me to wait. But she never came back. I hung around half an hour, then turned it in. But if you say she's been home all night, then I been dreaming.'

Dr. Morelle spoke calmly, his tone restrained.

'I believe I know what has transpired,' he said. 'I am most grateful to you for taking the trouble to telephone.'

'Not a bit, Dr. Morelle. If she's all right, then it's all right.'

Dr. Morelle hung up slowly. He stood for a moment as if turned to stone. Then galvanised into action he went out of the study and up the stairs. Miss Frayle's bedroom and sitting-room were at the top of the house. Dr. Morelle pounded on the bedroom door. There was no reply. He opened the door and looked in. Miss Frayle was not there, the bed had not been slept in.

He descended to his study trying to

imagine what fantastic motive had been responsible for her deliberately to disobey his explicit instructions. What had driven her to take the foolhardy step of following him to his rendezvous with a dangerous criminal? And where was she now?

The fact of her having instructed the driver of her car to await her return suggested to him she intended to return to Harley Street before he did. That was the explanation for there being no message, which otherwise she would surely have left him, explaining her absence. What blindly insane adventure had she embarked upon? What dreadful trap had engulfed her?

Dr. Morelle drew a deep shuddering sigh. Then he noticed the edge of the drawer in his desk. It was open a bare half-inch, but it was sufficient, for him to bend with a swift movement and wrench it wide.

The automatic pistol which was always kept there had gone.

Remembrance of Inspector Hood's advice that he should arm himself for his dangerous rendezvous came back to him.

He recalled how impressed Miss Frayle had been by the Inspector's warning. At once the realisation of what lay behind Miss Frayle's unprecedented disobedience struck him. Convinced he should not go to his appointment unprotected she had secretly resolved to follow him with the gun.

Unthinking, foolish Miss Frayle. She had been determined to act as his guardian-angel. Blithely, unwittingly, she had placed herself in appalling danger.

The door-bell jarred into the grim turmoil of his mind. Could it be her? He pictured her woebegone and guiltily waiting outside, the sole result of her wild-goose chase a lost handbag containing her frontdoor key. Swiftly he strode along the hall. The vitriolic flow of words intended to disguise his relief at her return rose to his lips as he wrenched open the door.

But it was not Miss Frayle who stood there with bowed head before him.

The bulky figure of Inspector Hood faced him. Dr. Morelle glimpsed a police-car drawn up at the kerb. The light from the hall showed the Inspector's face sunk between his hunched shoulders. Dr. Morelle had never before seen those genial features carved in such bitter lines.

'Afraid, Dr. Morelle,' Inspector Hood grunted. 'I've got bad news for you.'

20

Double Disaster

Inspector Hood slumped in a chair in the study making no attempt to relight his cold pipe. Dr. Morelle had made no comment as, closing the front door, he had followed after the Inspector. Now he stood waiting for the other to tell him what disaster had overtaken Miss Frayle.

'It was just sheer bad luck,' the Inspector mumbled lugubriously. 'One of those things it's impossible to guard against. Chap in the belfry's walkie-talkie packed up at the crucial moment. Burnt-out transmitter valve.'

Dr. Morelle stared at him. Then he realised he had mistaken Hood's remark at the front door. It had been a reference not to Miss Frayle, but to the plan for trapping the individual at St. Julian's Church.

261

'Everything went exactly as you foresaw,' Inspector Hood was saying. 'Our man in the belfry was able to see the chap arrive, then you. He saw him grab the package you chucked over to him, and you push off. After a few minutes he saw our man nip over the gate and hurry away.' He paused and then exploded: 'And not one ruddy word of his running commentary came over. Just because of some flaming little thing going wrong which was nobody's fault.'

Inspector Hood's bulky frame reverberated with a great sigh. Dr. Morelle remained silent, and the other continued:

'It was five minutes before the chap in the belfry realised none of us were getting a thing,' he said bitterly. 'By then, of course, it was too late. Only thing we've got out of the whole flaming business is we know it's a man all right. Our chap in the belfry's damned sure it wasn't a woman dressed up.'

Dr. Morelle, only half-listening to what the other was saying, nevertheless grasped the significance of what had happened. His scheme for unmasking the kidnapper and rescuing Doone Drummer had been an utter fiasco. It struck him that the plan's collapse might account for Miss Frayle's failure to return to her waiting car.

Was it possible, he wondered, that by some means she had become aware of what had transpired and had decided to set off on her own investigation? None knew better than Dr. Morelle that beneath her feather-brained timidity Miss Frayle could rise to moments of courageous action. She might faint with irritating frequency at a spot of blood, but she was also capable of calling upon sources of hidden resolve and strength. Dr. Morelle found it easy to visualise her comforted by the possession of his automatic attempting to demonstrate that single-handed she was capable of succeeding where Scotland Yard had failed.

'I was waiting in my car,' Inspector Hood burbled on, oblivious of the Doctor's divided interest. 'When we realised the belfry walkie-talkie had packed up it was about ten minutes past twelve. I was pretty certain you and the blighter in the graveyard had gone — I had to take the chance, anyway — and we drove round to the church. As I expected the bird had flown. Got well away and none of the others, waiting with their walkie-talkies, with the faintest idea which direction he'd taken.' He paused and sighed again. 'We gave the graveyard and all round as thorough a once-over as we could by torch-light. Just in case he'd left behind any clue. But there was nothing. Sorry, Dr. Morelle,' he wound up, heavily apologetic. 'Afraid I've let you down.'

Dr. Morelle gave him a glance of sympathy, but said nothing. The other regarded him for a moment, then gazed round the study. He stood up slowly.

'Miss Frayle gone to bed, eh?' he said, then added glumly: 'What do we tell Drummer?'

'I am afraid,' Dr. Morelle said, 'I have some disconcerting news for you.'

'About Drummer?'

'Miss Frayle.'

'Miss Frayle?'

'You will recall your fear that I might be walking into a trap tonight, and that I should arm myself. So deeply was Miss Frayle impressed by your warning that she took it into her head to follow me to St. Julian's Church. With her went my automatic pistol which I keep in that drawer. *Unfortunately, however, she omitted to note that it was unloaded.*'

'Good God,' Hood exclaimed. 'Where is she now?'

'That is something I wish I could tell you,' Dr. Morelle replied.

'You mean she hasn't come back?'

Dr. Morelle nodded. He went on:

'The driver of the car she hired was the last person to see her. He telephoned just before you arrived. He explained that he put Miss Frayle down a short distance from the church. It appears she anticipated being away only a few minutes, instructing him to wait for her. He waited some thirty minutes before finally returning to his garage.'

'What the devil can have happened to her?'

Dr. Morelle stubbed out his cigarette.

'I can only assume that in some way she learned tonight's scheme had gone awry,' he said. 'Knowing Miss Frayle it is quite conceivable that she determined to achieve what we had failed to do.'

'And thinking she was armed with a loaded gun,' Inspector Hood nodded. 'I wouldn't put it past her.'

'Either she is at this moment still trailing the individual concerned, or she has fallen into his clutches.' With a glance at Hood, he went on: 'I cannot but help feeling she is, in fact, in his hands. Otherwise she would have found some means of allaying my not unnatural anxiety by communicating with me before now.'

The Inspector had been chewing on his pipe-stem in obvious agitation. Now he threw a shrewd glance at Dr. Morelle from beneath his shaggy brows. It was plain to him the Doctor was shaken to the very roots by this catastrophic twist to the night's events In all his experience of his varied moods the Inspector had never known Dr. Morelle appear so emotionally affected. The hand that was lighting a fresh cigarette was unmistakably trembling.

It flashed across the mind of that stolid

man from Scotland Yard he was now receiving demonstrable proof that Dr. Morelle's outward manner to Miss Frayle was merely a pose concealing his secret regard for her. Hood had always suspected Miss Frayle's romantic inclination towards her employer; had been amused by the apparent hopelessness of her affection. The possibility that her feelings were, in fact, reciprocated came to him as a tremendous revelation.

'What in hell do we do?' he growled, his heavy jaw thrust forward. 'And what about Drummer?' he added. 'He's going to go up in a sheet of flame when he knows what's happened.' His voice rose in desperation.

'We shall contribute nothing to the solution of the problem by adding to the conflagration,' he was reminded in familiarly calm tones.

The other gave Dr. Morelle a glance of frank admiration. Shattered as he was by what had happened the Doctor was keeping a grip on himself. He wasn't going to let himself fly off the handle. The Inspector took his cue accordingly and pulled himself together.

'Suppose he's parked by his 'phone waiting for news,' he said. 'Or has he already 'phoned you?'

'He is expecting me to telephone him immediately I have any information.'

'Glad it's you who's got to tell him and not me.'

'I think we shall agree,' Dr. Morelle was regarding the other coolly through a cloud of cigarette smoke, 'that nothing will be gained by informing Drummer of both reverses we have suffered.'

'We don't have to tell him about Miss Frayle,' Inspector Hood agreed. 'But we can't keep him in the dark about the rest of it.'

'No reason why we should not be perfectly frank,' Dr. Morelle returned. 'Make it clear to him that because our part of the scheme failed it need not necessarily prevent his daughter's return. We have kept our bargain to the extent of paying over the ransom demanded. I fail to see why the criminal should not keep his part of the bargain and return Miss Drummer.'

'That's true enough,' the other muttered. 'Anyway, let's hope it'll work out that way. But assuming he has got Miss Frayle in his hands, how's he going to play that card?'

'It is unprofitable to speculate on the card one's opponent will play,' Dr. Morelle murmured, 'if one isn't even aware of what cards he holds. We can but trust we shall, in the final game, be in a position to trump him.'

'Drummer was counting on getting his diamond bracelet back as well,' the Inspector went on despondently. 'Still if his daughter does turn up safe that'll be something for him to be thankful for.'

'While there still remains the chance both will be returned to him,' Dr. Morelle pointed out.

'Hadn't you better 'phone him now? While we really believe what we're saying,' Inspector Hood grunted with grim humour.

Dr. Morelle gave him a look and lifted the receiver.

For the second time in the space of a

few moments Inspector Hood's admiration for the Doctor knew no bounds as he listened to the reassuring manner in which he gave Harvey Drummer a brief account of what had happened. Drummer was obviously bitterly disappointed at the turn events had taken. But Dr. Morelle contrived to buoy him up, emphasising the belief he had expressed to Hood that there was no reason why the kidnapper should not keep his bargain and return Doone Drummer safe and sound.

'Perhaps you're right after all,' Inspector Hood said, when Dr. Morelle had hung up. 'The blighter will keep his word.'

There was a sudden ring at the front door, and once again Dr. Morelle's heart leapt with hope. Inspector Hood glanced at him and muttered:

'Could be her, Doctor. Miss Frayle.'

Dr. Morelle remembered how his hopes had been dashed before.

'I'll go and see,' he said.

Inspector Hood followed him eagerly into the hall. It was the police-sergeant driver of Hood's car who was at the door.

He spoke to Hood standing behind Dr. Morelle.

'Message for you, Inspector Hood. Just come over the radio from Scotland Yard. Want you to 'phone them right away. Somebody's been on to them about a mystery woman on an old house-boat.'

The man returned to his car, and Dr. Morelle followed the Inspector back to his study.

'May be something in it,' he told Dr. Morelle a minute or two later, as he replaced the telephone receiver. 'They've had a call from a chap in Chelsea. Says there's some queer goings-on on one of those converted house-boats moored off the Embankment.' He shrugged. 'Could be something, could be nothing. Chap who tipped us off will be waiting outside a pub nearby. Want to come along?'

Dr. Morelle reached for a piece of paper on his writing-desk.

'I will leave a note for Miss Frayle. In the event of her returning during my absence.'

Inspector Hood watched Dr. Morelle rapidly scrawl a message. He had to confess he would dearly have loved to have looked over the Doctor's shoulder and seen what he'd written to the absent Miss Frayle. Hood would have been disappointed, however, and his conjecture regarding Dr. Morelle's secret affection, for Miss Frayle received somewhat of a set-back.

Dr. Morelle's note read briefly:
'Back soon.'

21

The Secret Room

Miss Frayle opened her eyes with a little moan.

She found herself in an enclosed space which pressed in on her from all sides. It was very dark. She felt for her horn-rimmed spectacles, but they were not there. After a few moments she realised she was huddled next to the driving seat of a small van, and with a rush of memory everything came back to her. The dark spectacled face looming towards her, and the sickening sensation as she pressed the trigger. She heard again the sound of the empty click; she remembered the man's hands reaching out to her. Then black-out. She had fainted.

The van was not moving, and she saw someone outside at the door beside her.

'So the patient's sitting up and taking notice.'

Miss Frayle met those dark spectacles again as the man opened the van door. Once more she found herself puzzling over the vaguely familiar tone in his voice. She tried to recall where she had heard it before. But it continued to elude her. She stared ahead of her and made out a wedge of dim light against the blackness. She turned her myopic gaze to the other window. It was pitch dark. She glanced back at the man.

'Where — where are we?'

'In a garage,' was the succinct reply.

A garage. She gave a little gasp. Was he planning to lock her in the garage with the engine running so that she would suffocate from the exhaust fumes? She froze with terror at the thought.

'Came in quite useful this van. Owner won't know I've borrowed it. Naturally. Fixed myself with a duplicate key.'

'What — what are you going to do?' she gulped shakily.

'Have to blindfold you,' he said pleasantly. 'Pity about your glasses. They fell when you passed out. Smashed.'

'Blindfold me?'

'That's the idea. Precautionary measures. So you won't see where I'm taking you. Get out,' he said. He pulled the van-door wide. She hesitated for a moment. He said: 'Shouldn't try any funny business; I've got a gun.' She caught the malevolent grin on his face as he added: 'And I made sure mine's loaded.'

She got out, swaying a little from the effects of her faint, and leant against the van to steady herself. She faced him uncertainly. His dark glasses seemed to glint evilly beneath the shadow of his hat pulled well over his eyes.

'Turn round.'

She turned obediently. She felt something like a handkerchief being placed over her eyes. He tied it securely at the back of her head, and she was effectively blindfolded. Her hands were forced behind her back, and a cord cut into her wrists as he bound them together.

Then she found herself being carried in his arms. She heard the scrape of the garage door opening and closing behind her. There came the dull sound of his footsteps and she realised he was wearing rubber heels. She took in gulps of fresh night air.

He stopped suddenly and she could feel him tense. His words hissed in her ear.

'One squeak out of you, and it'll be your last.'

'At once she closed her mouth tightly hardly daring to breathe. The man still stood taut, listening, then he relaxed. She heard him draw in his breath between his teeth and he was off again. From somewhere came the sound of a car in the distance. It drew nearer and then faded away. He stopped again and put her down. There was the scrape of a key in a lock, followed by the sound of a heavy door opening. He gave her a push and she stumbled forward. The door closed after her and the key scraped again. He grasped her arm and led her forward. Her heels clicked sharply on the stone floor.

'Walk on your toes,' he muttered.

At once she bounced along on tip-toe.

His grip tightened on her arm and halted her. There was the sound of another key being turned, the faint squeak of a door opening, and she was pushed forward again. The door squeaked behind her, the lock clicked.

Once more he was urging her forward. This time her footsteps were deadened by what felt like matting on the floor. Again he stopped her, a door opened, she was pushed forward, the door closed. Now the sound of the footsteps were muffled by a carpet. She felt his grip tighten again on her arm. He whispered in her ear:

'Stairs. Watch how you go up.'

It occurred to her to tell him that as she was blindfolded she couldn't very well watch how she went. Then she felt the jab of something hard in her back and decided perhaps this was not the time for such comments. They reached the landing and a sudden pressure on her arm warned her to stop. They stood for a few moments and she could hear his quiet breathing.

Obviously he thought he'd heard something. She thought she detected a creak which might have been a door opening or someone on a stair, but she couldn't be certain. After a few moments he seemed satisfied all was clear, and they went on up another flight of stairs, the carpet still muffling the sound of their footsteps.

Another landing and he urged her along it. They stopped, a door-handle turned, she went forward and the door closed behind her. She heard a light switched on, and there was a brightness edging her blindfold. She heard him move away from her, then a drawer opened and closed.

He stood beside her again and took her arm. A door creaked open again before her. Then it was as if she was going through the darkness of a cupboard, and yet another door opened and closed behind her. Another click of a light switch and she was breathing in an atmosphere that was stuffy and airless. She was urged forward once more, and now she was treading on wooden boards.

A door opened again, another click of a light switch and the door closed behind her. She felt his fingers at the back of her head, and her blindfold was removed. He was standing staring at her, his hat still over his eyes and still wearing dark spectacles.

She glanced round the small room. Facing her was the only window, small and high in the wall. It had been covered with some dark paint, making it impossible for anyone to look out. In one corner was a small iron bed with some blankets thrown on it and a chair and cupboard beside it. In the other corner was a fitted wash-basin. Another chair and a piece of worn linoleum in the centre of the bare boards completed the furniture.

'Not exactly the Ritz,' he grinned at her. 'But then you shouldn't be staying long.'

'Where have you brought me?' she asked.

'Just a little hide-away I'd prepared,' was the reply. 'Though I didn't expect two guests.'

Her short-sighted eyes widened.

'You mean you've got someone else

here? Doone Drummer?'

'In the next room,' he nodded.

She had found Doone Drummer, all right, she thought bitterly.

Her thoughts turned to Dr. Morelle. He would have got back to Harley Street by now, of course. She tried to imagine what his reactions would be when he discovered that she was missing. But her imagination boggled at the attempt.

She wondered how long the driver of the car she had hired would wait before he gave her up. Would he get in touch with the Doctor to find out what had happened to her? Or would he decide it was none of his business and just put it down on the bill in the ordinary way? Fervently she prayed he'd think there was something odd about her not returning, and would inform Dr. Morelle of what had happened. It was the only clue the Doctor would have to give him any idea where she had gone.

Then she recalled his automatic she had taken. But it might be any time before he realised it had disappeared. It was probable he might guess immediately that for once she had disobeyed him and followed him to St. Julian's Church. What a fool she had been, thinking she could follow in his footsteps, pretending to be a detective.

She consoled herself with the thought that perhaps hers hadn't been the only failure that night. Her intuition that Dr. Morelle's scheme had somehow come unstuck had been justified. That something must have gone wrong was proved, she thought ruefully, by the fact that the wanted man had not only escaped, but had added a second to his list of victims. She wondered if the man facing her had also collected the diamond bracelet.

She wondered about Doone Drummer. Poor thing, she thought, she wouldn't be looking so glamorous now. What a dreadful business it must have been for her. How had she coped with it? Miss Frayle focused her gaze on the figure before her.

'Is that the truth?' she asked. 'Is Miss Drummer really in the next room?'

'She's there all right.'

'Alive?' Miss Frayle queried after a moment.

'Alive,' was the reply. 'Though she's not exactly herself.'

An icy hand clutched at Miss Frayle's heart.

'What have you done to her?'

'Just kept her quiet,' he said casually. 'Same as I've got to keep you quiet.'

As he moved towards her the hand he had kept behind his back came forward, and she stood stricken with terror.

'Don't get scared,' he told her. 'You won't feel a thing.'

The hypodermic glinted evilly in the light of the unshaded bulb overhead. In one movement, her bound wrists were grasped, the sleeve of her right arm pushed up, and a stab of pain brought a quick gasp from her.

'Not quite the methods used by Dr. Morelle,' his voice mocked her. 'But, I flatter myself, just as effective.'

Miss Frayle fought off a feeling of sickness that swept over her. The sensation suddenly gave place to one of overwhelming terror. Had he injected her with a drug that would not merely make her unconscious but would kill her? Had he already murdered Doone Drummer that way? Her head swam with shock, the palms of her hands ran with sweat. She lurched back towards the bed in the corner, gritting her teeth against the black horror that enveloped her and sharpened by the pain in her arm.

Why, why, she cried to herself, had she disobeyed Dr. Morelle? He who'd always been so right in the past. Why had she been so foolish ever to doubt him? Now she would never see him again. She was dying. The drug was already beginning its dreadful work.

'Pull yourself together,' the man's voice cut in to her chaotic thoughts. 'You'll be dropping off into a nice sleep presently.' He interpreted the expression on her face and added: 'You'll wake up all right. Tell me something,' he went on. 'What was the bright idea Dr. Morelle and this Inspector Hood you mentioned had worked out for me?'

Miss Frayle made no answer for a moment. Then:

'I — I don't know.'

She wondered if Dr. Morelle would ever learn how she had died without giving away the information her murderer had tried to drag from her. The man watching her shrugged and smiled thinly.

'Think nothing of it,' he said. 'It flopped anyhow. I was just curious. Must say I can't figure out why he let you run your head into a spot.'

Once again she was puzzled by the tone in his voice. Where had she heard it before? She was finding it difficult to bring her mind to bear on the problem. All she could do was to protest loyally:

'It was my own fault. I — I disobeyed him.'

Her voice sounded as if it was someone else speaking.

Her eyelids drooped and she tried to push away a tremendous desire to let herself collapse on to the bed. Now she heard her own voice coming as if from a great distance. She couldn't make sense of the words, and then suddenly a bright ball of light was blazing down at her. For a moment she managed to get it into perspective, and she knew it was only the electric light bulb in the ceiling. Then it was a blazing sun again.

There was a movement beside her, and an enormous figure loomed over her. It grew larger and larger; it became darker and darker as if it was smothering her, and she remembered no more.

The man looked down at the inert figure on the bed with a little smile of satisfaction. He crossed to the light and snapped it out. Opening the door he glanced back into the room, which was in darkness except for a faint glimmer from the painted-out window. He closed the door after him, turned the key in the lock and pocketed it.

He stood on the small bare landing at the head of the uncarpeted stairs leading to two empty rooms below. It was a damned lucky accident he'd stumbled on this place. He recollected how almost from the moment he'd found it he'd realised it would make an ideal spot for dumping someone you wanted to hide. It was finding it which had probably sown the first seed of this kidnapping business in his mind. The most useful thing about the place was that it was so marvellously near where he'd installed himself.

After a moment he crossed to the door next to the one he had just closed, looked in and snapped on the light. He stood there for a few moments staring into the room, then switched out the light and closed the door again.

His fingers closed over the package in his pocket. The diamond bracelet. He frowned slightly as he wondered what the scheme was Dr. Morelle had cooked up with the cops. He would liked to have known. In case they might be planning another trap on similar lines for him. Had Miss Frayle been lying when she'd said she didn't know what the plan had been? He decided he'd give her a going-over about that when she recovered consciousness and before he gave her another shot of dope.

Anyhow, he congratulated himself, the luck had been with him all along.

Whatever throw of the dice had wrecked the combined efforts of Dr. Morelle and Scotland Yard to nail him, he had to thank his lucky stars for it. Result: he'd come out of it not only with the bracelet — he still had to check it added up to ten thousand pounds, though something told him Dr. Morelle wouldn't have tried to fool him — but also with Miss Frayle as an added string to his bow.

He grinned to himself. Maybe he'd give Dr. Morelle a ring. He should be back at Harley Street by now all right. Feeling pretty hot under the collar over Miss Frayle.

22

Aboard the 'Aloha'

The police-car drew up outside the Jollyboat Inn and a short figure stepped forward eagerly. Inspector Hood got out, followed by Dr. Morelle.

'You the cops, ain't yer?' the little man muttered from the side of his mouth.

'I'm Detective-Inspector Hood from Scotland Yard. This is Dr. Morelle.'

'Blimey. Toffs on the job, eh?'

'You are Eddie Rice who telephoned Scotland Yard just now about some funny business you witnessed on a house-boat down here?'

'I'm Mrs. Rice's little boy,' the other replied perkily. 'And that stuff I told 'em about wot's going on at the house-boat is true. Every word of it.'

Dr. Morelle scrutinised Eddie Rice from beneath the shadow of his hat. He was a man of about fifty-five, with a thin pinched face above the dirty-looking choker. An old cap with a broken peak was stuck over one ear, and his expression was foxy.

'Why didn't you tip off the local police?' Inspector Hood was asking.

'I was afraid you'd ask that,' the other confessed. 'It's like this. Me and the local cops — police, I mean — don't hit it off too well.'

'Sorry to hear that,' Inspector Hood sympathised not without a sarcastic edge to his voice.

'I'll live,' was the jaunty retort. 'Unless of course they pins a murder rap on me.'

'Why should they pin anything on you?' Hood demanded.

'They did before. And you know what cops — police — are.'

'Tell me,' Hood said pleasantly.

'All this promotion they're after,' the other explained. 'I'd be the same if I was in their boots. I'd want promotion. To get it you've got to make a pinch often as yer can. Only way you can show you're keen on yer job.'

'You appear to have been making a

close study of police precepts,' Dr. Morelle interposed dryly.

'I speaks from bitter experience,' was the retort.

'So you've been inside,' Inspector Hood said. 'Unjustly, of course.'

'Unjust isn't the word. I tell you, Inspector — ' the other began, but Hood interrupted him.

'Too bad. But tell us what d'you expect to make out of this tip-off you've given us tonight?'

'You pays for information received, don't yer?'

'If it's any good.'

'This is the goods, believe me.'

'Where is the boat?' Hood queried.

Eddie Rice jerked his thumb over his shoulder.

'Lying off the Embankment she is, about a hundred yards down.'

Inspector Hood instructed the sergeant at the wheel to wait where he was with the car. As a precaution he told the man to contact other police controls in the vicinity, asking them to keep in touch in case their assistance might be required.

He and Dr. Morelle followed Rice across the road and they proceeded in the direction the little man indicated.

That portion of Chelsea Embankment called Cheyne Row continues a few hundred yards past Battersea Bridge. It comes to a stop against a wall behind which lie boat-houses and boat-makers' yards. The Jollyboat Inn is about two hundred yards from where Cheyne Row terminates. Across the road from the public-house runs a low wall beyond which the muddy beach is crammed with boats of all shapes and sizes, from dinghies to sea-going barges. Many of the larger craft are converted into dwellings, superstructures having been built on to them.

'Called *Aloha* it is,' Eddie was saying. 'My first idea was that all the hanky-panky I'd noticed was to do with smuggling. Then tonight I spotted this woman on board. She looked as if something was wrong, and it was that decided me to give Scotland Yard the buzz.'

'As a matter of interest,' Dr. Morelle

inquired, 'what business causes you to range the streets at this late hour?'

'Insomnia,' replied the other simply. 'Ever since I come out after doing that stretch I've had insomnia something cruel. You being a doctor might know a cure.' He looked up at Dr. Morelle hopefully.

'Insomnia is frequently a symptom rather than a disease in itself,' Dr. Morelle pointed out. 'In which case the cause requires eliminating in order that the effect may be remedied.'

'I know what caused my insomnia,' said Eddie Rice. 'Being unjustly jugged, that's what.'

'I wonder you don't apply to the police for compensation,' growled Inspector Hood.

'Compensation,' the other snorted. 'More likely they'd jug me again for having the cheek. Anyway, finding it impossible to sleep of a night, I goes out and walks around. I find it makes me drowsy by early morning, then I goes back home and drops off for a few hours.'

'How do you occupy yourself during

these nocturnal perambulations?' Dr. Morelle asked.

'Thinking. Thinking what an unjust world it is for anyone wot's never got the chance of a proper start in life. Supposing I'd had a decent education and had been wearing a decent suit, d'you think the cops would have pinched me when they found me in that garden outside the house? You bet your life they wouldn't. I'd have only got to say I was tying up me shoelace and I'd have got away with it. But just because I was — '

'Save it,' Inspector Hood said wearily. 'Which of these is the boat?'

Ahead of them was the high wall which brought Cheyne Row to an abrupt stop. The low wall between them and the river had now given place to some even lower railings. At their backs lay attractive Georgian houses, balconies over small front gardens, jostling with converted blocks of flats.

'That's her.'

Eddie Rice pointed to one of the vessels lying on the gleaming mud. The *Aloha* lay apart from the others.

293

There was not a sign of life on any of the miscellany of boats. Only the glimmer of a light here and there. The curtained windows of the *Aloha* were edged with light. Between her and the Embankment lay an old hulk, a gang-plank leading from one to the other.

'There's a door further along you can nip through,' Rice said. 'Into the builders' yard. That's how you gets on to the hulk.'

'You seem to know your way around,' Inspector Hood said. 'You wouldn't happen to have a grudge against the owner by any chance?'

The other assumed an aggrieved expression.

'Never met 'im,' he protested. 'Don't hardly know what he looks like. Whenever I've seen 'im it's been late at night. He's been out there on the deck and when he's spotted me he's nipped back, as if he didn't want to be seen.'

Inspector Hood chewed dubiously on his pipe-stem and glanced questioningly at Dr. Morelle.

Dr. Morelle had been staring across at the black mass of buildings on the other side of the river. They mingled into the darkness of the sky, with the pointing finger of a chimney-stack barely discernible. Here and there squares of light from the factory windows dotted the dark blackcloth. The surface of the river was black and oily, catching the reflections of the street lamps strung out along the Embankment.

Further downstream the outline of Battersea Bridge could be made out, and here and there port and starboard lights glowed against the shadowy shapes of moored vessels. From the direction of the Pool the notes of a ship's sirren hovered mournfully on the air.

'D'you think it might be worthwhile investigating?' Inspector Hood asked the Doctor. 'The woman I'm thinking of?'

Dr. Morelle stared at Eddie Rice.

'You are unable to describe this woman?' he queried.

The little man shook his head.

'Only got a quick glimpse of her. Then suddenly the curtain was pulled over again.'

'You were not able to discern whether,

295

for instance, she was wearing spectacles?'

'Couldn't say,' was the reply. 'It was just a woman's face and that's all.'

Dr. Morelle's gaze rested on Inspector Hood. Dragging at his cigarette, he said:

'Since we have made the journey we might as well inquire further into the matter.'

'All right,' Inspector Hood said briskly, 'let's pay 'em a call.' He turned sharply on Eddie Rice. 'Think the woman's still there?'

'Never seen her come off. And I was keeping an eye on the boat while I was waiting for you.'

He led the way through a small door let into two taller doors that were the entrance to the boat yard. He produced a torch and led the way between half-completed boats to some steps leading down to the hulk.

Cautiously the Inspector and Dr. Morelle followed him and gained the rickety gangway to the *Aloha*. They paused for a moment, Inspector Hood breathing somewhat heavily from his exertions. The *Aloha* had once been a sea-going barge. Now a wooden super-structure several feet high rose from her decks. Facing them was the front door. On either side of it light still glimmered round the edges of the curtained windows.

'Looks as if it might be quite comfy inside,' Inspector Hood muttered beneath his breath. He put one foot on the gang-plank. 'Shall I lead the way?'

'Watch out,' Rice whispered hoarsely. 'If you don't want a mud-bath hang on to the rail tight.'

Inspector Hood moved cautiously across the narrow, slippery planks with Rice and Dr. Morelle following him. The rickety gangway swayed and creaked ominously beneath their weight, but they gained the deck safely. Now there came to them the murmur of voices from within the house-boat.

'They're there all right,' Rice whispered, his voice filled with satisfaction.

Inspector Hood took his pipe from between his teeth, squared his burly shoulders and moved towards the door. He banged on a small brass knocker shaped like a life-belt. The murmuring stopped abruptly. There was complete silence until Hood knocked again. The echoes died away and then silence fell again. Then there came the sound of slow footsteps within. After a moment the door opened cautiously.

The man staring at them suspiciously was of medium height. Dark hair brushed back. Shirt collar open. Sports jacket.

'Forgive us bothering you like this,' Inspector Hood said affably. 'But we thought you might be able to help us.'

'This is one hell of an hour to want help,' was the caustic retort. The man's voice was curiously metallic. 'Who are you?'

'I am Detective-Inspector Hood of Scotland Yard.'

Dr. Morelle caught an unmistakable gasp from someone beyond the man at the door. Hood was saying, his tone still genial:

'Please don't be alarmed — '

'Why should I be? I'm not scared of the cops.'

'I'm sure of that,' the Inspector

continued agreeably. 'I was thinking of whoever else was with you — your wife would it be?'

'What business is that of yours?' the other snapped.

'I'm afraid,' Inspector Hood said in his most apologetic voice, 'we are causing you some annoyance. Believe me, we shouldn't be bothering you if it wasn't that we thought you could give us some help. We are anxious to trace a young woman,' he went on quickly. 'She is missing. We've received information tonight that a woman has been seen on board here with you.'

'What the hell you getting at?'

Inspector Hood gave a little chuckle as if to say he was well aware he was of course on a fool's errand.

'I know your — er — wife can't possibly be this woman,' he said. 'But I'd just like your corroboration. Just a matter of routine — er — Mr — ?'

'My name's Goodwin. Dave Goodwin.'

The Inspector nodded smilingly.

'Have to make all these silly inquiries just for the record.'

Dr. Morelle watched the mixed emotions pass across the man's face. It was obvious Hood's visit was not welcome. Goodwin gave the impression that he was weighing up his chances of getting away with defying the Inspector's authority. Why, wondered Dr. Morelle, if he had nothing to hide? The man at the door stood, his face working indecisively, his eyes glittering as they darted from Inspector Hood to Dr. Morelle and Eddie Rice, then back to the Inspector. Finally he grumbled:

'I don't see what right you've got to come nosing into my affairs.'

Some of the affability dropped from Inspector Hood's manner. His tone hardened slightly, and his heavy jaw jutted forward as he replied ponderously:

'I have already explained this is merely a routine inquiry. I'm asking for your help. If I can report that whoever' — he hesitated delicately — 'whoever is occupying this boat with you is not the missing woman, that's all I want.'

'She doesn't occupy this boat,' the other admitted grudgingly. 'I live here alone.'

'Then it's not your wife?'

Goodwin stared at him sullenly.

'No,' he said slowly. 'A friend.'

'I am sure your — er — friend must be wondering who it is that's disturbing you at this hour,' Dr. Morelle insinuated.

'May even think,' Inspector Hood added with a touch of humour, 'it's the police who've called.'

There followed a further pause while the man who called himself Dave Goodwin stood there irresolutely.

'I'm sure,' the Inspector said persuasively, 'you don't want a bungling policeman like me hanging around. Strictly between you and me,' he added, 'we want to be getting back ourselves.'

The other finally made up his mind. Pulling the door back wide, he said: 'You can come in.'

Dr. Morelle followed Inspector Hood, Eddie Rice closing the door behind them. The light from a large oil-lamp on the table illuminated the comfortably furnished interior. Beside the lamp was a tray with the remains of a supper, and there were a tea-pot and two cups and saucers beside it.

The woman who faced them across the table stood in an aggressive attitude. Then she saw Dr. Morelle behind the burly figure of Inspector Hood, and her mouth opened in a gasp.

'Dr. Morelle,' she exclaimed.

It was Rosie Huggins.

23

The Liaison

As Rosie Huggins continued to stare incredulously at Dr. Morelle the man Goodwin moved to her side. He threw a glance at the Doctor and then said to the woman:

'You know him?'

Rosie Huggins nodded.

'How d'you know him?'

Inspector Hood was also looking at Dr. Morelle, his expression full of surprise tinged with faint amusement. Eddie Rice was glancing open-mouthed from one to the other. Finally he concentrated on the tall, dark figure who was regarding Rosie Huggins. This was something he certainly hadn't expected. The woman was interesting the sawbones all right. And the cop seemed to think there was something in the air too. Eddie Rice hoped that whatever the outcome of it all, there'd be something in it for him.

So this, Inspector Hood was thinking, was Harvey Drummer's housekeeper. Although Dr. Morelle had given him some idea of what she looked like, and he had pictured someone who wasn't at all typical of a housekeeper, the Inspector was nevertheless surprised at her appearance. He took in her *svelte* rounded lines, and the attractive face, shadowed as it was by a mixture of fear and defiance, then glanced at Dave Goodwin.

The relationship between them was pretty obvious, Hood decided. A woman doesn't visit a man in the early hours of the morning just to talk about the weather. He wondered what it was about the liaison that had driven the woman deliberately to lie about it to Dr. Morelle. Probably this Goodwin chap was married or something.

'Dr. Morelle is a friend of Mr. Drummer's,' Rosie Huggins found her voice.

'What?' Goodwin exclaimed, and shot a bitter look at the Doctor. 'So that's your game.' His attitude grew threatening as he went on: 'Drummer's found out about Rosie.'

'Found out what?' Dr. Morelle asked quietly.

Rosie Huggins' voice suddenly rose shrilly.

'That's why you questioned me the way you did about how I spent my hours off yesterday.'

'What business is it of anybody's?' Goodwin demanded aggressively.

'Pretending you'd lost something,' the woman added jeeringly.

'There would appear to be some misunderstanding,' Dr. Morelle murmured imperturbably. 'Permit me,' he said, fixing Rosie Huggins with a level gaze, 'to assure you that meeting you here is entirely fortuitous.'

'You don't expect me to believe that,' she said.

'Anyway, now you've found out you can get back to Drummer and tell him how smart you've been,' the man beside her put in. 'Come on, clear out all of you.' He stepped forward belligerently.

'Just a minute,' Inspector Hood said

patiently. 'Let's get one or two things clear. And for a start,' as Goodwin began to say something, 'you shut up, sit down and be quiet.'

Goodwin glowered at him for a moment, and then relaxed his attitude.

'What Dr. Morelle's said,' Hood went on, 'is on the level. Neither he nor I had any idea that you,' turning to the woman, 'were here. This little call was my idea. As I said to your pugnacious friend, we're looking for a missing woman.' He looked at Goodwin. 'Don't know how secret you've been trying to keep your friend's visits, and I don't know for what reason. Probably wouldn't be particularly interested if I did. But when Scotland Yard was tipped off tonight a woman had been seen here, and the circumstances sounded slightly suspicious, you'll understand it was my duty to investigate.'

The other gave Eddie Rice a sharp look and commented:

'I suppose that little copper's nark was responsible?'

Eddie Rice responded to the accusation with a protest.

'Copper's nark nothing. I never did no more than anybody else would have done — '

'It's a pity certain people haven't got something better to do with their time,' Goodwin sneered. 'Snooping round causing innocent people trouble.'

'How was I to know — ' began Rice, but Hood interrupted him curtly.

'Shut up, both of you,' he growled. 'If anyone thinks he sees something suspicious it's his duty to report it.'

'That's all right,' muttered Rice. 'I'm a good citizen. Allus have been.'

'I warned you it was risky,' the woman told Goodwin. 'Coming down to see you here so late. I was afraid people might see me and think it was funny.'

'What's wrong with it?'

'We know there's nothing wrong in it, Dave. But you know how people are.'

'I wouldn't have thought anything myself,' Eddie explained. 'Only I happened to see you through the window, and you looked upset. Thought perhaps you were being kept a prisoner or somethink. After all, it does happen sometimes. You've only got to read the papers.'

Rosie Huggins gave him a wry smile.

'Very thoughtful of you, I'm sure. I was only looking upset because Dave and I had a bit of a quarrel. Nothing more.'

'Sorry,' muttered Rice, 'but for all I knows, he might have been going to do yer in.'

'Perhaps I might inquire,' Dr. Morelle asked the woman quietly, 'if your — ah — relationship with Mr. Goodwin is the reason for your lying to me regarding your visit to the Oriental Cinema?'

She stared at him for a moment. Then she gave a little shrug.

'Since you've found out so much,' she admitted, 'you might as well know the truth.'

'Why should you tell him anything?' Goodwin cut in.

'May I inquire,' Dr. Morelle ignored the interruption, 'if it is your intention to return to Park Lane presently? It occurs to me that if you have any explanations to offer, this atmosphere is not altogether conducive.'

She gave Goodwin a worried look. She realised his aggressive attitude would, in fact, make it difficult for her to tell her story uninterrupted. She patted his arm affectionately.

'Perhaps it would be better if I went,' she said placatingly.

'Only too delighted to give you a lift back,' Inspector Hood told her cheerfully.

'That's very kind of you,' she said. She turned again to Goodwin. 'I'd better go really, Dave. It's very late in any case.'

'All right,' the other muttered grudgingly. 'Though I don't like it, and that's a fact. Then I never was keen on coppers, anyhow, let alone riding about with 'em in their ruddy cars.'

'Perhaps what Dr. Morelle says is true,' Rosie admonished him. 'It's just coincidence that they came here tonight.'

'It's quite a comfortable car,' Inspector Hood put in. 'You might find it difficult getting a taxi.'

Dave Goodwin stood framed in the doorway staring after them as Dr. Morelle and the others made their way back across the gangway and over the hulk. He was still standing there, a grim, implacable figure, watching them as they disappeared along Cheyne Row, towards the police-car waiting outside the Jollyboat Inn.

Rosie Huggins turned for a moment to wave to him. Dr. Morelle noticed that he did not return her wave, and then the door closed behind him.

'He's taking this rather badly,' she said in a subdued voice.

'Our arrival, under the circumstances,' Dr. Morelle replied, 'must have come as somewhat of a shock.'

'It certainly was a shock when I saw you. I really did think Mr. Drummer had found out. Just shows what a small world it is. Especially,' she added unhappily, 'when you start telling lies.'

''Oh what a tangled web we weave when first we practise to deceive,'' quoted Dr. Morelle.

Her glance in the light of a street-lamp was full of admiration for him.

'You do put things neatly, don't you, Doctor?' she murmured. Dr. Morelle made no further comment and she went

310

on: 'I suppose it's pretty obvious to you now why I lied to you the way I did?'

'An inkling of your motive is beginning to dawn on me,' he answered smoothly.

They had reached the waiting police-car, and Hood took Eddie Rice aside and muttered in his ear for a few moments. The little man's face was wearing a disappointed look as the Inspector left him. His dreams of remuneration for the under-cover work he had taken upon himself on behalf of the police had faded miserably.

Eddie Rice stood watching the police-car disappear into the darkness of Chelsea Embankment. With a muttered curse, he turned towards the back streets. Once more the world had turned against him. Never again, he decided, would he condescend to give the police the benefit of any information he picked up. Next time, if he saw someone being murdered in cold blood he'd keep it to himself and let the cops find out for themselves.

The police-car headed Park Lane-wards.

Inspector Hood sat next to the driver,

and behind him were Rosie Huggins and Dr. Morelle. Hood leant back, one ear cocked as the woman began to unfold the story of her association with Dave Goodwin.

At first she talked in disjointed phrases, and Dr. Morelle had difficulty in catching what she said. Then she grew more confident, as if Dr. Morelle was inspiring her confidence, and was soon speaking clearly and concisely.

She had met Goodwin, she explained, very soon after her husband's tragic fishing-trip. Goodwin had attracted her from the first, she said. Even when he told her he was married, living apart from his wife, she still found herself unable to give him up. He had made this confession very early in their acquaintance, telling her his wife refused to divorce him.

She had realised from the start it was a hopeless love-affair, and from time to time she had made up her mind to break it off. Then she had started visiting him on the *Aloha*. She had kept her friendship with Goodwin a secret from Drummer. She feared that if her employer learned of her association with a married man he would almost certainly take exception to it. She might even lose her job. She couldn't risk that.

Inevitably the strain of the liaison began to tell on her. At her last meeting with Goodwin the day before — that was the occasion about which she had lied to Dr. Morelle — she had suggested more strongly than ever they should never see each other again.

'I suppose, by the way,' she said ruefully, 'you just rang up the Oriental; they told you the film I said I'd seen wasn't on at that time, and you knew I was a liar?'

She sighed. Dr. Morelle murmured inaudibly, and she continued her story.

When she said good-bye to Goodwin he had begged her to reconsider finishing with him. Next day she had received a letter from him imploring her to slip out that night and meet him on the *Aloha*.

It was a desperately worded letter. Frightened he might come up to Park Lane and be seen hanging round the house, or worse still, commit suicide

— he had threatened to do so when she had talked once before about their breaking up — she had slipped out of the house that night and gone down to Chelsea.

'I'd just agreed,' she concluded, 'to continue meeting him on condition he made even greater efforts to free himself from his wife so we could be married, when you turned up.' She smiled wryly in the darkness.

The police-car swung into Park Lane towards Drummer's house. At Rosie Huggins' direction it turned off along a side-street. A few yards along it stopped by the entrance to a mews. Down the mews was Drummer's garage. There was an entrance from the garage into his house, the woman explained.

Hood watched her figure melt into the darkness of the mews. If by any chance her absence had been discovered she would say that being unable to sleep she'd decided some fresh air would do her good. Inspector Hood said over his shoulder to Dr. Morelle:

'What d'you think of her?'

'You heard almost as much of her story as I did,' the Doctor replied, leaning back smoking a *Le Sphinx*.

'Seemed to make sense to me,' Hood said. 'Didn't quite catch what you told her before she got out.'

'I merely reassured her that her relationship with Goodwin was no concern of ours, and her wishes about it remaining a secret would certainly be respected.'

The burly figure in front of him nodded.

'Let's hope it all works out for her,' he said. 'Nice woman. Deserves to be happy.'

Little could Inspector Hood foresee how his hopes for Rosie Huggins' happiness were destined to be answered.

24

Dilemma

The man heard the car pull up at the entrance to the mews, and he darted quickly across into the shadows. He could see the car, dark and shining in the lamp-light, then a woman get out. There was a slam of a door and the car drove off. The woman stood staring after it for a moment. Then she turned into the mews.

The man hugged the shadows more closely and glanced at the luminous dial of his wrist-watch. It was approaching two-thirty. He watched the figure, never taking his eyes off her as she approached. The tap-tap of her heels on the cobblestones drew nearer. She stopped outside Drummer's garage. She looked cautiously up and down the mews, and her eyes rested on the shadowy corner where he stood. He held his breath as he waited for her to challenge him.

His hat was tilted well over his face, hiding his eyes. His hands were thrust deep into his pockets, one hand loosely curved round the butt of his automatic. He knew he couldn't use it; that if she did discover him he would have to bluff his way out of it.

But the darkness hid him and she turned away. She dipped into her handbag and he heard a key turn in the lock, then a click and one of the garage doors swung open creaking slightly. The woman drew the door open wide. It was then the man, relaxing a little, allowed one foot to press heavily on a small piece of brick. The piece crunched loudly beneath the sudden pressure. The woman whipped round, hand to her throat, and stared in his direction.

'Who's there?' she challenged.

He flattened himself against the wall, but after a pause the woman moved slowly towards him.

'Who is it?' she called. 'Show yourself, or I'll scream the place down.'

He cursed silently. Another moment and she'd have been in the garage. He pulled off his dark glasses, pushed them into his pocket and stepped out of the shadows. Forcing a laugh into his voice he said:

'Why so scared? Take it easy.'

She gave a gasp of mingled amazement and dismay as he advanced towards her.

'Oh,' she found her voice and muttered apologetically, 'I thought it was somebody hiding. A — a burglar or someone.'

'Sorry if I startled you,' he returned pleasantly.

He was holding the garage-door open for her. She eyed him curiously, and he knew she was waiting for him to offer her some explanation. He said nothing. There was nothing he could say that would sound like anything but an attempt to bluff her. They stood for a moment staring at each other. He could see clearly reflected in her face the questions that were battling round her mind.

Then without a word she went into the garage.

He pushed the door shut after her, and after a moment went swiftly and silently along the mews. Too bad, he told himself, it had to be like this. But it was just one of those unlucky breaks that came up. You had to take the bad with the good. There was nothing he could do about it. Nothing except the obvious thing. His face suddenly became cruel and evil as he turned out of the mews.

Somewhere a clock was chiming the half-hour.

★   ★   ★

The police-car turned back into Park Lane and prowled along until Inspector Hood spotted a call-box. Dr. Morelle watched him while he telephoned. After a few moments the burly figure hung up and walked ponderously across the pavement. His face was heavy as he got back into the car.

'Not so good,' he said.

'No news of his daughter's return?'

The other shook his head and sighed wearily.

'Drummer wants us to go round there. Sounded as if he's feeling pretty low, I'm afraid.'

'It is not in our power to bear him better news,' Dr. Morelle replied. 'However, we may be able to give him some reassurance.'

'That it's only a matter of time before his daughter will be safely restored to him?' Inspector Hood struck a match and re-lit his pipe, drawing at it noisily. He stared at the glowing tobacco for a few moments before he ventured: 'Don't you think we'd better tell him about our flop tonight? And Miss Frayle getting — er — involved?'

'I was considering it,' Dr. Morelle murmured. 'He is almost bound to ask after Miss Frayle. If he detects I am being evasive it may lead him to conclude that we are withholding information in order to allay his anxiety.'

'We don't have to say anything about Chelsea and Rosie Huggins,' Inspector Hood said. 'That wild-goose chase got us nowhere fast, anyhow.'

They drew up outside Drummer's house. Harvey Drummer himself opened the door and led the way to his study. His face appeared grey and drawn with anxiety. He handed a cup of black coffee he had poured from a percolator to Inspector Hood. As he was giving Dr. Morelle a cup he told him what Inspector Hood had learned over the 'phone. His daughter had still not turned up. Stirring his coffee Dr. Morelle related what had happened at St. Julian's Church. Harvey Drummer listened in complete silence. Inspector Hood put in a word here and there, and in conclusion took upon himself the entire blame for the disastrous turn of events.

'Whatever happens to Doone,' Drummer said heavily, 'I shall never forgive myself for getting Miss Frayle dragged into this ghastly business.'

'You have nothing to reproach yourself with,' Dr. Morelle reassured him. 'Had the misguided young woman obeyed my instructions — '

'I think it was damned courageous of her,' Harvey Drummer said warmly. 'I hope she'll be rescued safely so that I can tell her so.' He paused and then looked at Dr. Morelle squarely. 'You telling me this now,' he queried sombrely, 'to prepare me for the worst about Doone?'

There was a little silence while Inspector Hood cleared his throat noisily.

'Personally,' replied Dr. Morelle, 'I see no reason to suppose your daughter's safety is menaced any more now than before. In fact, her captor must be even more confident that he holds the whip-hand. Not only has he obtained the ransom he demanded, he also holds another hostage in the person of mis-guided Miss Frayle. As I see it, the worst that could happen is that in his confidence he may demand more ransom in excess of that you have already paid for your daughter's safe return.'

The other appeared to give a faint sigh of relief.

Inspector Hood drained his coffee cup and growled:

'What we've got to decide on is our next move.'

As if in answer to his question the telephone rang. Harvey Drummer glanced at Dr. Morelle and then at the Inspector interrogatively.

'Maybe it's — it's Doone,' he muttered.

Inspector Hood moved forward, picked up the receiver and held it out to him. Drummer's hand was trembling visibly as he took it and spoke into the mouthpiece. Dr. Morelle and Inspector Hood watched his expression as he listened. After a moment, he looked at the Doctor and, covering the receiver with his hand, said:

'It's for you.' He added: 'A man. Might be — '

But Dr. Morelle had already taken the receiver and was speaking into it.

'Dr. Morelle here.'

Once again the familiar voice reached him over the wire.

'Tried to 'phone you at Harley Street. But there was no reply.' Behind the muffled tones Dr. Morelle caught the suggestion of mocking triumph. 'So I guessed you might be commiserating with your client.' Dr. Morelle made no reply, and the other went on: 'Thank him for the bracelet. Just what I ordered.'

'When are you fulfilling your part of the bargain?'

Hood's shoulders hunched as he watched Dr. Morelle. At his words

Drummer had already moved slowly forward, realising whom the Doctor was speaking to.

'That's a little thing,' the man was saying to Dr. Morelle coolly, 'which I'm turning over in my mind. You see, you didn't keep your part of the bargain. Remember?' The voice added: 'Maybe I should consult Miss Frayle. On second thoughts, her opinion might be biased in your favour. Only natural.'

Dr. Morelle responded with deliberate calm: 'I am fully resigned to the fact that as a result of foolishly disobeying my orders Miss Frayle is in your hands.'

'You'll be glad to hear she's enjoying good health,' the other said. 'At the moment.'

Dr. Morelle made no comment, and the voice went on:

'It wasn't only her butting in I objected to. I was disappointed to hear you'd set out to trap me, aided by your pal, Inspector Hood.'

'I am waiting to learn what purpose you have in mind regarding both your captives,' the Doctor said quietly.

'Frankly, I don't quite know how to play it. When a chap's faith has been destroyed he needs a little time in which to build it up again. I trusted you, Dr. Morelle, truly I did. That trust's been betrayed. I called you to let you know Miss Frayle was in good hands, which, considering the circumstances, is pretty big-hearted of me.'

'I am suitably impressed.'

'What happens next you'll have to leave to me. I won't keep you in suspense too long. You'll be hearing from me. Soon.'

The line went dead, and Dr. Morelle replaced the receiver.

'What's he say?' Inspector Hood grunted.

'Did he mention Doone?' Drummer said. Dr. Morelle tapped the ash off his cigarette. 'He gave me to understand that your daughter is still unharmed.' He continued: 'He asked me to thank you for the bracelet, which meets his requirements.'

Harvey Drummer gulped and then said: 'Miss Frayle?'

'It would appear he holds her a

325

prisoner,' was the reply. 'She, too, it seems is unharmed — ' Dr. Morelle broke off as the other moved quickly towards the door. 'Where are you going?'

Drummer swung round at him impatiently. 'This is a chance to see if it's Pearson or Mrs. Huggins,' he said. 'Using the telephone in my office. Come on.'

'By God, he's got something — ' Inspector Hood began, then he broke off as he saw Dr. Morelle's face.

'Whichever it is, even if they've left the office,' Drummer was saying excitedly, 'we still might catch 'em in their room.'

It was obvious to Hood, however, that Dr. Morelle remained unimpressed by Drummer's enthusiasm.

'I must remind you,' he told Drummer coolly, 'of one important fact.'

'What?' Harvey Drummer spoke impatiently from the door. 'We shall be too late in a minute.'

'If Mrs. Huggins and Pearson are innocent,' Dr. Morelle said, 'they should still be unaware that your daughter has disappeared. Supposing we find both of them asleep, what explanations have you

326

in mind to offer for disturbing them?'

'We can make some excuse,' Drummer said quickly.

Dr. Morelle regarded the tip of his cigarette, murmuring:

'You obviously have supreme confidence in your powers of invention.'

'What d'you mean?'

'You'll have to think up a pretty good story,' Inspector Hood said. 'If they are genuinely asleep they're bound to start wondering what's wrong, and maybe put two and two together.'

'But surely, if one of them is the kidnapper — ?' Harvey Drummer frowned and left the question unfinished. He said: 'We know Mrs. Huggins is a liar. Then there are those gloves of Pearson's — by the way, they've gone from his drawer, I can tell you that — '

'All of which point to both your housekeeper and secretary as being possible suspects,' Dr. Morelle conceded. 'But until we are convinced these circumstances offer no other explanation it would be rash to assume either person's guilt.'

Inspector Hood regarded Harvey Drummer anxiously. Drummer was only half-convinced by Dr. Morelle's argument, and Hood feared the other would at any moment charge off, intent upon investigating his suspicions. The Inspector had promptly realised the dilemma in which Dr. Morelle found himself. As a result of their visit to the *Aloha*, both Hood and Dr. Morelle were satisfied Rosie Huggins was not implicated in the kidnapping. But Dr. Morelle could not inform Drummer accordingly without revealing the liaison which the woman had begged him to keep secret.

It was more than likely that if Drummer rushed up to the housekeeper's room at this moment he would discover she was in fact not in bed. In which case, her prearranged excuse might not convince him, and in order to prove conclusively she was not concerned in his daughter's disappearance the story of her association with Goodwin would have to be revealed. The danger of her being forced into such a damaging confession must be prevented. Obviously, therefore,

Dr. Morelle had decided that even if Pearson's behaviour did invite investigation, this — for Rosie Huggins' sake — was not the moment to put it into operation.

'If a simple explanation is forthcoming,' Dr. Morelle was telling Drummer, 'for your secretary's black gloves — which are now missing — and Mrs. Huggins' falsehood, your action might result in their suspicions being aroused regarding your daughter.'

'Supposing they did guess something's happened to Doone?' Drummer protested. 'I don't see how it matters now. They could be sworn to secrecy — '

Inspector Hood glanced quickly at Dr. Morelle. How would he wriggle out of that one? Pausing only long enough to tap the ash of his cigarette, Dr. Morelle replied coolly:

'I must remind you of a further aspect of the case. Which is that though Mrs. Huggins or Pearson may not be the actual kidnapper, the possibility still remains that one — or both of them — may nevertheless be implicated in some way.

So far,' Dr. Morelle continued persuasively, 'we have contrived not to disclose our hands. Though at this stage circumstances may appear dark, we shall not lighten our task by revealing to anyone more than is absolutely necessary.'

Harvey Drummer's attitude relaxed somewhat. He turned away from the door and shook off his aggressive eagerness with a fatalistic shrug.

'You don't think it'd be a good idea, then, to check with my 'phone,' he said. 'Just in case we might pick up some clue?'

Noting the change in his demeanour Dr. Morelle pressed home his advantage. Shaking his head he said:

'It seems to me unlikely it could have been either Pearson or your housekeeper on the telephone. The voice which I have had the opportunity of hearing upon three occasions, although disguised, has nevertheless none of the characteristics of either Mrs. Huggins' speech or Pearson's ingratiating tones.'

'You certainly should know about that,' Drummer agreed. 'Come to think, if it was either of them they'd be running a bit of a risk, making the call from my office.'

The Inspector had been thoughtfully massaging his heavy chin.

'I suppose,' he put in, 'our friend on the 'phone was telling the truth?'

'So far as Miss Frayle is concerned,' Dr. Morelle replied, 'there seems little doubt she is his prisoner. He is fully cognisant of the snare we laid for him; he even mentioned your name in its connection. He must have obtained the information from Miss Frayle. How else could he have come by it?'

'And you think he's telling the truth about Doone?' Drummer asked anxiously. 'You don't think he's killed her? After all, he's already got one murder on his hands. Rolf, I mean.'

Dr. Morelle drew thoughtfully at his cigarette.

'I favour an optimistic view,' he declared. 'If your daughter was alive before tonight's ill-fated attempt to rescue her, I see no reason why she should not be alive now. The kidnapper is in no greater danger. In fact, Miss Frayle's capture must give him greater confidence than ever that he can achieve his purpose to his complete satisfaction. Doubtless Miss Frayle, in his view, provides him with a powerful pawn in the game he is playing.'

Inspector Hood saw Drummer's face lighten at Dr. Morelle's optimistic words. He thought he detected a shadow of pessimism at the back of the Doctor's eyes. Shrewdly he detected that behind the façade he was succeeding magnificently in putting up, the capture of Miss Frayle had struck Dr. Morelle a shattering blow. He promised himself that at the first opportunity he got he'd tell Miss Frayle all about Dr. Morelle's growing anxiety for her. Anxiety — glancing again at Dr. Morelle — even his inscrutable countenance couldn't altogether mask. He imagined she'd feel it was almost worthwhile being kidnapped just to be told that. It never occurred to him he might never have the chance of imparting this heart-warming information to Miss Frayle.

It never entered Inspector Hood's mind that in fact he might never see

Miss Frayle again.

A little later Dr. Morelle and the Inspector left the house in Park Lane to return to their respective homes, Tired, but resolutely refusing to admit their spirits were low, they had decided they could do little more except patiently await whatever news the next few hours would bring.

25

Nightmare

Dr. Morelle scowled irritably as he watched the slim familiar figure drawing further away from him.

Soon, he knew, she would be lost to sight among the gravestones that stretched on and on into infinity. It was bright moonlight. Across the graveyard tall cypress trees threw long black shadows into which Miss Frayle kept disappearing, reappearing in the moonlight once more. Dr. Morelle felt a tap on his arm and Leo Rolf materialised before him, sipping from his glass of bourbon whisky. Rolf moved round and obscured the Doctor's view of Miss Frayle. Irritably Dr. Morelle pushed him aside and tried to hurry away, but his feet were entangled in the roots of one of the cypresses, and he found it impossible to move.

Rolf's pale blue eyes wore an aggrieved

expression, and he shrugged and hurried off, Dr. Morelle staring after him at the ghastly knife wound in his back. The Doctor turned again to look for Miss Frayle. He was gratified to see her approaching him. He observed she was wearing black silk gloves, and both her bare arms were covered with diamond bracelets. She was looking anxiously from side to side, stopping every now and again to peer behind the gravestones, and he knew she was looking for Pearson's pince-nez.

Again Dr. Morelle tried to free himself from the cypress tree roots, but without success. He tried to call out, and then discovered that he was smoking three *Le Sphinx* at once and he couldn't speak.

Miss Frayle drew nearer, still searching for the pince-nez. Suddenly Dr. Morelle became aware that Doone Drummer was in the church-tower behind him preparing to leap down and show Miss Frayle a selection of photographs, all of them of himself. If only, he thought, he could order Miss Frayle away before Doone Drummer landed in her path. Why

wouldn't she leave the churchyard without bothering her silly head about
Pearson's pince-nez? If he could disen-
tangle his feet he could lead her out of the
churchyard. Inspector Hood was waiting
in his police-car to drive them back to the
Aloha off Cheyne Walk.

With mounting anger and frustration
Dr. Morelle knew that there was no need
for her to worry about the pince-nez. It
was only her ridiculous intuition which
made her believe they were a vital clue.
The church-bell began to ring behind
him. Now Dr. Morelle could see Miss
Frayle was wearing the pince-nez herself
all the time, and the *tempo* of the
churchbell became a continuous staccato
jangling, and he woke up to find the
bedside telephone ringing in his ear.

As he lifted the receiver he glanced at
his bedside clock. Seven forty-two a.m.
Harvey Drummer's voice reached him
agitatedly over the wire.

'It's Mrs. Huggins. She's dead. Committed suicide.'

Dr. Morelle had been idly speculating
about the dream from which he had been

awakened. He had been impressed by its Gothic atmosphere of terror and fantasy. Drummer's words drove everything out of his mind. He sat up in bed, his jaw-line grim and taut as he listened.

Hurriedly Harvey Drummer described how Mrs. Huggins had been discovered a few minutes before by Brethers. Apparently the housekeeper habitually brought a morning cup of tea to Brethers at seven o'clock. Half an hour after she had failed to give her usual knock on his door he had gone along to her room. She was in bed. She was dead. On the floor was a glass that had contained orange-juice.

'It was cyanide,' Drummer asserted. 'Her face was definitely cyanosed, and there was a smell of almonds round her mouth.'

'Did you try artificial respiration?'

'Yes,' was the reply. 'I happen to know a bit about this sort of thing. Brethers and I did all we could. Ammonia. Brandy. But it was hopeless.'

'I will come round at once,' Dr. Morelle rapped.

'Should I 'phone the police?'

'I will speak to Inspector Hood,' Dr. Morelle told him. He hung up. He then dialled the number of Inspector Hood's home.

What was the meaning of this unexpected and sensational development? he wondered as he listened to the burr-burring of the telephone at the other end. Was Rosie Huggins' death another twist to the already tangled skein in which he had become involved?

The receiver at the other end was lifted and a woman answered it. He recognised Mrs. Hood's voice. He had met the Inspector's wife when he had visited their garden flat at Belsize Park, one Sunday afternoon. He had found the Scotland Yard man in a hut in the garden indulging in his hobby of carving old sailing-ships. Hood had always nursed a boyhood ambition to run away to sea.

Her husband, Mrs. Hood told him, was in the middle of shaving. But he came to the 'phone promptly.

'Right, Dr. Morelle,' he said on hearing the news. 'Pick you up in twenty minutes, and we'll go on to Park Lane.'

Dr. Morelle rang off and slipped on his dressing-gown. He shaved and showered with miraculous speed, allowing himself only a brief moment of regret that Miss Frayle's absence would mean his having to go out without even a cup of tea. He was consoling himself with a *Le Sphinx* when the doorbell rang. Inspector Hood was waiting for him in a police patrol-car which had picked him up at Belsize Park.

'You could have knocked me down with a mink coat, as the chorus girl said,' Inspector Hood grunted as they drove off. 'What on earth induced her to commit suicide? Couldn't have been because of last night, surely?'

Dr. Morelle gave a slight shrug, and there was silence between them for the rest of the journey. Only the inevitable gurglings from Inspector Hood's pipe as he slumped back in the corner of the car, chin sunk on his chest.

Brethers opened the door to them, his face set in suitably grave lines. He led the way to the breakfast-room where Harvey Drummer was waiting. After exchanging a few brief words Drummer took them up to Rosie Huggins' rooms. They went through a small, neat sitting-room and found themselves in a bedroom of about the same size. The curtains were drawn, and the cold light of the morning showed up the figure in the bed. The bedclothes were drawn up to the face, distorted and ghastly.

'Poor thing was half-covered by the bedclothes when Brethers found her,' Drummer said to Hood. 'After we tried all we could I drew the clothes over her. The glass,' he went on, 'was on the floor. The remains of her drink had spilled from it.' He pointed to a small patch beside the bed. 'I picked the glass up in case it got smashed while we were trying to revive her.'

Hood muttered between his teeth :

'Never saw a more typical cyanide poisoning. Face that blue colour — '

He broke off as he realised Dr. Morelle had moved away from the body over which he had been bending. He was looking at something on the dressing-table.

'Brethers tells me she was in the habit

of having a glass of orange-juice every morning when she awoke,' Drummer was saying. 'Prepared it overnight apparently.'

He broke off also to follow the Inspector's gaze. He moved to Dr. Morelle and indicated the envelope which was propped on the dressing-table, at which the Doctor was staring.

'Didn't open it,' Drummer said. 'Although it's addressed to me. Thought I'd better wait until you arrived.'

Dr. Morelle nodded and picked up the envelope.

'Be her farewell message no doubt,' Hood said as he joined them. 'What's it say, Doctor?'

Dr. Morelle handed the envelope to Drummer, who gave him and then the Inspector a questioning look.

'See what it says,' Hood nodded.

The other tore open the envelope and read the letter aloud.

'I can't go on any longer without my beloved Bill. Tried to be brave but am desperately lonely. I go to him now. Forgive me — Rosie Huggins.'

There was a little silence. Inspector Hood was staring at Dr. Morelle with one heavy eye-brow raised. The pale, ascetic features were as inscrutable as ever, but the Inspector had no doubt about what must be passing through the Doctor's mind. Hood took his pipe out of his mouth to say something and then put it back without speaking. Better leave it to Dr. Morelle. The situation was just about his cup of tea.

'Might I see it?'

Harvey Drummer handed the letter to Dr. Morelle, who read it through carefully. After a few moments he asked :

'Are you familiar with the deceased's handwriting?'

The other hesitated for a moment. Then:

'Wouldn't say I know it all that well. Though I must have seen it before.' He seemed to be searching his memory before he went on: 'I can't remember when exactly. Why?'

'It will be necessary to establish that this is, in fact, her handwriting.'

Drummer glanced at the Inspector, his expression somewhat puzzled. He turned back to Dr. Morelle.

'But of course it's her handwriting,' he said. He frowned at the Doctor for a moment and then asked : 'What are you getting at? You suggesting she didn't commit suicide?'

'I am of the opinion,' was the reply, 'that she did not take her own life.'

Drummer regarded him in blank amazement.

'But this is fantastic,' he gasped. 'You mean — you mean somebody murdered her?'

'It appears out of the question that it could have been an accident. Murder offers itself as the only reasonable alternative.'

Drummer turned appealingly to Inspector Hood.

'Can this be right?'

'Never knew Dr. Morelle to be wrong yet,' Hood answered heavily. 'You see, we happen to know a bit more about the poor woman than you do.'

'This is like some nightmare,' the other exclaimed. 'That she should have committed suicide was a big enough shock, but murder!' He shook his head help-lessly. 'I just can't believe it.'

'I suggest,' Dr. Morelle put in, 'we continue this talk elsewhere. Inspector Hood will wish to make necessary arrangements with Scotland Yard.'

'Yes,' Hood said. 'I'll speak to the men in the car.'

Harvey Drummer led the way down to his study, while Inspector Hood hurried ahead to the police-car waiting outside. Automatically Drummer filled his pipe from the tobacco jar on the writing-desk. Then he slumped into an armchair.

Dr. Morelle gave him a penetrating glance. Drummer appeared utterly crushed by Rosie Huggins' death. He looked up and found the Doctor's gaze on him. Interpreting it, he managed a wry smile.

'Just about the last straw,' he muttered. 'My daughter, Miss Frayle and now Mrs. Huggins.'

'The vital difference being,' Dr. Morelle reminded him, 'that both the former are alive.'

'Yes.' But Drummer failed to hide the feeling of doubt in his voice. He said: 'There's Leo Rolf, too.' He glanced at Dr. Morelle suddenly. 'How could this have anything to do with all the other?'

'That,' returned Dr. Morelle, examining the tip of his cigarette, 'is a matter for speculation.'

'What did you and Inspector Hood find out about Mrs. Huggins that makes you so sure it wasn't suicide?'

'The motive for her deliberate falsehoods the day before yesterday.'

'You mean you discovered where she was that time?'

'She was visiting a man on his converted barge, where he resides, off Chelsea Embankment. An individual with whom she had formed an illicit attachment.'

'Good God!'

'He is married,' Dr. Morelle proceeded. 'His wife, it appeared, was unwilling to divorce him. But he had renewed hope that he would be able to free himself from her and marry Mrs. Huggins.'

The other drew at his pipe for a

moment and, expelling a cloud of tobacco-smoke, said:

'So that stuff about her killing herself on account of her late husband was obviously phoney.'

'Mrs. Huggins emphasised to me last night the depth of her love for this man, and her hope that they would be able to marry. As you have perceived, the note supposedly written by her to the effect that she found it impossible to continue living without her husband is therefore palpably suspect.'

Drummer was staring at him with a puzzled expression.

'Last night?' he queried. 'You saw her last night?'

'Between the hours of approximately one-thirty and two-thirty,' Dr. Morelle replied. 'Inspector Hood and I visited the vessel of the man in question.'

'How the devil did you know she'd be there?'

'We were as much surprised as she was at the encounter,' was the reply. 'Inspector Hood had received information concerning the presence of a woman on board this particular craft. The circumstances appeared to require our investigation. Accordingly Inspector Hood and I proceeded to the scene. To our amazement we discovered the woman involved was none other than Mrs. Huggins.'

'I can't imagine Mrs. Huggins down in Chelsea on some man's boat at that hour,' the other exclaimed.

'At her last meeting with the man — the occasion upon which she was supposed to have attended the cinema — she told him that unless he could hold out greater hopes of freeing himself from his wife and marrying her, they should end their relationship. Subsequently he wrote begging her to visit him that night — this was yesterday — to convince her he would re-double his efforts to ensure that they could be married. I elicited this information from Mrs. Huggins during the journey back in the police-car in which I accompanied Inspector Hood down to Chelsea. The Inspector also heard the gist of her story.'

'And you last saw her when you

dropped her here?'

'She was put down at the entrance to the mews. She intended making her way into the house by way of the garage.'

Harvey Drummer shook his head in bewilderment.

'I still can't believe she was murdered,' he muttered. 'Yet after what you've said the letter's obviously a forgery. Incidentally,' he added, 'Brethers might be able to give you more information about her handwriting. Shall I call him in?'

Dr. Morelle gave him a nod of acquiescence, and the other pressed a bell on his writing-desk.

'I had intended questioning him,' Dr. Morelle said. 'He may have heard something in the night which may prove helpful.'

'I asked him about that myself,' Drummer replied. 'But he's a pretty sound sleeper, I gather.'

The door opened and Inspector Hood came in, followed by Brethers.

'Been having a chat with Brethers,' the Inspector announced. 'In case he heard anything during the night. Routine questions, that's all.'

'I'd just rung for him so the Doctor could ask him the very same thing,' Harvey Drummer said.

'Also seen your secretary,' Hood went on. 'Pearson, isn't it?'

'Yes,' Drummer said. 'I told him what had happened after I rang Dr. Morelle.'

'Heard nothing suspicious, either,' the Inspector said. 'Though he didn't get to sleep till just after midnight.'

'Pearson didn't come in till after eleven,' Drummer put in. 'He went out after dinner to see some friends.'

The manservant stood there regarding Dr. Morelle expectantly.

'One of these chaps with no worries,' Inspector Hood said genially to Brethers. 'Sleeps like a log. Right, Brethers?'

'That's true, sir,' Brethers replied. 'I went to bed at my usual time. About eleven o'clock, and I must have been asleep half an hour later. I didn't wake until my alarm went off at six-forty-five.'

'You enjoyed an undisturbed night?' queried Dr. Morelle.

'As the Inspector says,' Brethers

nodded, 'it needs a lot to wake me.'

'According to Mr. Drummer you found Mrs. Huggins dead some time after she did not arrive as usual with your morning cup of tea.'

'Yes, Dr. Morelle. Always used to look in at seven o'clock. Just after I'd finished shaving. I was puzzled when she didn't turn up at the usual time, but didn't think much about it until half an hour later. I wondered if perhaps she'd overslept, or was ill. I went along and knocked on her bedroom door. There was no reply, and after I'd knocked and called two or three times I went in. There she was, exactly as I described it to Mr. Drummer.'

Brethers' voice had taken on a tremor, and Dr. Morelle said:

'It must have been something of a shock to you.'

'I couldn't believe my eyes,' the other shook his head. 'It's still impossible to realise it's happened. What can have made her commit suicide, I can't think,' he said. 'She was always so lively and cheerful. It doesn't make sense.'

Drummer gave Hood a look. He

realised that while questioning Brethers the Inspector had shrewdly withheld the fact that it was no longer suicide, but murder.

'Doubtless,' Dr. Morelle was asking Brethers, 'you noticed there was an envelope addressed to Mr. Drummer on the deceased's dressing-table?'

'Yes.'

Dr. Morelle handed him the letter.

'It explains why she so tragically took her own life,' he said smoothly. 'Merely for the benefit of Inspector Hood here, you can of course identify the writing as hers?'

Brethers gave him a sharp look and hesitated.

'Just a matter of routine,' Inspector Hood put in with elaborate casualness. The other took the letter and read it through carefully.

'Poor woman,' he muttered half to himself. 'I know she was very cut up about her husband.' He looked up at the Doctor and went on: 'I don't remember ever having noticed her handwriting before. But I suppose this would be hers.

Must be, of course.'

Dr. Morelle took the letter from him. He gave Inspector Hood a quizzical glance.

'All right by me,' the Inspector grunted.

Dr. Morelle had no further questions to ask, and the manservant went out.

'Photograph and fingerprint boys are on their way,' Hood said. Then: 'Thought it was as well to let Brethers go on thinking it was suicide.'

'I had rather gathered as much,' Dr. Morelle said dryly.

Inspector Hood gave him a look. He said:

'That's what the other chap still thinks, too.' He paused for a moment and then went on: 'One thing, it looks like an inside job all right.'

Harvey Drummer started. Slowly he took his pipe out of his mouth.

'Good God,' he said. 'That means you must suspect either Pearson or Brethers or' — his voice dropped — ' or myself.'

'That's about it,' Hood replied cheerfully.

Drummer swung round with a panic-stricken movement, to find Dr. Morelle eyeing him narrowly.

'For heaven's sake,' Drummer choked, 'you can't think I did it.'

Dr. Morelle drew at his cigarette and observed quietly:

'I fear Inspector Hood is on occasion inclined to leap to conclusions.'

'What d'you mean?' Hood grunted a trifle truculently.

'We have yet to receive indisputable proof,' was the reply, 'that the murder could *not* have been committed by someone from outside.'

26

A Scrap of Evidence?

There was a long pause, then Inspector Hood, frowning, asked Dr. Morelle:

'Don't you think this murder is connected with our kidnapper — ?'

'Who murdered Leo Rolf,' Harvey Drummer put in. 'And for the same reason.'

'You've been saying all along it's an inside job,' Hood went on, and Drummer added:

'That it must have been a guest at the party — '

'I have intimated,' Dr. Morelle replied, assuming a long-suffering air, 'that whoever abducted Miss Drummer was present on the evening in question, is acquainted with the topography of this house and, it seems, inevitably implicated in the murder of Rolf and the abduction of Miss Frayle.' He turned to Drummer.

'You agreed the criminal must be one of a circle including members of your household and several of your closer friends.'

Drummer nodded. 'It certainly looks that way.'

'I agree,' Inspector Hood chimed in. 'That's roughly the picture.'

'A picture,' Dr. Morelle pointed out, 'which includes persons other than those resident here. Someone who, for example, could have waited in the mews for Mrs. Huggins' return. Who could have followed her, gaining admittance to the house by some means, poisoned the glass of orange-juice, knowing she would drink it when she awoke, and as stealthily made off again.'

'By cripes,' Inspector Hood exclaimed inelegantly, 'it could be.'

'Why pick on that poor woman?' Drummer queried.

Dr. Morelle eyed him thoughtfully.

'The most obvious answer to that,' he replied, 'would appear to be that the murderer and the person responsible for the other crimes are one and the same.'

'And he killed her,' Hood grunted,

'because she knew too much. Same as Rolf.'

Dr. Morelle nodded and then, glancing at Drummer, indicated the letter he was holding.

'Might not your secretary have some opinion concerning the handwriting's authenticity?'

The other hesitated for a moment before he said:

'We can ask him. Though I don't know that Pearson will be any more helpful about that than I've been.'

'I could ascertain that for myself on our way to the garage,' was the reply.

'You want to take a look at the garage?' Hood queried.

'Also the mews outside,' Dr. Morelle told him.

They found Pearson in his office. Taking the letter from Dr. Morelle he scrutinised it carefully.

'Just a routine matter, of course,' Inspector Hood explained easily.

Pearson raised his pince-nez, shaking his head mournfully.

'What a dreadful thing,' he said. 'To the

best of my belief,' he went on, 'this is her writing.' He frowned slightly. 'Though I can't honestly remember having noticed her handwriting at all before.'

'That's all right,' Inspector Hood said. 'Just a formality.'

Pearson handed the letter back to Dr. Morelle. He held the door open as Drummer led the Doctor and Hood out of the office.

The man in pince-nez closed the door and, returning to his desk, sat down with a thoughtful expression.

'Unless we find another specimen of hers,' Inspector Hood muttered in Dr. Morelle's ear as they followed Harvey Drummer, 'it's going to be tricky proving it is a forgery.'

'A factor of which the forger was doubtless equally aware,' Dr. Morelle returned quietly.

'You mean he knew he was on a good thing because there wasn't much likelihood of anyone knowing what her handwriting did look like?'

'I have maintained all along,' was the reply, 'that we are at grips with an adversary of calculating cunning.'

'I think you've got something there,' Inspector Hood said.

Harvey Drummer had led them into the kitchen, and they followed him across to a door, the key of which was in the lock.

'This is the garage,' he said. 'Also the tradesmen's entrance, only way in from the mews. This is how Mrs. Huggins came in.'

'Like all criminals, however,' Dr. Morelle said musingly, 'our friend has also made one miscalculation.'

'Eh?' queried Harvey Drummer, frowning at Dr. Morelle.

'I refer to a conversation between Hood and I,' Dr. Morelle returned, 'regarding the forgery.' He turned to the Inspector, continuing loftily: 'The criminal in this case was unaware of Mrs. Huggins' liaison with Goodwin, who, as it happens, may very well possess specimens of her handwriting proving indisputably this letter is forged.'

'Goodwin,' Hood muttered. 'I'd forgotten about him.'

'Before you rush off to Chelsea,' Dr. Morelle said, smiling thinly as he handed over the letter, 'to confirm the fact, let us proceed to examine the garage and the vicinity outside.'

'Come to think of it,' Inspector Hood ventured, 'he could have murdered Rosie.'

'Doubtless you will satisfy your curiosity upon that interesting speculation during your interview with him,' was the cryptic response.

Hood started to say something, then Harvey Drummer turned the key in the lock. He was about to open the door when Dr. Morelle stopped him.

'This door is habitually kept locked?'

'It's only unlocked for tradesmen, or whenever the car's taken out,' the other said.

Dr. Morelle glanced at his watch. It was sixteen minutes past nine. To Drummer he said:

'Have you had occasion to use the door this morning?'

'No.'

'And have any tradesmen called?'

Drummer shook his head. He glanced down at the key he had just turned.

'I'm pretty sure the door hasn't been unlocked since last night.'

'No doubt Brethers would corroborate that?' Dr. Morelle queried.

'I'll go and find him and check it,' Inspector Hood promptly volunteered, and marched off.

Drummer watched the burly back depart, then he opened the door. The garage was dark. He snapped on a switch. The garage was fairly large, most of its space being taken up by an American-made, dark blue coupé. Drummer unlocked the double doors and swung one back as Dr. Morelle, skirting the car, heard Inspector Hood returning through the kitchen. The Scotland Yard man followed Dr. Morelle and Drummer into the mews. Puffing at his pipe a trifle breathlessly, he said:

'Brethers positive door locked last night. Hadn't unlocked it this morning.'

'I was pretty sure he hadn't,' Drummer said.

Inspector Hood ambled into the centre

of the mews and stood, a burly figure, glancing up and down. Drummer joined him.

'Dark enough at night,' he said. 'If you're thinking about someone lying in wait for Mrs. Huggins.'

Both their backs happened to be turned on Dr. Morelle as he suddenly picked up a small object which lay between two cobblestones near the garage-door which was closed. He gave the fragment a cursory glance and slipped it into his pocket. Slowly he crossed over to the other two. With his head bent Inspector Hood started pacing the ground round about, his pipe gurgling furiously. After a few moments he returned to Dr. Morelle and Drummer and shrugged his heavy shoulders.

'Not even so much as a cigarette-stub.'

'Perhaps he doesn't smoke,' Drummer suggested, with a faint smile.

'Not cigarettes, anyway,' Hood replied shortly.

Dr. Morelle's expression remained inscrutable as from the corner of his eye he observed Harvey Drummer unconsciously push his pipe into his pocket.

'Better take a look round the garage,' Hood was saying, and he moved away. Drummer followed him and Dr. Morelle into the garage. The Inspector stood staring at the stone floor for a few moments. The highly polished surface of the car glimmered beneath the powerful bulb overhead.

'Got a torch?' the Inspector grunted.

Drummer opened the car door and took out a torch from the inside pocket. Grunting and wheezing Inspector Hood got on his hands and knees and flashed the torch under the car. With more wheezing and grunting and puce in the face, he stood up. He pushed his trilby hat which had slipped over his eyes back on his head. He handed the torch back to Drummer who returned it to the car.

'Not a sign of anything,' Hood said. 'Didn't expect to find much, but you never know.' He pushed his hat to one side to scratch his head, and offered: 'One thing about our friend, whoever he is, he hasn't been very obliging. Left behind no handkerchief with his name on or anything.'

'Are criminals often as obliging as that?' Drummer queried.

'How d'you think we flatties manage to be so successful?' was the rejoinder. 'Because we're so smart? Not a bit of it. Because the crooks are such mugs. But this chap isn't running a bit true to form.' And he gave a rueful sigh.

Drummer was locking the garage door when Brethers appeared from the kitchen.

'Inspector Hood,' he said. 'Some more gentlemen from Scotland Yard have arrived.'

'I'll come along,' the Inspector said, and Brethers went away.

'Be the photo and fingerprint boys,' Hood explained to Drummer. 'Better go and take 'em upstairs.' He glanced questioningly at Dr. Morelle. 'What's your next move, Doctor?'

'In the direction of Harley Street,' Dr. Morelle replied. 'For some breakfast.' He glanced at Drummer's haggard countenance. 'You might do worse than follow my example,' he said.

The other said with a shrug of weariness:

'I suppose I'd better have something. Won't you stay and join me?'

'It is imperative that I should return to Harley Street. Some news may come through.'

Drummer nodded. Turning to the Inspector: 'You'll have some coffee, I'm sure. Or tea?'

'A nice cup of tea won't come amiss,' Inspector Hood promptly accepted. 'I'll just have a word with the boys first.'

As they made their way out of the kitchen, Hood muttered to Dr. Morelle:

'Then I'll be getting down to Chelsea for a chat with Goodwin.'

Dr. Morelle picked up a taxi in Park Lane and returned to 221B, Harley Street. Hanging up his coat and hat he went and abstractedly put on a kettle for some tea. Then he foraged in the breadbin, cut himself some bread and made toast. He found the butter and marmalade, and methodically prepared himself a tray.

The tea made he carried the tray into his study and sat down and thoughtfully poured himself a cup of tea. From a drawer he took a magnifying glass. Taking the small object he had picked up in the mews out of his pocket, he placed it on the table. Carefully he scrutinised it beneath the powerful glass.

Satisfied from his examination his original surmise was correct, he slipped the fragment back in his pocket. With narrowed eyes he began to eat his toast and marmalade. Suddenly he gave a tiny sigh. The flow of his thoughts were interrupted as he realised how empty his study seemed without Miss Frayle. His sharply-etched features softened perceptibly as he glanced across at her chair. In his mind's eye he pictured the small slim figure, her horn-rimmed spectacles balanced precariously on her nose as they bent over her note-book. Then he gave a scowl as if irritated by this intrusion of his cogitations. With a restless movement he poured himself another cup of tea.

Lighting a cigarette he leaned back in his chair and blew a speculative cloud of smoke towards the ceiling. He reached for the batch of type-written notes Miss Frayle had completed. They amounted to a précis of the events following Harvey Drummer's disclosure of his daughter's failure to arrive for the party in Park Lane.

The notes were reasonably detailed, and Dr. Morelle perused them carefully while he finished his cup of tea. Pushing the breakfast-tray aside he proceeded to scratch out the names of Leo Rolf and Mrs. Huggins with his pen. Next he scored a thick line beneath the names of Drummer, Neil Fulton and Pearson. As he reached the last name the telephone rang.

It was Neil Fulton.

'Been trying to 'phone you several times, but couldn't get any reply. I'm speaking from my flat before going down to the studio. Not working early today. Just as well; I was out late last night. I know Miss Frayle told me,' the film-actor went on hurriedly, 'you'd let me know at once if there was any news about Doone. But there's this ghastly

Leo Rolf business — '

'I gather Inspector Hood visited you in that connection,' Dr. Morelle said.

'I wasn't able to tell him much. Didn't mention anything about Doone, of course. Are the two things mixed up? Incredible to think they could be — I mean it was I who introduced him to Doone — and yet — ' He broke off uncertainly.

'The assumption is that Rolf's murder may have a bearing on the abduction of Miss Drummer,' Dr. Morelle replied.

'I'd have rung up her father,' the other said, 'only I don't think he'd exactly welcome it.'

'He can give you no more information than I.'

Dr. Morelle hung up, dragged deeply at his cigarette and slowly expelled a spiral of smoke.

Neil Fulton.

Dr. Morelle recalled his conclusion that Doone Drummer's kidnapper must have possessed inside knowledge of her father's house. Fulton was not included in Drummer's circle of close friends, and had never been a visitor to Park Lane. Nevertheless he could have learned something about the house from Doone Drummer herself.

On the other hand Fulton had not apparently been present at the party. How, therefore, could he have known it was Dr. Morelle who had answered the telephone in Drummer's study? But the young actor had just said something over the telephone which was causing Dr. Morelle to reconsider him from a fresh angle. Neil Fulton's remark to the effect that he had been out late last night. Fulton was an actor. Trained in the art of simulation. Who would find it simpler than most to assume a disguised voice.

Dr. Morelle stirred in his chair. Was it possible, he wondered, that Fulton had telephoned with the object of deliberately drawing suspicion upon himself? Had there been some subtly ulterior motive behind that apparently casual reference to last night?

Was it Fulton whom Rosie Huggins had encountered in the shadows of the dark mews?

Dr. Morelle scored a thicker line under Neil Fulton's name, and then began reading his notes where he had left off when the telephone had rung. It was Pearson he had been considering then.

Pearson.

Dr. Morelle conjured up a mental picture of Harvey Drummer's secretary furtively quitting the house by way of the garage to telephone his announcement that Miss Frayle was now his captive. Supposing on his return he had encountered Rosie Huggins? His presence in the mews would certainly arouse her curiosity. Curiosity which, if she pursued, it might lead to her denouncing Pearson. What would have been easier than for him subsequently to visit her room while she was asleep and poison her drink?

Dr. Morelle cupped his chin in his hand. His gaze moved to Harvey Drummer's name in the notes before him. He began to speculate on the possibility of Drummer still being the motivating force behind his daughter's kidnapping, when the front door-bell rang.

Dr. Morelle glanced at his watch.

Inspector Hood would hardly have had time to conclude his arrangements at Park Lane, proceed to Chelsea Embankment to interview Goodwin and return by now. Slowly he ground his cigarette-stub into the ash-tray. He went along the hall and opened the door.

A familiar figure stood there blinking nervously up at him.

27

The Tip-Off

'I do hope I haven't disturbed you,' the man in pince-nez said going through the motions of washing his hands. 'But I had to see you.'

Dr. Morelle held the door wide, and the other preceded him to the study. Pearson clutched his black Homburg agitatedly and sat down. The Doctor eyed him curiously over the flame of his lighter as he lit a fresh cigarette.

'I've slipped away,' Pearson explained, 'on the pretext of seeing my dentist. I hope you won't think I'm troubling you unnecessarily. I'll be as brief as I can.'

He glanced at Dr. Morelle as if awaiting a word of encouragement. There was no response. Only the dark basilisk-like stare fixed on him through a cloud of cigarette-smoke. Pearson cleared his throat nervously.

'I don't have to tell you,' he said, 'how very ill Mr. Drummer's been looking these last few days. I've come to the conclusion something's terribly wrong. For one thing the fact that you, Dr. Morelle, have been there so frequently started me wondering if something was amiss. Then Mr. Drummer's preoccupied manner. Not a bit like his usual self, I assure you. Always so brisk and business-like. Full of enthusiasm.' The pince-nez shook from side to side, and Pearson gave a heavy sigh. 'Now this ghastly business this morning,' he went on. 'Poor Mrs. Huggins, taking her own life like that.'

He paused and again waited for Dr. Morelle to speak. Still no response and, clasping and unclasping his hat, he continued:

'I have hinted to Mr. Drummer to confide in me. After all I have been his confidential secretary for many years now. I know most of what goes on. But I'm afraid I was rebuffed. Gently, but none the less firmly, rebuffed. And so, Dr. Morelle, you're the only one I can turn to.'

'What information do you expect from me that your employer refuses to give you?'

The other regarded Dr. Morelle for several moments. A subtle change came over him. His manner grew less servile, the eyes behind the pince-nez hardened and assumed a shrewd expression. His tone when next he spoke was firm and controlled.

'Tell me frankly if you know him to be involved in deeper waters than I imagine. My object in asking this,' Pearson went on, 'is that if I know what is wrong I feel I might help you to help Mr. Drummer. You'll agree that sometimes help secretly given can prove the most effective.'

'There have been cases in which that has been so,' Dr. Morelle conceded.

'On the other hand, Mr. Drummer may be making it difficult for you to do your best on his behalf. He may be hiding his troubles from you. For instance, I think you should know he's suddenly had to realise ten thousand pounds' worth of his holdings. Then there's something mysterious about his daughter. She's supposed to be staying with a relative who's ill. So far as I know she hasn't written or telephoned her father since she failed to turn up at the party that was given for her.' He shook his head. 'They've always been most affectionate. Hardly a day without them seeing each other or at least 'phoning. That alone strikes me as odd. Don't you agree?'

'From what you say,' Dr. Morelle replied, 'the circumstances appear somewhat disturbing.'

'There's something wrong,' the other said. 'I wondered if it was a question of money? Some secret deal Mr. Drummer's conducting unknown to me. Perhaps on his daughter's behalf. I'd be only too glad to help him in my small way. I have a modest nest-egg tucked away. I was going to dip into it soon for some treatment for my hands.'

He glanced at the curiously deformed fingers gripping his hat. With a look at Dr. Morelle:

'Expect you've noticed they're badly arthritic. I've become very self-conscious about them. I've thought of wearing black gloves.' He gave an ashamed smile. 'Silly of me. But we all have our little vanities, I suppose.'

'I can reassure you so far as the financial aspect of Mr. Drummer's anxiety is concerned,' Dr. Morelle said slowly. 'It is true he needed a large sum of money urgently, but finance is not the fundamental cause of his distress. What it is I am not at the moment at liberty to divulge.'

The secretary had reverted to his former attitude. A hesitant cough was followed by nervous movements of his fingers; the eyes behind the pince-nez blinked and wore their usual subservient look.

'There's one other thing,' Pearson mumbled, 'that I feel I ought to mention.'

Dr. Morelle who had been apparently gazing abstractedly out of the window at the sky above Harley Street turned, one eyebrow raised questioningly.

'It's about that poor woman,' Pearson went on tentatively. He hesitated and then blurted it out: 'I did hear someone creeping about the house. Early this morning. My room isn't far from Mrs. Huggins, and just before three o'clock something woke me, as if it was someone creeping along the passage. I listened, wondering who it might be. But I must have dropped off to sleep. I deliberately didn't tell the Inspector.'

'Why?' Dr. Morelle rapped out.

Pearson returned his probing glance with an expression of faint surprise.

'I had a feeling it might have been something to do with Mrs. Huggins' death. I — I suppose I was afraid it might have implicated Mr. Drummer. I don't know why. I just, had a feeling — ' He stuttered on, then burst out: 'And that suicide note. I know Inspector Hood's suspicious it isn't her handwriting.'

Dr. Morelle regarded the other with narrowed eyes. He glanced at the tip of his cigarette and observed:

'Your concern for Mr. Drummer has caused your imagination to run away with you. Though your intentions were naturally of the best, you should not have withheld any information from Inspector Hood. Assuming, of course,' he added insinuatingly, 'that what you believed you heard last night was not in fact a remnant of a dream you had been experiencing.'

Pearson opened his mouth as if to say something, but fell silent again. Dr. Morelle had crossed significantly to the door. The other stood up, fumbling with his hat, and blinking agitatedly.

'I must advise Inspector Hood forthwith of what you have informed me,' Dr. Morelle said suavely. 'He will fully appreciate your most understandable motive for remaining silent.'

The other began to mutter something, but Dr. Morelle was urging him out of the study.

'Meantime,' he told Pearson, 'I advise you not to give way to further anxious speculation upon the matter.'

Dr. Morelle opened the front door as the other mumbled his apologetic thanks. Pearson stood for a moment indecisively, and then started to put his hat on. It seemed to slip in his nervous clutch and, catching the side of his head, revealed his luxuriant and glossy hair to be an unmistakable toupee. Pearson's pale features reddened with embarrassment as he pushed the toupee back into place. He contrived a rueful smile as he caught Dr. Morelle's sardonic glance.

'Another example of my vanity, I'm afraid,' he said. Then he asked anxiously: 'It's a very good one, don't you think? Nobody ever notices it.'

'I should never have detected it,' Dr. Morelle lied dutifully.

'Had it made in America,' the other volunteered. 'When I was there on business for Mr. Drummer last autumn. I have three. I change them as my hair is supposed to grow longer. Cunning device, isn't it?'

'Remarkable,' Dr. Morelle said.

He stood at the door for a moment watching the dapper figure hurrying off down Harley Street, looking for a taxi.

Back in his study Dr. Morelle leaned against his desk, his jaw sunk thoughtfully on his tie. What had been behind Pearson's visit? Was there some ulterior motive? Was Pearson afraid that in some way he had revealed he knew more about

Rosie Huggins' death than he had admitted? Was his visit an attempted pretence at frankness to divert any suspicion from him on to someone else? On to Drummer himself?

If it was that, Dr. Morelle decided, it had been a decidedly crude attempt. It occurred to him this apparent crudeness might be part of some subtle game Pearson was playing, when the telephone jarred into his ruminations.

'I'm at Scotland Yard,' Inspector Hood's voice boomed against Dr. Morelle's eardrum. 'Back from interviewing the great lover. Knocked all of a heap he was when I told him about poor Rosie. Said he couldn't help on the letter. Said she'd only written him one or two brief notes which he'd destroyed. Seemed to think the one I showed him might be her handwriting, but he was too shaken up to be really coherent. I been checking up on him here, but there isn't a thing about him. However, we found a letter in her room from her late husband's sister. Lives in Essex. Where he used to go fishing apparently. She might be able to give us a lead. Tell you one little thing I've got for you.'

'Which would be?'

'A tip-off about a character known as Bertie Herberts. Englishman. Known in America. To the Los Angeles police especially. Blackmail used to be his racket.'

'Why should I be interested in this individual?'

'Been putting in some work over the 'phone with Los Angeles,' Hood said. 'He knew Leo Rolf in Hollywood. When I say knew, I mean Herberts had put the bite on him. Rolf left Hollywood eighteen months back. A little while later our Bertie was last heard of heading in this direction. If he's in London it could fit. He could have forced Rolf to line-up the Drummer girl for him. Then when Rolf got panicky and threatened to spill the beans he bumped him off.'

'Is there any possibility of this man being located?' queried Dr. Morelle.

'Just what I'm working on,' Hood replied. 'Soon as I've got anything I'll be on to you.'

Dr. Morelle replaced the receiver. He glanced down at Miss Frayle's notes and at what he had absently scribbled while Inspector Hood was talking to him. Suddenly his eyes narrowed. A great wave of exultation uplifted him. As he rode on the feeling of triumph, bitter anger tightened his jaw into a grim line. Anger against himself. Anger that he had failed until now to pierce the mystery. As mentally he fitted the last piece of the jigsaw into place he spoke briefly into the telephone. Slamming the receiver down, he swept out of the house like an avenging angel, brandished his swordstick so alarmingly at a passing taxi it cowered immediately to a stop.

The taxi pulled up outside the house in Park Lane and Dr. Morelle got out. Brethers opened the door to him; his usually unruffled features exhibited some slight surprise at the tall forbidding figure looming before him. He closed the door and murmured uncertainly:

'Mr. Drummer's in his office. I'll tell him you've come back.'

'You will kindly refrain from announcing me to anyone,' Dr. Morelle snapped, and Brethers, catching the unmistakable ring of command in his voice, gave him a startled glance.

28

Unmasked

The man paused at the bedroom door.

'Go in!' Dr. Morelle's voice rasped behind him.

The man's body suddenly tensed as if he was about to turn on Dr. Morelle. But the swordstick blade pressed inexorably into his back. He could almost feel the point penetrating through his clothes to the skin. He decided this was not the moment for him to try any tricks. He opened the door. Dr. Morelle followed him into the room. The door remained open.

'Proceed as far as the cupboard.'

Once again the figure in front of Dr. Morelle hesitated. A tremor seemed to shake him as if he was filled with some icy dread. The swordstick urged him forward until he was forced up against a large built-in cupboard and he could go no farther.

'Keep your hands above your head and turn round.'

Slowly the other raised his arms.

'Higher.'

The man reached higher.

As he faced Dr. Morelle there was a thin flash of steel, and he could feel the point of the swordstick searching his throat just above the knot of his tie. Blinking involuntarily, he contrived to force a derisive smile to his lips.

'Acting tough, eh, Doctor?'

Now the man's eyes were lidless and cold and wary as the eyes of a snake.

'Move a fraction of an inch,' Dr. Morelle retorted through his teeth, 'and you will discover I am indulging in no histrionics but am deadly serious. Deadly for you.'

The other made no reply. His mouth tightened into a cruel bitter line.

It was as if a mask had been snatched suddenly from his face. His personality seemed to have undergone a complete metamorphosis. Even his appearance had altered. His voice was somehow different, pitched on a grating note which had not been apparent before. Had he been attired in a different suit of clothes it would have been possible for mere acquaintances to have failed to recognise him.

'Where are your prisoners?' Dr. Morelle demanded.

The other stared back at him. Then with an insolent shrug he replied coolly:

'Don't know what you're getting at.'

Dr. Morelle's smile was warm and friendly as an iceberg.

'You feel you have nothing to lose by a stubborn refusal to reveal where you have hidden them? You intend remaining defiant to the last?' Dr. Morelle's lip curled. 'Unfortunately for you I anticipated such might be your attitude. That you would have the audacity to offer the police the information I ask in exchange for your freedom.'

'Quite the bright one, aren't we?'

'You are the typical monomaniac. Buoying yourself up in the belief you can successfully defy society, triumph over law and order. Supremely confident that you are in a position to strike a bargain with Inspector Hood.'

'Go on talking.'

'That is why,' Dr. Morelle continued obligingly, 'instead of awaiting the arrival of the police I propose taking the matter into my own hands.'

The other's expression underwent a change. An apprehensive look flickered in his eyes.

'I somehow fancied my unconventional tactics might upset your calculations,' Dr. Morelle commented.

'What's the idea? What's on your mind?'

'The intention to drag from you the information I want. Here and now,' the Doctor continued grimly. 'I must warn you I shall dispense with any niceties you would have received from Scotland Yard. It is you *versus* me — and I happen to hold the trump card in the contest. A flick of my wrist and you die where you stand.'

The point of the blade pressed threateningly against the man's throat, and his head was forced hard against the cupboard. Drops of perspiration began to shine on his brow and on his upper lip. He made as if to say something, and then his mouth tightened in a thin line again.

'No need to inform you that this blade is razor sharp,' Dr. Morelle told him blandly. 'You can appreciate the fact for yourself.'

'You wouldn't dare do it,' the man muttered. 'You couldn't.'

Dr. Morelle measured him with a cold stare.

'You forget,' he said, 'that one of your captives happens to be Miss Frayle. Stupid, blundering fool that she may be, nevertheless I hold myself responsible for her well-being and safety.' His mouth closed like a trap, and he said through his teeth: 'Where is she?'

'I tell you I don't know what you're talking about.'

Dr. Morelle's grip on the swordstick handle tightened.

'Still trusting in your capacity to brazen it out? Still calculating that you might as well be hanged for a sheep as a lamb?'

The other's cold stare faltered for a fraction of a second. It was enough for

Dr. Morelle to fling at him:

'Hanged — for the murder of Leo Rolf and the woman Huggins.'

Once more the other blinked. The tip of his tongue moistened his lip.

'You're crazy,' he gasped.

'Leo Rolf, whom you had been blackmailing,' Dr. Morelle went on relentlessly. 'And whom you induced or forced to assist you to abduct Doone Drummer. You murdered him for reasons best known to yourself, but I hazard the suggestion it was because, fearful of the consequences, he threatened to denounce you. Just as you administered poison in Mrs. Huggins' drink because, I surmise, she accidentally met you in the mews last night. You were either on the way to telephone me or returning from having already done so.'

The other's eyes blinked again. The perspiration was running down his face. Dr. Morelle leaned forward, his voice harsh and compelling.

'Miss Frayle — whom you brought back to this house last night — where is she? And your other victim?'

The man's mouth twisted in another sneer.

'Brimful of newsy items, aren't you? Why so sure they're here?'

'It is not unreasonable to suppose,' Dr. Morelle retorted, 'that where one is the other will also be found.' He plunged his free hand into his pocket and held out a fragment in his palm. 'I picked it up,' he said, 'a short while ago. Outside the garage.'

The other's jaw sagged as he stared at the object before him.

'You may recognise it,' Dr. Morelle continued smoothly, 'as a broken piece of Miss Frayles horn-rimmed spectacles. Obviously dislodged from her apparel in which it had caught when the glasses were broken.' His voice rose suddenly in an enraged snarl. 'Where is she? Answer me — before I skewer your throat to the cupboard-door behind you.'

The man uttered a choked cry of terror as the needle-sharp point at his throat drew a spurt of blood which trickled down to his collar.

'For God's sake, don't — '

'Where is Miss Frayle?' Dr. Morelle's voice lashed him. 'For the last time.'

'Behind here,' the other gasped. 'Through — through this cupboard. A secret door that had been covered over. Leads into some empty rooms over the mews.'

Dr. Morelle's eyes blazed with triumph. Then suddenly the other gave a moan and slid slowly to the floor in a crumpled heap.

'You scared the swine into a dead faint,' a familiar voice boomed out, and Dr. Morelle swung round to find Inspector Hood framed in the doorway.

Two other plain-clothes men were crowding behind the Inspector. They sprang towards the unconscious figure on the floor, and there came a click of handcuffs. Inspector Hood shook his head at the inert heap, the blood oozing over his collar.

'All very reprehensible,' he turned to Dr. Morelle rebukingly. 'But ruddy successful.'

Dr. Morelle was wrenching open the cupboard-doors facing him. He crashed his shoulder against another narrow door at the back of the cupboard. There was a splintering sound as the light wood gave way before his attack, and he plunged through. He found himself in another large cupboard the doors of which were unlocked. He stood on a bare landing with a flight of uncarpeted stairs leading below. The air was musty, the place echoed to his footsteps and had an unlived-in atmosphere. He realised he was in an empty two-storeyed flat above Harvey Drummer's garage. He recalled having noticed two storeys over the garage, the windows dirty, and dark, the iron stairway to the front door broken and dilapidated, the door itself heavily boarded up.

Dr. Morelle crossed to two doors facing him. Both were locked. Inspector Hood at his back jingled a key-ring he had taken from the man still insensible in the room behind them. He said to Dr. Morelle, who was eyeing the locked doors aggressively:

'No need to go overdoing breaking up the happy home. Try if one of these keys will do the trick.'

Miss Frayle lay stretched out on the bed in the corner. She was unconscious, moaning faintly now and then under the influence of the narcotic.

In the next room Doone Drummer was just recovering from the last injection she had received. She was muttering incoherently as Hood and one of the plain-clothes men carried her carefully through to Harvey Drummer's house. There a police-surgeon and nurses who had been called in against any such emergency swiftly attended to her.

After assuring himself that she was in no danger Dr. Morelle himself carried Miss Frayle into the house and down to a waiting police-car. Inspector Hood followed and gave a hand settling the pathetic-looking figure comfortably in the back seat. He stood back and grinned broadly at Dr. Morelle.

'Never forgive herself, she won't,' he said. 'Being unconscious while she was in your arms.'

Dr. Morelle glanced at him sharply.

'I shall esteem it a favour if you will

forget ever having witnessed the incident,' he replied stiffly.

Inspector Hood chuckled, but Dr. Morelle's face was uncompromisingly stern.

'I have your word?' he pressed.

'Anything you say,' the other laughed. 'I'd promise you the earth after what you've pulled off this morning.' Shaking his head ruefully. 'If only I'd got that tip-off about Bertie Herberts earlier — '

'And deciphered the anagram he had chosen as an alias,' Dr. Morelle insinuated, recalling the name he had doodled on Miss Frayle's notes when Hood had telephoned him about Herberts.

'Colossal nerve of the so-and-so,' Hood grunted. 'Rearranging the same name to make it 'Brethers'. Herberts . . . Brethers,' he rolled the names round his tongue. 'What a blighter. Got to admit he looked the part too. References were faked, of course. Drummer's just told me he took 'em for granted. But Drummer's so excited over having his precious daughter back that's all he can think of.'

'Not to mention the diamond bracelet

also safely recovered,' Dr. Morelle reminded him.

'Everything's sewn up neat and tidy,' Inspector Hood beamed, giving the Doctor a wide grin of gratitude.

Dr. Morelle offered no comment, but merely permitted a smug, self-satisfied expression to settle on his face as he stepped into the car and sat beside Miss Frayle. She gave a little moan and seemed to slide sideways so that her head was nestling against his shoulder. He was about to push her away, and then appeared to recall that she was not conscious of what she was doing. He gave Inspector Hood a somewhat uncomfortable look and leaned as far away from Miss Frayle as he could. Somehow her head still contrived to nestle firmly against his shoulder, Hood noticed, as he closed the car-door.

Had he detected Miss Frayle's eyes flutter open for one brief moment? the Inspector wondered. Just before she had re-settled herself comfortably close to Dr. Morelle? Inspector Hood's pipe gurgled and spluttered as, chuckling aloud, he watched the car drive off, bearing Dr. Morelle and Miss Frayle back to 221B, Harley Street.

THE END

We do hope that you have enjoyed reading this large print book.

Did you know that all of our titles are available for purchase?

We publish a wide range of high quality large print books including:
Romances, Mysteries, Classics
General Fiction
Non Fiction and Westerns

Special interest titles available in large print are:
The Little Oxford Dictionary
Music Book, Song Book
Hymn Book, Service Book

Also available from us courtesy of Oxford University Press:
Young Readers' Dictionary
(large print edition)
Young Readers' Thesaurus
(large print edition)

For further information or a free brochure, please contact us at:
Ulverscroft Large Print Books Ltd.,
The Green, Bradgate Road, Anstey,
Leicester, LE7 7FU, England.
Tel: (00 44) 0116 236 4325
Fax: (00 44) 0116 234 0205

THE CLEOPATRA SYNDICATE

Sydney J. Bounds

Maurice Cole, the inventor of a mysterious new perfume, is found murdered. But his employer's only concern is to recover the stolen perfume . . . He hires Daniel Shield, head of I.C.E. — the Industrial Counter Espionage agency — who is aided by Barney Ryker and the beautiful Melody Gay. The trail leads them to Egypt, where Shield must find international criminal Suliman Kalif and recover the perfume before the Nile runs red with the blood of a Holy War.

DR. MORELLE TAKES A BOW

Ernest Dudley

Miss Frayle, no longer employed by psychiatrist and detective Dr. Morelle, now works as secretary to Hugo Coltman, head of a drama school. Endeavouring to entice her back, Dr. Morelle accepts an invitation to lecture at the school, only to become entangled in the sinister schemes that threaten the lives of students and teachers. After a brutal murder, tension mounts as Dr. Morelle and Miss Frayle find themselves targeted by the killer. Can Dr. Morelle's investigation be successfully concluded, and the murderer unmasked?